WINTER BEACH DOG TROT

WINTER BEACH DOG TROT

A Novel

Richard Haight

iUniverse, Inc.

New York Lincoln Shanghai

Winter Beach Dog Trot

iUniverse books may be ordered through booksellers or by contacting:

iUniverse
2021 Pine Lake Road, Suite 100
Lincoln, NE 68512
www.iuniverse.com
1-800-Authors (1-800-288-4677)

Because of the dynamic nature of the Internet, any Web addresses or links contained in this book may have changed since publication and may no longer be valid.

This is a work of fiction. All of the characters, names, incidents, organizations, and dialogue in this novel are either the products of the author's imagination or are used fictitiously.

ISBN: 978-0-595-47875-0 (pbk)
ISBN: 978-0-595-71490-2 (cloth)

Printed in the United States of America

For Denise

From the Author

Although the characters of *Winter Beach Dog Trot* are purely fictional, the setting, with the exception of a few literary liberties, is not. I am grateful for the inspiration of the residents of Florida's Treasure Coast who struggle to make a living in an economy dominated by tourism and home health care. Seasonal employees, who comprise the bulk of the work force, often lack basic human rights such as health insurance As if that's not enough, there are always hurricanes like Buzz lurking offshore waiting for the chance to humble even the wealthiest of our inhabitants.

I would like to thank my wife Denise, first and foremost. Without her skillful and diligent editing, this project would never have been completed. I would also like to recognize my late parents. My father taught me all I know about veterinary medicine while my mother inspired me to read everything from *The Pink Motel* to *The Red Pony*. To my children and their spouses, you have been encouraging and supportive despite your embarrassed snickering at Lucinda's sex scenes. Finally, I would like to thank Brindle and Dodger, our Boston terriers, for reminding me daily that true love is unconditional. (No dogs were abused or injured in the making of this book.)

I would also be remiss for not acknowledging the hard-working staffs of the Ocean Grill, Mr. Manatee's, Dell's, Chelsea's, and Captain Hiram's for their exceptional food and impeccable service.

ONE

The night sky over Winter Beach, Florida, was cloudless, and the light from May's full moon splayed over the open blinds and onto the disheveled bed where Gidget slept fitfully. An almost imperceptible breeze rustled through the live oak in the back yard and awakened her. It was 2:00 a.m. With the oppressive air that drifted from the direction of the Indian River came the mixed odors of fish, rotting wood, and gasoline fumes from the boats, but tonight they held no interest for Gidget. She was in season, or in heat according to the vulgar vernacular, and craved the kind of companionship only a male could offer.

Gidget sat up, stretched, and looked over at the man sleeping next to her. She sighed as he rolled onto his back and gave a snort, which would invariably lead to a chorus of snores if he were allowed to remain in this position. The corners of Gidget's mouth turned up as if to smile. She did love this man dearly and knew he would take her out, trolling as he liked to call it, as he had the other times when this urge consumed her. She stood on all four legs and stretched, then shook her twelve-pound, brindle-and-white frame. Satisfied the night was ripe for adventure the Boston terrier climbed across the rumpled sheets and the striped shadows created by moonlight on the blinds and proceeded to lick her master's ear.

Spencer Hawley, doctor of veterinary medicine, dreamed he had arrived late for his poultry anatomy test and had forgotten his pen. In fact, he had forgotten everything and stood naked before his class and professor. The wizened professor extended a bony finger and approached him, his twitching nose almost touching

Spencer's. Spencer could hear his short rapid sniffs. Suddenly, the professor thrust his wet tongue into Spencer's ear and gave him a wet Willie. Spencer awakened and stared into Gidget's pleading brown eyes, her damp pug nose just inches from his own.

"Jesus, Gidget, I wish you wouldn't do that. What is it? Do you need to go outside?"

Just then the alarm rang and brought it all back to Spencer. "Oh yes, it's time to take baby trolling." Spencer sat up on the edge of the bed and rubbed his eyes as he searched the floor with a bare foot for his underwear. "I've got to quit sleeping in the nude, Gidget; I keep having the damndest dreams."

Gidget sat in the middle of the tangled sheets and cocked her head first to the right then the left. Finally she perked up her ears and directed a soft yip at Spencer.

"All right all ready, let me pee first." Spencer picked up his Jockey shorts and scratched his bare butt as he ambled into the bathroom with the *savoir faire* of a spent coon hound and shut the door. Gidget jumped off the bed and pawed the door as Spencer loudly relieved himself into the middle of the bowl. "No, Gidget, lie down."

Gidget obediently slumped to the floor and placed her wet nose against the door to listen as Spencer ran water in the sink and brushed his teeth with the toothbrush he kept in his *Star Wars* glass on the cluttered counter.

Spencer, reeking of peppermint, eventually reappeared dressed in the tennis shorts and Braves T-shirt he had worn the evening before. He hadn't bothered to tuck in his shirt or put on socks before slipping into his deck shoes. "Let's go, Gidget."

Gidget jumped to her feet, yipped again, and dashed for the back door. Still only half awake, Spencer followed turning on the light in his bungalow's living room as he crossed the tiled floor to the kitchen table still cluttered with last night's dirty dishes. He found the keys to his aging Suburban under a paper napkin which partially obscured a column of sugar ants commuting to and from the remains of last night's pork chop and canned beans. At the back door he reached for Gidget's harness and slipped it over her head.

The terrier in the Boston breed loves to run, but the bulldog genes in the original cross leaves the Boston terrier with the typical pug nose and tapered trachea. Therefore, Gidget couldn't tolerate a choke chain no matter how stylish it looked. She was much more comfortable when she trotted behind the faltering Suburban in her harness, which consisted of a neck collar connected by a dorsal and ventral strip to a thoracic collar secured behind her front legs. This arrangement reduced the pressure on her windpipe and allowed her to trot merrily behind Spencer for blocks at a time before she required a rest.

Once harnessed, Gidget bounded out the door and bolted to the Suburban. Sitting on the driveway she pawed the passenger side door and looked over her shoulder impatiently at Spencer. Spencer struggled to unlock the door, and Gidget leapt onto the seat as he quietly closed the door and walked around to his side of the cab. Gidget promptly scooted over and began to lick his face in appreciation.

"Okay, Gidget, stop it now; we're going." He slipped the key into the ignition and turned the engine over. The Suburban shuddered as the engine roared to life. Spencer looked around furtively to see if he had awakened anyone, but his neighbors' houses were dark. Then he laughed. "What am I worried about, Gidget? I'm a veterinarian and we're called out at all hours of the night to save lives. No one will think twice about you and me driving off at two in the morning." He shifted into reverse and backed out onto the street, which was really just a soft dirt lane bordered by ancient drooping live oaks and barely wide enough for two lanes of traffic.

When he first arrived in Winter Beach from Iowa, the dusty side streets struck him as quaint and he justified their not being curbed or paved by the fact that it didn't snow in Florida—thank God. He soon became annoyed with the thin layer of dust covering everything in his house in January and was amazed at his street's near impassable state during the fall monsoon season. During a downpour he'd shift into four wheel drive and push the pedal to the floor as he fishtailed up Flamevine Drive praying he wouldn't encounter anyone slip sliding from the other direction.

Tonight the road was dry, and the Suburban kicked up a soft cloud of dust in the moonlight as Spencer and Gidget headed west toward the new subdivision aptly named Citrus Trace. Gidget stood with her forepaws planted on the dash and whined anxiously every time Spencer slowed for an intersection. "We're almost there, girl."

Spencer didn't know what made him feel more guilty, the fact that Gidget would be disappointed and depressed when she didn't get what she really wanted, or the fact that what he was doing was both unethical and illegal. But they had to eat, and he had tried everything he could think of to make his practice successful including radio and newspaper ads, discounts on his kennel service, talks at the Lions Club, and even a heartworm presentation complete with graphic slides at the DAR luncheon. Despite the Chamber of Commerce's glowing reports of new growth and development on the mainland north of Vero Beach, the area simply didn't need another vet.

The wealthy residents across the river on Premiere Island preferred the longer drive south to Vero rather than cross the Wabasso bridge to see him. In Vero, Poopsie could see any number of vets while her master shopped for exotic wine and key lime pie at Chelsea's or dined on a grilled grouper sandwich at the Ocean Grill.

Winter Beach by contrast offered a drive-thru liquor depot that only recently upgraded its beer selection to include Michelob. For lunch there was always an overcooked cheese dog at the new Quickstop, which also proudly offered the first video rentals and ATM machine in Winter Beach.

The prospect of remaining in Indian River County had almost faded completely until several months ago when Spencer noticed three of the neighbors' dogs as they scrambled frantically between the hibiscus and the oleander in his backyard, their noses to the ground and their tails working back and forth furiously. He smiled because he realized that Gidget had ovulated and the hormones released in her urine could be detected by males several backyards away. Fortunately, he had kept her in the house, although some day he hoped to breed her and show Boston terriers as a hobby. He might even write it off on his tax forms as a promotional expense for his vet clinic.

Over the next few days the idea evolved to use Gidget's condition to attract business. Trolling Gidget through a newly developed neighborhood late at night would attract any untethered male. Spencer simply had to cage them, dispose of their tags, and escort the dogs back to his boarding kennel. Then he would wait for an ad to appear in the paper and phone the grateful owner to inform him that he had found the dog, hungry and languishing, by the roadside. He would accept his standard kennel fee but no reward. His selfless act would undoubtedly net a new client while word of his good Samaritanism would spread.

Spencer slowed as he approached the white façade that marked the entrance to Citrus Trace. The sign proclaimed that a few choice lots remained in Phase I, and that Phase II, which included a community pool and clubhouse, was about to begin. Gidget began to whine as her white stockinged feet traversed the dash. Her fluid brown eyes beseeched Spencer to stop and let her out.

"I'll stop once we clear the entrance, Gidget. Your wanton sexual behavior embarrasses me, dear." Spencer pulled over to the side of the road and shifted into park. Then he climbed out and opened the tailgate to check his three cages. The suffocating night air enveloped the petnappers like a wet cotton blanket. Gidget's red trolling leash lay in the back next to Spencer's faded Braves cap. He pulled the cap down and habitually tilted the brim to favor his right eye, as was his father's habit, and walked back to Gidget. "Well, girl, it's time to go to work."

As Spencer rolled the Suburban along at an imperceptibly slow pace Gidget raced behind with her head held high and her ears pointed skyward. Her four white stockinged paws blurred in a stiff legged trot as if to say, *Here I am boys. Let's go; I don't have all night.*

Suddenly a shadow loomed from behind a white stucco ranch. Gidget wasn't sure if she saw or smelled him first, and she skidded sideways briefly startled. The golden retriever lunged into full view in the moonlight. *My, you are a big one.* Gidget found herself at once both frightened and excited at the possibility. *God, I love this.*

Spencer finally noticed the ardent suitor and stopped the truck. Gidget slowed down exposing her backside to the retriever as he caught up and sniffed. His tail wagged eagerly as his nose confirmed his hopes. Like most Bostons, Gidget lacked a tail and settled for wagging her hind quarters in a most inviting manner.

"Gotcha!" whispered Spencer as he swept up the seventy-pound lovesick puppy and pushed him into the large wire cargo cage. "Nice job, Gidget." Spencer leaned over and offered her a Cheesie Treat.

It wasn't exactly what Gidget had hoped for, but in typical Boston terrier fashion she turned up the corners of her mouth as if to smile and swallowed the treat whole.

"We've gotta move on, girl, before someone hears us."

Gidget jumped up and licked Spencer's face to signal her readiness, and they set off again.

As he drove, Spencer rehashed in his mind the same justification for his crime that he had conjured after their first fateful run. In the first place, he was a superbly trained small animal vet with extensive postgraduate experience in surgery. Secondly, these dogs were obviously not well secured, and he was doing their owners a service by saving their dear companions from a worse fate, like being flattened by a citrus truck. These folks were getting a lesson in proper pet restraint as well as a good vet at a convenient location with Saturday morning hours.

Forty-five minutes later Gidget and Spencer had bagged a Westie and a Jack Russell terrier when they heard a loud bark followed by a crash as a dark hulk burst through a screened lanai and bore down on Gidget. Spencer had heard the bark and turned to see a German shepherd closing on Gidget like Rin Tin Tin on a rustler. He slammed on the brakes and Gidget, apparently sensing this was the dream date from Hell, took one final look then leapt up onto the tailgate.

Spencer hit the accelerator just as the beast reached the bumper, but for nearly a hundred yards the dog kept pace with the truck. Gidget looked anxiously over her shoulder at Spencer then back at the snarling menace. "Hang on, girl. We're almost out of here," he shouted .

Spencer failed to notice Delwood and Clayton as they sat in Delwood's pickup in an alcoholic stupor behind a brush pile on one of Citrus Trace's unsold lots. They had bought a twelve pack of Glades beer when the bar closed and drove up here hoping to catch a breeze off the river.

"Did you see that, Delwood?"

"That big goddamn truck? So what?" Delwood stuck his head out the window trying to catch some breeze in his face.

"No, I mean that wild animal chasing it."

"Didn't see it, Clayton." He reached under the seat for another beer. "Dammit the beer's gettin' warm. We shoulda' brought the cooler."

"It looked like one of those jockaroondies they been seein' down in Vero Beach."

"Drink up, Clayton. There ain't no such think as a jockaroondy. Not around here anyways."

Clayton downed his beer and threw the empty can out the window. "I bet it was," he muttered.

"You don't know shit, Clayton."

TWO

Spencer swept the vet journals and junk mail off the couch onto his office floor. He had just finished neutering a cat from the Humane Society and planned to catch a nap next to Gidget before his next appointment. The cat's new owner had presented the voucher, which was only half Spencer's usual fee, but he couldn't afford to turn any work away. He still owed a thousand dollars a month to Dr. Gifford Watts for the building and the practice. Unfortunately the practice was slower than Watts had implied, and the building was in constant need of repair. The roof leaked, its paint was peeling, and the asphalt parking lot was so cracked and potted it resembled a Bosnian mine field.

Yesterday, the kid from Poole's Pest Control pointed out the drywood termites. A quick trip on the Internet confirmed the pock-faced adolescent's prescription. Spencer would have to remove his medicines from the clinic, at which point Poole would enclose his entire building in a tent and fumigate. He would be closed down at least three days and Poole demanded five hundred dollars down payment. The little bastard termites were reprieved; Spencer didn't have the cash.

Just as Spencer was about to shove his financial worries aside and slip off to dreamland he heard a soft knock at his office door. "Dr. Hawley?"

"Yes, Missy."

"There's a man here that would like you to take a look at his dog."

"Is it urgent? I'm rather busy." Spencer knew he wasn't going to get out of this so he sat up.

"He's afraid he's been injured."

"All right, Missy. I'll be right there." Missy served as Spencer's receptionist, records keeper, dog walker, and surgical assistant. He couldn't afford to lose her, even if he couldn't afford to pay her what she was worth.

The former Alabama Peanut Princess had walked away from a lucrative vet practice in Melbourne because she sensed the doctor hated animals. They were always biting or scratching him, and he responded by calling them cruel names. As if that wasn't enough, her arms-dealing uncle had been killed on Premiere Island during an ATF gun bust, and her boyfriend had run off to Boca with a gay writer. She mentioned all of this casually one noon as she washed down her second peanut butter and jelly sandwich with a Mountain Dew. She didn't offer any further details, and Spencer shouldered too many problems of his own to inquire more about hers.

Walker Braddock III stood at the counter waiting for the vet's perky receptionist to return. Braddock was the proprietor of three funeral homes stretching from Winter Beach to Ft. Pierce where, unlike at this clinic, first impressions defined the business. From the carefully manicured hibiscus and bougainvillea draped entrance to the soft classical music emanating from the sequestered Bose speakers, his plush carpeted mortuaries impressed upon the grief stricken that their dearly departed had found peace in this final resting place. They were like the posh homes that rich and poor alike dreamed of owning, and in a subliminal manner said, *You don't want to display your beloved here in just any plain casket. This setting dictates the solid burled walnut or the brushed pewter with the gold handles and trim.*

It was no accident. Walker Braddock orchestrated that first impression not only to soothe the grieving but to encourage them to spare no expense for grandma, even though in life she might have been a blue-haired manipulative bitch making grandpa's life a living hell. Walker contended everyone deserved a proper burial, and "proper" meant coaxing every dollar he could from the next of kin. As long as he got the money, he didn't give a damn about their motives. Guilt paid his mortgage just as well as grief.

Spencer appeared in the doorway and appraised his wealthy-appearing client. "What can I do for you, Mr …?"

"The name is Braddock, Walker Braddock." Walker extended a beefy right hand bearing his Masonic ring.

Spencer shook Walker's hand and smiled. "I'm Spencer Hawley, the vet. Can I help you?"

"I wondered if you'd take a look at my German shepherd. Somethi
him last night and he broke through the screen in our lanai. I want to be sure he's
okay. He's quite valuable."

"Sure, bring him in and we'll have a look."

"Ajax is out in my Lincoln Navigator; I'll go get him." Walker returned to his
SUV and wrestled Ajax from the back seat. He dragged him into the clinic by his
choke chain. "Here he is." Walker slid a stiffened Ajax across the tiled floor. "I
must have forgotten his leash."

The vet stepped forward and nonchalantly extended a hand for the growling
Ajax to sniff. "He's a beautiful animal, Mr. Braddock."

"His mother was a grand champion. He cost me three grand."

"Do you plan to show him?"

"Hell, no. I own some valuable Greek antiquities. The security company rec-
ommended I get a watchdog, so I got the best."

"Greek antiquities? Thus the name Ajax, the huge and courageous hero of the
Trojan Wars."

"Are you a student of the classics, Doctor?"

"No, just an intro course in college. You know a pricey pedigree doesn't necessarily translate into a great watchdog."

"Maybe you don't think so, but I assure you I got the best of the gene pool
right there. He'd tear the heart out of a stranger."

"He doesn't seem to be after mine."

Ajax was licking Spencer's right hand as Spencer carefully examined his flanks
with his left. Spencer stood up straight and walked around the room as Ajax trotted at his side still trying to lick his right hand.

"Amazing. He took to you right away. I don't believe it," Walker grumbled.

"It's no big deal. He's fine physically but he needs to be trained. A good
watchdog will hold his ground and defend the premises, not bound through the
screen."

"Good point I suppose. You don't look old enough to be a vet. How long have
you been practicing?"

"Five years up North but just eight months here. It's been a bit slow."

"That shouldn't be the case, Doctor. You're good with animals. What you
need is better marketing."

"Thanks, but I've tried the ads and all the usual stuff."

"Have you used your full line of credit at the bank?"

"Just about but I've got some repairs due on this place."

"Well, I hope to God you do something about this reception area. I've seen better décor at a ten-minute oil change. It makes a lousy first impression, no matter how pretty your receptionist." Walker pulled a business card from his pocket and handed it to Spencer. "You come over and see me and we'll talk. I could use your advice and maybe help you out in return."

"How's that, sir?"

"I want to branch into pet crematoriums and a pet cemetery. There's a ton of money in it."

"My association would be construed as unethical." Spencer glanced over his shoulder at Missy.

Walker threw his head back and laughed. "Haven't you heard the old saying that doctors bury their mistakes? Come see me. I've learned there's a way around everything." Walker reached into his pocket and produced a gold money clip thick with cash. "How much do I owe you for Ajax's exam?"

"Ten should do it."

"Ten? You're kidding."

"He's okay. Just remember to mention me to your friends and neighbors, and, if you like, Missy can start a chart on Ajax."

Walker peeled off a ten and handed it to Missy. He smiled as he slipped his money clip back into his pocket. "With a little help you just might make it, Dr. Spencer Hawley." Then he laughed out loud and opened the door. "Come on, Ajax."

Ajax, obviously disappointed with their abrupt departure, hung his head and padded slowly toward the door.

The door slammed and Spencer looked down at the card Mr. Braddock had pressed into his hand. "Funeral business," he muttered and shook his head. He knew funeral directors back in Iowa who could sell grandma a burial suit for grandpa with two pair of pants. Then they'd view grandpa with just the top half of the casket open and him wearing no pants at all. "Like I'm so much better," he said aloud as he shoved the card into his pocket.

A smiling Lucinda Vickers, Treasure Coast realtor, extended her hand to the elderly couple from Illinois as they struggled to extract themselves from their car. "You'll have to admit this is an exquisite place."

The elderly couple slowly nodded their gray heads in unison. Earlier in the day they had responded to Lucinda's sales pitch like two bobble-head dolls, but after the seventh property their enthusiasm had faded like the Dodgers in September. Lucinda suspected that they had missed their afternoon naps.

"It's a rare day when we get a thirty-eight-hundred square foot ranch on two acres. And it's only four miles from the hospital."

"It's beautiful but it would be a lot to keep up," Mrs. Destasio ventured.

"Good help is so easy to find down here. And cheap too. Of course it doesn't hurt if you speak a little Spanish, if you know what I mean."

Mr. Destasio smiled weakly. "The pool is nice, and I've always wanted a three-car garage."

"All important when the kids and grandkids come down, Mr. Destasio. Very perceptive on your part."

Mr. Destasio hesitated. "Marge and I will have to think about it." He started for his Cadillac. Marge sensed his plan to extricate himself from the situation and leapt for the car door. "Marge and I will talk it over and call you in the morning."

"So many properties. It's just overwhelming," whined Marge. The leather seats of the Cadillac exhaled with a whoosh as her enormous butt came to a rest. "I thought it would be more like Evanston, Virgil."

"We're not in Chicago anymore, Marge. You go ahead and lock up, Ms. Vickers. We'll find our way back to the motel."

"I do have more treasures over on the island our agency can show you tomorrow."

Virgil smiled and waved. He had already started the car and turned on the air conditioning and couldn't have heard Lucinda's last remark. He slipped the car into reverse and backed away.

"Ass wipes," muttered Lucinda as she returned to the house. "Damn Northerners come down here for sunshine and orange juice expecting *Leave it to Beaver* neighborhoods with maple-lined streets. If you don't want to experience anything new, Marge, then why don't you just buy a goddamn sunlamp and a can of orange concentrate and stay in Evanston? It would save both Virgil and me a lot of time and trouble."

Lucinda stood in the tiled foyer and scanned the house. She had at least half an hour before T. Pascoe Redstone, the county supervisor, returned. Plenty of time to learn all about Tip. Friends called him Tip for short because the tip of his prominent nose curled downward like a cormorant's beak. She proceeded down the hall toward the master bedroom where she always started. Experience taught her that most dirty secrets are kept in the bedroom.

Her motivational tapes emphasized that it was always crucial to know everything she could about her client, her competition, and her associates, but Lucinda had already learned that in college. She caught her roommate, the sorority president, in bed playing fruit roll up with Ms. Atkins, the women's softball coach. All it took was a wink and a nod and two weeks later she had a single room on the first floor with her own key to the service entrance. Unfortunately, Ms. Atkins did not have the pull to get her football season tickets on the fifty yard line and was forced to resign from the university when Lucinda floated the rumor about her sexual preferences.

Finding something to hold over the chairman of the county zoning committee would be a real plum for a realtor, especially one who worked for a boss like Ian, a former interior decorator who ruled like an iron butterfly. He forbid any of the associates except his partner Ken from showing the prestigious highly-commissioned beach properties. Immune to the charms of women, Ian didn't care what people knew about him, and until this property came along, Lucinda's career was drifting into the proverbial real estate dead end cul-de-sac.

Lucinda opened the bedside drawer and assumed it belonged to Mrs. Redstone for it contained a Nite-Glow vibrator and a tube of K-Y Jelly neatly tucked behind two Danielle Steele novels. Tip's drawer contained a red hairpiece and a Johnny Wad video along with a small spiral note pad and two pens from her real estate office.

Lucinda gingerly lifted the note pad out from under his red rug and opened it. It contained two phone numbers, the name *Tom,* and the words *Island Orchard Estates.* Lucinda copied the numbers down on her Palm Pilot and returned the book and pens to the drawer.

She scanned the bedroom and master bath but learned little else. The medicine cabinet revealed that Tip needed Viagra to get it up, and his wife took Darvocet for her chronic headaches. Lucinda stared briefly into the mirror, then plucked a tissue off the counter and blotted her lipstick.

Her examination of Tip's sweater drawer unearthed two sheer negligees, one sea foam and the other black. Lucinda stroked the expensive material but she shuddered and shoved them back into the drawer when she realized they might actually belong to Tip himself.

In the back of Tip's sock drawer Lucinda felt a small plastic object. When she pulled out an unlabeled 3 ¼ inch floppy disk she cursed herself for not having some way to download it onto her Palm Pilot and made a mental note to look into it. Reluctantly she placed it back behind Tip's argyle socks and monogrammed handkerchiefs.

Just then Lucinda heard the front door open and someone enter the foyer. "Are you still here, Miss Vickers? Is it safe to come back?"

"Yes, Mr. Redstone. I'm back here in the bedroom just confirming some measurements." Lucinda fumbled through her purse for her tape measure. "The prospects just left and I was about to lock up." Lucinda found her tape measure and started down the hall toward Tip.

"Tell me, Lucinda, what did they think?"

"They were very impressed, Mr. Redstone."

"Call me Tip." Ever the politician, Tip extended a puffy hand and shook Lucinda's. He wore Italian loafers and argyle socks which offset aqua walking shorts and a red, green, and yellow swirled golf shirt that reminded Lucinda of a hurricane pattern on The Weather Channel. He also sported a white Miami Dolphins cap and a pair of geriatric wraparound sun goggles. The overall effect proffered a cross between Mr. Magoo and Elmer Fudd. "They were impressed, huh?"

"Absolutely, Tip. The Mrs. said she was reminded of some of the show places back home in Evanston."

"They make an offer?"

"Not yet. It may be too upscale for their budget. But I can assure you, they're excited and giving it careful consideration."

"Well, they better come close to our asking price." He pointed a pudgy finger at Lucinda. "You folks low balled it as it is."

Lucinda noted that Tip was approaching sixty, the age when everything he owned was a priceless treasure and everything he wanted to buy should cost what it did twenty-five years ago. "We just priced it to sell, Tip. Since you're building that new home on the beach you don't want to be sitting on two properties with mortgages."

"Don't worry how I'll handle it. You just get me my price." He wagged his finger at Lucinda as she smiled through clenched teeth, resisting the temptation to bite it off.

"Have you and the Mrs. thought any more about an open house on Sunday?"

"I told you, no goddamn open houses. I won't have the whole neighborhood in here snooping through our personal stuff. We have a lot of valuable antiques here."

Including the Mrs., thought Lucinda as she scanned Mrs. Redstone's outdated décor. "Tip, I'll be on site the entire time. I can assure you nothing like that would happen while I'm here."

"No thank you, Miss Vickers, and don't ask again."

THREE

"Mrs. Helseth, I can assure you that my staff and I will do everything in our power to make Leonard's—I'm sorry—Mr. Helseth's memorial service and interment a tribute befitting his exemplary life." Walker Braddock smiled as he brought his hands together in the prayer position. It was a pose right out of his funeral director's manual which stated: *This is a most difficult position to hold. One must be extremely careful not to be caught rubbing ones hands together lest it be construed as anticipation of a large recompense.*

Mrs. Helseth was a frail, blue-haired lady propped up by her guilt-ridden daughter. "We didn't realize how sick he was, or we would never have kept him out all day in the hot sun at the Magic Kingdom with the grandkids."

Mrs. Helseth nodded in dazed agreement. A green pillbox hat sat askew on top of her head, and her red lipstick looked as if it had been smeared on with toilet paper. Clearly she had been sedated. "The little fuckers kept demanding he take them on the Mad Hatter's tea cup ride," she slurred.

"Mom, they're just kids," pleaded the brunette.

"Six fucking times. I could tell he was sick."

"It sounds like he was a wonderful father and grandfather," interjected Walker as he reached out and ushered Mrs. Helseth into the soft peach-colored leather side chair next to his desk. "I'm sure you'll all want the best for him." He smiled at the brunette daughter as if he felt her pain, but his focus was on the full breasts under her sheer white blouse.

"And he was a Shriner. The Masons will attend you know."

Walker took a seat at his desk. "In that case you'll want to consider the walnut casket with the burled side paneling and hand-carved fez." Assisting the remorseful family of a Shriner was like picking a winning lottery ticket.

"That's so thoughtful, Mr. Braddock. We heard you were the best, and that's what we want for Papa." The brunette sobbed softly into her handkerchief as Walker shifted in his chair to adjust the arousal developing in his pants.

"That's quite all right, Ms....?"

"I'm sorry," she blubbered. "It's Helseth, too. I'm divorced and took back my maiden name."

Walker blushed and reached under the desk and again adjusted himself. It was as if he'd died and gone to funeral directors' heaven. He resumed the prayer position with his hands on top of the desk and shook his head as he clucked, "You two have to be strong for the children. I'm sure he was a father figure to them."

"More like a fucking ATM machine," snorted grandma.

"Yes, Mrs. Helseth. You're angry and that's good. It's a normal part of the grieving process." It was the only salient feature Walker remembered from his Elizabeth Kubler-Ross audio tapes. "But let's continue with the practical matter at hand."

Mrs. Helseth dozed off so Walker turned his attention to her daughter and focused on her breasts. "The base price for the walnut casket funeral is eighty five hundred dollars. That includes the use of the Shriner sanctuary, the crypt, the Shriner embossed order of service, acknowledgement cards, and interment. In honor of the community service Shriners provide, I include the armadillo protection at no extra charge."

Walker paused and cleared his throat, waiting for someone to speak, then proceeded. "It will be five hundred dollars extra for the hand carved Shriner emblem and I'm sure there will be a few other extras, although minor."

In truth, the emblem was carved with a computerized laser in Singapore and Walker bought them by the gross for twenty-five dollars apiece. The few other extras were actually a list of thirty items which would bring the cost of Mr. Helseth's funeral to over twelve thousand dollars.

"To avoid any financial hardship in your time of grief, we'll just bill the estate."

"You said something about armadillo protection?" the daughter asked.

Walker nodded. "A big problem here in Florida. Armadillos are natural burrowers and are particularly attracted to the final resting places of our loved ones where they do unspeakable damage."

"Cemeteries?"

"Yes, of course."

Ms. Helseth shuddered causing her bosom to quiver like a Jello mold at a Baptist potluck. "Fortunately our institution has developed a repellent that we apply to the crypt. Our usual fee is two hundreds and fifty dollars but waived in your father's case."

"And they seem so harmless."

"The damage can be irreparable," Walker sighed. As a matter of fact, Arnold Schwarzenegger Armadillo couldn't penetrate the concrete crypt required by Florida law, but the old legend of the necrophilic armadillo was one Walker Braddock could heartily embrace as well as capitalize on.

"My mother and I certainly appreciate your thoroughness, Mr. Braddock."

A small light on the base of the telephone began to flash. "Mrs. Helseth and Ms. Helseth, will you please excuse me for a moment. I have a call. Frederick will escort you to the display room where we have a model of Mr. Helseth's exquisite casket." Frederick, who seemed to have materialized from out of nowhere, solemnly extended his arm toward the doorway.

"Hello, Walker, how have you been?"

"Lucinda Vickers. Darling, it's been too long. How is your grandmamma?"

"I hate to disappoint you, Walker, but she's doing just fine. She lost her dog last night but that new vet found him."

"He's a handsome young man. I recommend you retrieve the dog yourself."

"Funny you should mention it. Mudge just called not more than half an hour ago and demanded I pick him up."

"I must stop in and see your grandmamma. I've been remiss with her living in the same subdivision and all."

"We'll have you to dinner real soon. Mudge would love sharing the family gossip with you. Unfortunately it usually involves me."

"If you'd just give up this career notion and settle down you wouldn't be the constant topic of scandal. You could be the wind beneath the wings of some up-and-coming executive and have ten times the money you are making now, Lucinda."

"Luncheons at Riomar Country Club, vanity plates on my convertible, Riverside Theatre, and weekends at the Gator games. Sounds like heaven and all for the low low price of producing a male heir and providing two blow jobs a month."

"Lucinda, I'm shocked!"

"No, you're not, Walker. You love it when I talk dirty. You've loved it since we were in high school."

"That was a long time ago," Walker added.

"And you just won't let it go, will you?"

His voice was a whisper now. "I can't forget that face—those eyes."

"We couldn't just leave her in your daddy's pool. You didn't mean for it to happen, Walker."

"But no one would have believed us."

"You're right, Walker. She was a beautiful girl and I saved your ass, but it's twelve years over. We don't need to rehash this every time we talk."

Walker sighed; his palms were beginning to sweat. "Why did you call?"

"I think a big real estate deal might be going down. Does the name Island Orchard Estates mean anything to you?"

"No, where did you get the name?"

"I can't reveal my source yet, but since you've attended the county board meetings to get your pet cemetery approved I thought you might have heard something."

"I can't say as I have."

"Actually that might give us more time."

"Us?"

"You don't get it do you?"

"What?"

"If developers are moving into this area with their eye on a particular property we can pool our resources and buy it out from under them."

Walker paused. "And sell it to them at a premium."

"That's the Walker Braddock I know and love. I can picture you now in that ludicrous undertaker pose rubbing your greedy little hands together."

"I've never been adverse to making obscene profits off the dead or the living. Let's work on it, hon."

Her talk with Walker reminded Lucinda that she had promised her grandmother she would stop by the vet's and pick up her errant dog. Every night before grandma retired she'd let the dog out but, with her failing short-term memory, she'd forget to let him back in. Lucinda usually spent three mornings a week scouring the neighborhood for Buster, the Jack Russell terrier.

"I must say your business certainly lacks curb appeal." Lucinda was in the lobby of Spencer Hawley's vet clinic waiting for his assistant to retrieve her grandmother's dog.

"I'm surprised to hear you say that, Ms. Vickers. *Southern Living* is planning to do a spread on us next month: "Treasured Animal Hospitals of the Old South.""

"And this is a Treasure Coast treasure?" Walker Braddock was right. Spencer Hawley was an attractive specimen who offered no apologies.

"Absolutely, and I understand they're going to include recipes, too: honey roasted retriever, key lime kittens, and my personal favorite onion crusted cocker."

He was playing with her, not intimidated by her initial insult. Lucinda liked that. "Maybe you'll invite me over the next time you find a spare cocker." She could play, too, and handed him her card.

The vet smiled and brushed back his brown hair as he read the card. "Lucinda Vickers, real estate associate," he recited then stuck the card in the pocket of his rumpled khakis. "If business doesn't pick up, I may require your services."

"I'll bet it's nothing a little paint and asphalt couldn't fix. You look competent."

"You're the second person today to recommend that, and I am competent."

Lucinda sensed she was pushing the game too far and decided to back off. Spencer Hawley might be worth stringing along. "My grandmother doesn't have a vet for Buster. Could I register him here?"

"Certainly. Buster's a healthy looking Jack Russell. He'd be welcome as would your grandmother."

He was all business now and not too bad at it. Polite. Not the hard sell she was used to. "What do I owe you for keeping him overnight?"

"Just my usual kennel fee—less twenty five percent since he plans to be a regular here."

"Thank you. Mudge will appreciate that, as well as the fact that you rescued Buster."

"Mudge?"

"That's what everyone calls Grandmother. It's an old family name she got tagged with. It's a Southern thing. I think it has to do with the Judge Mudge family up in Brevard County. We're related somehow. Mudge is the only one left in the family that cares about that stuff."

"So Mudge is old South while Lucinda is the new?"

He was teasing again. Although deeply tanned, Spencer Hawley obviously wasn't a native; but as he stood leaning against his own counter in loafers sans socks, khakis, and a white polo shirt, he appeared totally at ease flirting with this Southern girl, acting as familiar as if he'd lived here all his life. Lucinda was both charmed and resentful that he thought she could be won over as easily as if she were trailer trash.

Missy appeared at the door with a squirming Buster enveloped in her arms. He alternately licked Missy's face and yipped at Lucinda. Spencer watched as the two women assessed each other. Missy studied Lucinda in an attempt to match the owner's personality to the dog's. Spencer sensed Missy didn't perceive Lucinda as the Jack Russell type.

Lucinda, on the other hand, sized up Missy from more of a feline perspective. He watched her take in Missy's blonde hair then followed her eyes as they paused briefly at her breasts then took in her long firm legs. Content that Missy was not an immediate threat, she retracted her claws and forced a smile that conveyed all the warmth of Iowa's winter corn stubble.

"Thank you, miss." She reached awkwardly for the struggling dog and averted her face to avoid his kisses. Finally she released Buster who leapt to the floor and raced back and forth to sniff the feet of three adults trapped in an awkward silence.

Finally Spencer knelt down and calmed the dog by stroking him behind the ears. Buster regained his composure and began to pant. "I'll carry him out to the car for you. Jack Russell terriers are high energy dogs. They can be a handful."

"He's probably not the best choice for Grandmamma but she's not the kitten or poodle type. Come and visit us. You do make house calls don't you?"

"I have traveled to your neighborhood on occasion."

When they reached the car, Spencer dumped Buster unceremoniously into the back seat and Lucinda extended her hand. "Thank you again for rescuing Buster. Grandmamma might offer you a reward."

"Trusting me with his future care is enough reward; besides it's not my nature to let a valuable dog like that wander off into trouble." Spencer did his best to sound convincing, glad his father wasn't alive to see he had stooped to this.

"I'm sure we'll see you again real soon, Dr. Hawley." Lucinda smiled with the sincerity reminiscent of a cat rubbing against his leg.

Spencer Hawley had been around animals too long. He had developed a habit of categorizing everyone into one species or another. As a kid he worked long hours with his father, a large animal veterinarian in rural Iowa. Then he was off to Iowa State to study animal husbandry and vet medicine himself. A bitter divorce and bitterly cold winters drove him to Winter Beach after the death of his father.

He wasn't the first Hawley to seek his fortune in Indian River County. His great grandfather had followed the famous developer Herman Zeuch of Davenport, Iowa, to the area in the early nineteen hundreds when Herman developed the canal system that led to the growth of Vero Beach and the citrus boom. But he returned North to his farm after a few short years and never spoke about his family's experience or the daughter they left behind. He resumed raising corn and his Boston terriers while his neighbors smiled with the smug reassurance that indeed the grass wasn't greener outside Henry County.

FOUR

"Dr. Hawley, I'm Eldridge Stoval." Spencer, who'd been leaning on the counter reading a magazine, looked up as the towering black man swung his long arm forward in a slow arching loop and extended a rough hand. Spencer sensed the confident grace of a tiger as he witnessed his own hand being enveloped in a vise-like grip. Spencer also heard the clickety-click of a small dog's toenails on the tile, but before he could break eye contact with his imposing visitor the dog rounded the corner and disappeared down the hallway.

"O.J., come back here," the black man boomed.

"You didn't lose a dog did you?" Spencer asked cautiously. This was not a man he wanted to be caught stealing a dog from.

"No, but I hear you rescued a few."

"I seem to have found my share lately."

Eldridge paused for a moment, and Spencer sensed he was being stared down, as if Eldridge were a highway patrolman deciding between a speeding ticket and a warning. "I need some vitamins for my pups."

"No kiddin?" Spencer was relieved to change the subject. "I just got a new shipment in. How much do they weigh?" O.J. had disappeared into the bowels of the clinic but Eldridge showed no signs of concern.

"Twelve to eighteen pounds."

"Mixed breed."

"Boston terrier." Eldridge appeared mildly annoyed at Spencer's assumption.

"A solid breed. I've got one myself."

"I've been breeding them for years. If you got yours in this county, it probably came from my place."

"No, Gidget came down with me when I bought the practice. They've been part of the family since my great grandfather started raising Bostons in southern Iowa."

"Been in my family, too. I always brought them to Doctor Gifford, and I was sorry to see him go. He was a good vet, but he didn't take much pride in this place."

"You're not the first to point out the rustic nature of this place." Spencer handed Eldridge a bottle of vitamins.

"These will do," Eldridge responded without looking at the container. Then, as if anticipating Spencer's next question, he continued. "Tangela didn't need a cesarean her first time. Doc Gifford couldn't believe it."

"That is remarkable for a Boston terrier."

"Show quality markings, too. I'll show you. O.J., where the hell are you?" Eldridge bellowed down the hallway in the direction of Spencer's office.

Spencer suddenly remembered that Gidget was asleep on the couch in his office. "My God, I forgot my female is down there."

"That bitch in heat?"

"About ten days into it, dammit." Spencer started to run toward his office.

Just then a face peered around the door frame. Despite his apprehension Spencer couldn't help but admire the interloper's fine qualities. He had the requisite pug nose and proportioned square head with upright ears at the corners. His white blaze evenly split large milky brown eyes and led to a white shawl which encompassed both shoulders. Eldridge pegged it right; he was a show dog.

Eldridge smiled broadly, and Spencer could have sworn O.J. smiled back at Eldridge. "I've seen that look in his eyes before, Doc. If that's your office, I think O.J. just made you a granddaddy."

Gidget had curled herself into the corner of the worn brown couch against the arm where a cumulus cloud of stuffing erupted through the seam. She was sleeping soundly when she sensed another presence in the room. Keenly aware of the scent of a dog, she opened one weary eye to witness a male that looked much like the vision of herself in her master's long mirror.

He appeared in the doorway like a dreamy apparition with penetrating maple-syrup eyes and erect ears. He panted silently, his velvet pink tongue modestly exposed above a broad white chest. The overall effect was that of regal self-confidence.

Gidget cocked her head and shifted her weight as she prepared to rise and greet her guest. The stranger approached Gidget and without fanfare gracefully leapt onto the couch. He paused as Gidget rose to her feet half in protest to this intrusion on her nap, curious as to the intentions of this look-alike male version of herself.

At no sign of being rebuffed the handsome dog stepped forward cautiously and began to sniff at Gidget's private places. Gidget's heart pounded in her canine breast as she became acutely aware of what was about to happen. What she couldn't comprehend was the absence of her master, the tether, and his slow moving truck. *Was it possible that she was about to lose her virginity to this handsome prince?*

Before Gidget could even contemplate her own rhetorical question, it was answered. The regal specter took her there on the couch without so much as an introduction. It was as if he sensed the invisible tether of her intrusive master, and that his window of opportunity was as narrow as Gidget's introitus. Gidget had little choice but to succumb to her own animal instinct and the powerful thrusts of her mounted sovereign.

It was over as quickly as it began. The interloper withdrew from Gidget and leapt to the floor at the sound of a stranger's voice calling his name. "O.J., O.J.!" An already trembling Gidget shivered with sudden unexplained fulfillment and a vague sense that she and the dog named O.J. were forever bonded by this brief coupling.

FIVE

Walker Braddock, awakened by a recurring sense of suffocation, sat on the edge of his king-sized bed and struggled to regain his breath. The sound of his stridulant gasps filled the otherwise empty bedroom and his heart pounded like a cheap reggae band as perspiration soaked through his silk pajamas.

He wrapped his arms around himself and pleaded, "God, make it stop!" Logically he knew it would eventually stop whether he appealed to a divine being or not, but he feared for his heart. What if he had a heart attack here alone in the house before the panic attack subsided? He'd be fucked and headed for his own pre-selected solid teak casket which he proudly referred to as the Rolex. He wanted to go out in style but not yet, not for another fifty years.

Walker picked up the phone to dial 911 then stopped. "A shot of bourbon, that's all I need." Clutching his pounding chest he slowly walked over to the dresser where he kept bourbon and a glass for just such emergencies. Hands shaking he managed to pour two fingers then added a third for good measure and tossed it back quickly before it splashed out of the glass onto the Spanish-tiled floor.

"Jesus, Mary, and Joseph," he said as he shuddered and leaned forward supporting himself with both arms on the dresser. The security light in the backyard provided just enough illumination for him to assess the man in the mirror.

"What a sorry bastard you are. You're not even thirty five and you've got saddle bags hanging under your eyes, Gabby Hayes' cheeks, and an ass wider than Trigger's. Your gut sticks out so far you haven't seen your own six shooter in two years." The room was silent; no voice ventured forth to refute Walker's claims.

Walker felt his pulse slow as the pounding in his ears began to recede. Self deprecation usually had that effect, that and the urge to drink himself back into unconsciousness.

It was always the same dream, the dream of the drowning brown girl. She screamed the desperate scream of someone whose lungs were filling with water. It wasn't high pitched, but instead muffled by the water in the back of her throat as it eddied and bubbled before pitching down over her vocal cords.

Walker thrashed frantically to reach her, but the river's current pulled him further away until he could no longer hear or see the little brown girl. Then he washed ashore and was aware of the featureless faces of others surrounding him. He was suddenly aware of his own nakedness, but no one would hand him a towel.

Then the brown girl drifted ashore. She too was naked, but her skin had turned gray and cold, her lifeless brown eyes staring up at Walker through the tangled roots of the mangroves. Her head bobbed silently on the water as Walker frantically wrestled with the mangrove's tentacle-like roots. He tried to scream for help, but the words caught in his throat and he began to choke. That's when he would awaken. Always the same.

Eldridge Stoval didn't need an alarm because he always awakened at 4:00 a.m. and prepared to work his citrus groves. He could smell the strong aroma of coffee coming from the kitchen. His automatic coffeemaker had faithfully kicked on at 3:45 a.m., as it had every morning since his wife died.

Some of his own people said Eldridge was cursed because he had become an uppity boss with his own groves and his pure-bred dogs. *That's why God drowned his only child her senior year in high school then took his wife when she couldn't bear the grief no more. That's what God does when folks gits uppity. Sooner or later they gits it awright.*

Eldridge sat on the edge of the bed and rubbed his face as he asked God to help him get through another day alone. It was a short prayer, but he never asked for more because he didn't deserve even this one request.

He'd had plenty of chances to sell the groves and go to work for the conglomerates. Then he might have had more time to lend support to his grieving wife. But he kept the land that his grandfather had cleared and planted even after the white men returned north to their corn farms or moved onto the better land drained by Mr. Zeuch's canals. That new land was segregated from the old railroad camp they called Gifford and closer to the gleaming new white churches of Vero Beach.

When he wasn't invited to join the Indian River Citrus Growers, his grandfather studied whatever information he could get from Florida A&M by oil lamp at the kitchen table. But mostly he spent time in the orchards observing what the change of seasons revealed.

That's what Eldridge had done when he lost his daughter Jasmine. He immersed himself in his orchards in unspeakable grief, a grief he couldn't share even with his wife. When he retired to the orchards, she retired to her room relinquishing the rest of the house to the dynasty of Boston terriers.

Lucinda Vickers enjoyed her vivid dreams. She slept in the nude and consequently usually appeared nude in her dreams, but it didn't bother her. She'd skinny dipped with the boys since she was eight years old, and still enjoyed it on occasion. In tonight's dream she had spiked hair—purple at the tips. And a tattoo of a slender black she-panther whose cold penetrating eyes originated above her pubic area as its body wrapped around to her back where the tail proceeded up her spine.

Lucinda's dreams were never uniformly heterosexual. As far back as she could remember she was attracted to males as well as females, which made for endless erotic possibilities and pairings. Tonight she had gone to bed thinking about Spencer Hawley and had given little if any consideration to Missy, his receptionist.

Now as Spencer backed her naked body against his tilted stainless steel surgical table and began to tie her wrists upward to the corners where he strapped the little animals' paws, she caught a glimpse of Missy as she entered the room. She too was completely unadorned except for the small white poodle she clutched to her bare breasts.

Lucinda strained against the cold steel of the table not to escape but rather to reach out to Missy to caress beyond the poodle. Spencer tugged at the cords, causing her to wince in pain. Lucinda bit her lip and peered deep into Missy's bottomless sea-blue eyes.

Missy frowned then extended the little dog, who began dutifully licking at the tethers and Lucinda's wrists. His feathery tongue felt soft, moist. Then Missy smiled, leaning forward as she extended her tongue to caress Lucinda with her own small moist flicks. She moved slowly down Lucinda's sweating body as Spencer looked on.

Lucinda shuddered so hard the bed shook. With her head thrown back she clutched herself as wave after blissful wave washed over her body. When it subsided, she lay wide awake on damp sheets only partially satisfied, but calm in her resolve to get to know Dr. Hawley's receptionist better.

Spencer Hawley slept soundly on the living room couch as the portable television flickered in muted silence. A small army of brown ants marched single file from his half empty can of Pepsi across the tile toward the front door. He had barely made it through supper and the third inning of the Atlanta game before slipping into the dreamless sleep of the dead.

Gidget lay curled up in a chair in the corner. She had restlessly alternated between the warm chair and the cool tile floor. Finally she surrendered the tile to the little brown invaders and closed her eyes. Something had happened today that she didn't fully understand, but it felt right. Inside her changes were already in progress. She wasn't sure what they were, but was convinced somehow that her life and Spencer's would never be the same again.

SIX

Lucinda sat at her desk and looked at her stack of messages, then looked at the phone numbers she had found in T. Pascoe Redstone's drawer. One was a local number, but whose? She debated whether or not to just dial it and find out who it belonged to, but what if they had caller ID and it got back to old Tip? Even a county commissioner could put two and two together.

She fingered through her messages. Redstone wanted her to call about his house and demanded to know when she would show it again. Marge and Virgil had passed up this bargain. After viewing the secluded Redstone place, they had jumped at the chance to buy a condo in a gated community with twenty-four hour onsite surveillance.

Ian, her boss, had left her two messages directing her to cover the open houses on Saturday and Sunday up in Sebastian. The Refuge was a low-end development made up of cheap tract homes whose only attractive feature was their arched entrance. The septic systems were backing up in the first phase, and the last storm lifted off eighty percent of the shingles and deposited them in the adjacent trailer park. With the bad press and threatened lawsuits, the developer had put on a full court press every weekend including balloons, hot dogs, and a gray-headed trio hired to massacre Glenn Miller tunes. With all the charm of a high school production of *Oklahoma*, a platoon of agents in cowboy hats and fringed shirts rushed pale-skinned snowbirds from one building site to another in yellow surried golf carts.

Lucinda sifted through the messages until she came to the one from Missy at Dr. Hawley's office. It was a reminder to review Buster's shot record and bring him in for his boosters. Lucinda smiled and contemplated how she might connect with Missy. Buster could only get so many shots.

She looked again at the local number she'd found at Redstone's. "Fuck it!" she said and picked up the phone and dialed.

"Sebastian Inn, how may I direct your call?"

Damn, thought Lucinda. That wasn't going to help much. "Do you have conference rooms?"

"We do have a conference room, and food can be catered in from Captain Hiram's across the street. Would you like to speak to our manager?"

"Thank you, that's all I needed to know. I'll get back to you." Lucinda hung up the phone and leaned back in her chair. If Redstone had met with a developer named Tom at the inn, then Tom probably came from out of town. It could also mean this project was really big if it involved outside developers. A big outfit out of Miami or maybe even Disney from Orlando. Redstone would have been recognized in Sebastian even if it was on the north end of the county, and maybe someone saw something. A cocktail at Captain Hiram's would certainly ease the pain of donning a cowboy hat and passing out hot dogs at the Refuge.

At 5:15 Spencer had just finished putting Beebee, a twelve-year-old, champagne-colored toy poodle, back into her kennel for the night. Her octogenarian owner had boarded Beebee with Spencer for the next month while she cruised the Mediterranean. She had proudly confessed that Beebee was very socially sought after by the other canines at Premiere Island. Of course she was clueless to the fact that Beebee was in heat.

Spencer was reaching for the closed sign on the front door when he noticed a woman in a BMW convertible brake hard on U.S. 1 and careen into the parking lot. The car stopped an inch short of the rear bumper of his Suburban. As the woman approached the door, Spencer's first reaction was to point at the closed sign, but then he recognized Lucinda and unlocked the door. "Good evening, Miss Vickers. I've just closed. Can I help you?"

Gidget scurried out from behind Spencer and began to sniff Lucinda's shoes. "Hello, Spencer. And it's Lucinda by the way." She stepped back from the advancing dog. "I was driving up to Captain Hiram's for happy hour, saw a car, and thought you or your assistant might like to tag along."

"Get down, Gidget," Spencer commanded. Then he smiled at Lucinda like a first grader who's just been picked by his teacher to take the bat and ball out for recess. "It would be immoral to let you drink alone. Why not?"

"Let's take my car, and leave the impression that the dedicated doctor is working late."

"Fine." Spencer studied the convertible. "I'll just put Gidget in the office." Gidget, who had been eagerly sniffing the bushes for deposits of the day's patients, looked up at the mention of her name. "Come on, girl." Gidget trotted over and followed Spencer down the hall to his office. "I'll just be a minute," Spencer shouted over his shoulder.

Lucinda walked over to the reception desk and paused. The scent of Missy's perfume lingered. It was light innocence with just a hint of jasmine. "Captain Hiram's serves excellent crab cakes if we decide to have dinner," she shouted toward the empty hallway.

"I've never had crab cakes. Are they dessert, dinner, or breakfast?"

"What planet did you say you're from?"

"Iowa." Spencer stood in the doorway drying his hands and face with a towel. "Fish sticks are about as high as we go on the seafood chain."

Lucinda made a face. "You've got a lot to learn about Florida, Doc."

"Then let's get started." He threw the towel down on a chair and motioned toward the door.

They reached the car and Lucinda tossed the keys to Spencer. "You do know how to handle a straight stick don't you?"

"I hold my own," Spencer responded just before he caught Lucinda's double entendre.

"Sounds like you don't get out much, Doctor." Lucinda winked and quickly opened her own door and slid into the passenger seat. Her skirt slid up her thigh and she proceeded to smooth the material as if to draw Spencer's attention to her legs. He reached over to fasten his seat belt and briefly admired the view. He'd been without sex too long to turn down a tease.

Spencer eased the powder blue BMW into traffic and smoothly shifted into second gear. "Nice machine."

"Typical male response. Your Suburban is a machine, Spencer. This is a fucking work of art." Lucinda slipped on her sunglasses and tilted her head back against the headrest and closed her eyes.

Spencer laughed and shifted into third. They passed struggling strip malls, and convenience stations gave way to citrus groves interspersed between middle class condo projects on the river side of the highway. Korean War era mom and pop motels and trailer parks dotted the west side. "You make any money selling this stuff?" Spencer waved his arm in the general direction of a boarded-up convenience store.

"You'd be surprised," Lucinda shouted over the wind stream. "The real money is invested in development further east on the barrier island and A1A, but Disney's timeshare at the east end of the Wabasso bridge has prompted a twelve-pump filling station and a large Publix grocery store on this end. The real estate from Winter Beach to Sebastian is about to explode with new development. These old failing businesses and the struggling citrus groves near the Disney property are a developer's wet dream. A Wal-Mart was next, but unfortunately I couldn't convince a group of Vero businessmen to invest in some prime frontage property. These good ol' boys still don't trust a businesswoman, and I threaten the hell out of their little homemaker better halves."

"I don't find that hard to believe." Spencer stole another glance at Lucinda's thighs and speculated that legs like that would be a powerful threat to any marriage.

"Look out!"

Spencer looked up to see a big-ass blue Caddy stopped in his lane to make a left turn. "Damn." He swerved hard to the right kicking up gravel as he maneuvered around the blue whale.

"Better keep your eyes off the real estate and on the road, Doctor."

"Sorry, but I think I got some dust or something in my eye. I'll be fine now."

Lucinda smiled, just a bit too triumphantly for Spencer's taste, then leaned back against the headrest and adjusted her sunglasses.

When they arrived at Captain Hiram's the lot was half empty; it didn't offer an early bird special. Spencer pulled into a spot between two SUV's both sporting pro-life and Bush bumper stickers.

Lucinda looked into the rearview mirror and swept back her hair then reached over and casually rested her hand on Spencer's thigh. "This is going to take a minute, love. Why don't you go in and get us a table while I fix the damages."

Spencer looked down at the hand on his thigh then back at Lucinda. "Are you sure you'll be safe out here all by yourself?"

Lucinda smiled and retrieved her hand. "Something tells me I'll be even more safe. Now go get us a table."

Spencer reluctantly left Lucinda to fix what needed fixing. As he entered the restaurant he was greeted by a young girl dressed like a Jimmy Buffett groupie. She wore short shorts and a small Hawaiian print halter top that barely managed to contain her breasts. Spencer waved her off and pointed to the bar.

The bar also had a Key West appeal. The chairs, bar stools, table, and the bar itself were all either made or trimmed with bamboo. The ceiling was faux thatched roof and the east side opened onto a deck overlooking the Indian River. The deck was built for the winter tourist season. Only fools and scantily clad boaters would sit out there in July. Spencer chose a table in the corner where it felt the coolest.

A refreshed Lucinda appeared shortly and joined Spencer. "You own the cutest little dog. What kind is it?"

"It's a Boston terrier. My family has raised them for generations."

"Male or female?" She turned her attention to the other patrons as if she were looking for someone.

"Female and pregnant I'm afraid."

"That's bad?" Lucinda turned back to Spencer suddenly interested in his little soap opera.

"I don't think we're ready to start a family."

Lucinda laughed. "How long have you two been married?"

Spencer looked at her quizzically, then laughed. "I'm sorry. I guess I'm a little too emotionally attached. Bostons often have trouble with their litters and I've put off getting Gidget in a family way because I don't want to lose her."

"Do we know the father?"

"Sort of. It's O.J., another Boston owned by a man named Eldridge Stoval. Do you know him?"

Lucinda twisted in her chair and tried to get the bartender's attention. "Everyone knows of Eldridge Stoval, but I doubt anyone knows him well. He's got a citrus operation in Winter Beach, one of the few that hasn't caved into the conglomerates. It's also prime property right between Highway 1 and I-95. If that ever got rezoned residential and he decided to sell, who knows what he'd rake in."

"Would he do that?" Spencer spoke to the back of her head. Her auburn hair was styled short but feathered over her collar. She looked good dressed casual like this, but then she'd look good in a feed sack.

"Like I said, no one knows him well enough to say." She finally caught the bartender's attention. He smiled in recognition and returned an effeminate wave. Returning to Spencer she leaned forward and, like a teenager in the lunch room, looked from side to side before speaking in a low voice. "He lost his daughter and only child to a freakish drowning back when I was in high school just after Vero Beach integrated. His wife died a few years later—of grief they say. He pretty much keeps to himself and his groves."

"Did they think she was murdered, his daughter I mean?"

"It was a bit suspicious. They found her nude body tangled in some mangrove roots up on the Sebastian River, but she hadn't been molested. No one ever figured out how she got there."

"Is it a common place to swim?"

"Not that area, but she couldn't swim anyway." Lucinda shivered as the bartender approached. "Unwanted pregnancies and dead black girls. Dear God, let's talk about something else." She straightened and smiled at the bartender as if they were the only two in the room. "Stephen, how are you?"

"Not good, Lucinda. It's been slow and they want me to clean the kitchen in my spare time, but I won't have it." Stephen was a short plump twenty-something with thinning blonde hair and a voice that suggested toy poodles and interior decorating.

"You're wasting your talent here, Stephen. We should talk."

"I'll say. Hurricane season starts in a few weeks. I just may move inland until November."

"You should find some nice boy and settle down."

Spencer detected a blush before Stephen responded. "You should talk, girl. And who's this fine specimen you dragged in off the street?" he asked as he turned to Spencer.

"I'm sorry, this is Dr. Hawley. Dr. Hawley, this is my dear friend Stephen." She was laying it on thick like she wanted something.

Spencer extended his hand as Stephen withdrew clutching his breast in mock reverence. "A doctor, Lucinda. Good work, girl!"

"Just an animal doctor. Sorry to disappoint," Spencer responded well aware of Stephen's imminent disenchantment.

"And just a new friend, Stephen." Lucinda reached over and patted Spencer's hand.

"Oh well, the evening's young, love. What can I get you two?"

"Scotch on the rocks, dear."

"And for the doctor?"

"C.C. and seven," Spencer said.

"Careful, Lucinda, he must be from the Midwest. That's their drink, and he'll stick you with the tab, too." Stephen smiled broadly at Spencer and floated back to the bar.

"We need to talk business, Stephen," Lucinda said over her shoulder.

"I'll be back, hon."

A few minutes later Stephen returned with their drinks and, since the bar was nearly empty, pulled up a chair and sat down. "Now, how can I advance your real estate career? Short of sexual compromise that is."

Lucinda turned to Stephen as if Spencer had just melted into the floor. "I'm representing T. Pascoe Redstone. He's selling his place and moving to the island."

"That's big bucks. More than his daddy left him."

"That's what I'm thinking. Has he been around lately?"

"As a matter of fact he has. Comes in about once a week and meets with Tommy."

"Tommy?"

"He's a businessman from Miami who's been in here lately throwing his money around."

"What's his company?" Lucinda was looking very interested now. Intense. No more joking.

"I'll think of it in a minute. He's a looker. Dark and handsome. Real Miami with the silk shirts, linen slacks, Gucci loafers, and overstated gold chains. Too macho for my taste."

"Sounds Cuban."

"No, just trying to look the look. Empire ... something or other. That's the company. Anyway he and Pascoe always take the corner table. Maybe he's the architect for the new place."

"Could be." Lucinda didn't sound convinced. "What do they talk about?"

"I don't know. They clam up whenever I bring their drinks. Like I'm an irritation. I think Tommy's a homophobe, which is ironic since rumor has it T. Pascoe is a switch hitter."

"No kidding, Stephen. Intriguing." She brought her drink to her lips and paused to wink at Spencer.

"Just what I hear from the boys. No specifics."

Thank God for no specifics, thought Spencer as he sipped his drink and looked out over the river. He realized now that Lucinda's invitation to Captain Hiram's had been an afterthought. Her real purpose had been to come here and pump Stephen for information.

"Wait, Lucinda, Enterprise Promotions. That's the company." Stephen clapped his hands gleefully. "Sounds like something to do with rock concerts."

"I can find out easy enough, darling. Now why don't you get the doctor and me a fresh drink?" Lucinda sipped her scotch and winked over the top of the glass at Spencer. She was evidently done with Stephen and had returned her attention to her guest.

"I'm sorry, Spencer. Just some business I needed to clear up," Lucinda said when Stephen returned to the bar.

"I'm guessing it's the real reason you came here."

"Stephen's sweet," Lucinda responded wistfully as if she hadn't heard Spencer. "But he's let his sexuality define who he is, and he'll never get anywhere with that outlook."

"He complains but he seems happy enough working here."

"He has a powerful gift but he doesn't see it."

"I see," Spencer nodded. He considered himself liberal but had never considered homosexuality a gift, if that's what Lucinda indeed meant. When his second drink arrived he smiled at Lucinda, then Stephen, and decided to go with the flow. He'd contemplate this new paradigm later.

Several hours later Spencer sat staring into his glass as he contemplated his numb lower lip. He had gotten drunk and predictably morose. "What was I saying?"

"You mentioned something about needing to take out one of your boarders at the clinic," Lucinda replied.

"Business has been sooo bad." Spencer rested his chin on his chest as Lucinda waved her credit card at Stephen.

Stephen approached the table and reached for the card. "I said you'd get stiffed for the bill," he scolded.

"Just keep an eye on him, Stephen, while I go to the ladies room."

Stephen turned to leave. "I just hope you're the one driving, hon."

Spencer looked up. "Business is bad; I've got some work to do."

"I just hope it's not surgery, Doctor."

"Nooooo, I call it trolling. Where'd Lucinda go?"

"She'll be right back, sir. Just sit right there and don't move."

"Okay. Is my speech slurry?"

"Just a teensy."

Lucinda returned from the rest room just as Stephen arrived with her card and the bill. "Is he all right?" she asked as she focused on the bill.

"He says he needs to go trolling, but if it involves a vehicle I think you both ought to sleep it off."

"Thanks, Stephen, we'll be fine."

Spencer pushed back from the table and slowly stood up. He looked around as if he had just awakened and wasn't sure where he was. "Let's go, Lucinda. I think you'd better drive this time."

Spencer fell sound asleep the minute Lucinda started the car and slept all the way back to his clinic. He awakened and sat up straight as Lucinda pulled in next to his truck. "Spencer, are you sure you can drive yourself home from here? If something happened to you, I'd feel responsible."

"Thanks, but I feel better now. The night air always sobers me up." Spencer began to fumble for his keys. "Besides, I've got some work to do."

"Does trolling require a driver? Because if it does I'd better help."

"Who said anything about trolling?"

"You did to Stephen back at Hiram's."

"Oh."

"What's trolling?" she asked.

Spencer paused then asked, "Can you keep a secret?"

"You wouldn't believe all the secrets I keep, Doc."

Spencer stared at Lucinda and tried to focus on her face. Finally he smiled and said, "You take my keys and start the truck. I'll go get Beebee."

Once Beebee and the gear were loaded Spencer climbed into the truck and directed Lucinda to head north on U.S. 1 then west. As they drove he once again related his business woes and proceeded to explain trolling.

Lucinda, who had had her share of alcohol at Hiram's, began to giggle. "I can't believe you dragged that little dog of yours behind the truck."

"The trick is to drive very slowly."

"But she got pregnant."

"Not trolling. That was somewhere else; I didn't take precautions."

"That's what they all say."

"Just stop here in this subdivision if you still want to help."

Lucinda stopped and shifted into park. Spencer rolled out of the passenger side and slammed the door. "Shhhhh, Spencer." Lucinda put her finger to her lips and giggled again.

"It's not funny. We could get arrested." Spencer began to tether a perplexed looking Beebee to the back bumper. Once back in the truck he directed Lucinda to drive slowly around the complex. "And don't hit any dogs for Christ's sake."

"I won't. You just watch out your own window." Lucinda was into it now. Beebee resisted momentarily but found it futile, lest she choke, and began to follow at a trot.

For the next half an hour they slowly cruised Tropic Splendor subdivision. The buzz of the alcohol had worn off and a sleepy Lucinda began to lose interest. "I can't see a damn thing." She flipped on the headlights.

"Turn them off." Spencer snapped. He'd fallen asleep himself.

"How am I supposed to see?"

"Use the parking lights. And you're going too fast. Slow down."

"You're upsetting me, and I drive faster when I'm upset." Lucinda reached up and adjusted the rearview mirror.

"What are you looking for?"

"The dog."

"What dog?"

"The one we are trolling with. Beebop or whatever her name is."

"Sweet, Jesus," Spencer moaned. "We were supposed to give her a break. Stop the truck!" Lucinda hit the brakes and Spencer spilled out.

"Oh no," he cried as he broke into a run toward Beebee. Beebee wobbled like a newborn calf then braced herself on all four legs. Her tongue dangled from her open mouth as her depleted condition was beyond panting. Spencer reached out to her but her glassy stare showed no signs of recognition. At his touch her legs folded like a cheap card table and Beebee was dead before her head hit the street.

Lucinda arrived to find Spencer on his knees with his ear pressed against Beebee's chest. "What's her problem, Doc?"

Spencer looked up and said, "She's dead; we've killed her." He pushed himself away from the dog's lifeless body and sat on the road and buried his head in his hands.

"Bummer, Doc."

Spencer slowly raised his head. "Bummer? Is that all you can say?" He took a deep breath. "I've just willfully destroyed a pedigreed dog and could lose my license—not to mention the lawsuit, and all you can say is *bummer?*"

"You don't have to get all melodramatic about it. I was just thinking of all that money you stand to lose."

"Money?"

"Yes, the boarding fees for the next month as well as the incidentals like grooming and exercise sessions. It must add up to nearly a thousand bucks— more than that dog was worth."

"That money is the least of my problems."

"If she'd only died of natural causes the day before her owner returned. At least then you wouldn't be out your kennel fees or your license."

"Sure, and if my aunt had balls she'd be my uncle." Spencer rose to his feet and dusted himself off. He and Lucinda stood in silence as they gazed down at the poodle's lifeless carcass in the early gray light of dawn.

Finally Lucinda spoke. "Have you got one of those big free-standing freezers?"

SEVEN

Spencer forced one eye open and faced Gidget, who promptly licked his face and backed into a sitting position before emitting a short yelp. Spencer sat up and wiped his face with the sheet. "All right, I'm up. Oh, God, my head," he groaned.

Gidget yipped again and leapt from the bed for the kitchen where she promptly began to push her food bowl across the floor toward her approaching master. "I'm coming, Gidget. I'm coming." Since her pregnancy began, Gidget's appetite had become insatiable. Signs of motherhood already showed in her girth and teats, and she wouldn't be leaping onto or off the bed much longer.

Spencer poured a bowl of Materna Chow for Gidget, and for no particular scientific reason, poured some egg substitute over the top before pouring the rest into a fry pan on the stove. He turned on the burner and proceeded to retrieve his Saturday paper.

He opened the front door and waved half-heartedly to Mrs. Helseth, his neighbor, who merely scowled and stomped back into her house. Spencer attributed her attitude to the fact that her husband had recently passed away, that is until he realized he was standing in the doorway in his Jockey shorts.

He threw the paper on the counter and retrieved his running shorts and T-shirt from the floor of his closet. As he struggled to get the shirt over his head he stirred his scrambled eggs. Gidget, oblivious to the world around her, wolfed down her puppy casserole.

Last night's fiasco with Lucinda had been Spencer's first social engagement since he'd had lunch a month ago with the rep from Vet Surgical. His deep freeze stood accusingly in the corner and his tongue tasted like it had been dipped in kitty litter.

At the bar Lucinda seemed to recognize everyone who walked through the door. The men were genuinely glad to see her while their wives enthusiasm approached that of an enema recipient, which didn't surprise Spencer. Lucinda was a long-stemmed beauty with the cool marble complexion of a model. She had that quality that made any man she addressed feel like he was the only one in the room, and that guaranteed very few close women friends.

Spencer wasn't totally unaccustomed to Lucinda's style. Every small town and university faculty had a Lucinda. Yet something about Lucinda was different and he couldn't quite put a finger on it. She didn't just collect men, nor would she marry for power like his wife had. She wanted real power for herself, the kind she sensed men held.

Spencer's wife married him because he was a doctor, and naively thought all doctors made piles of money and ran their practices from the country club. Raised in the big city of Cedar Rapids, Iowa, she was clueless about the isolation and boredom of small town life. She was also clueless about what a large animal vet smelled like at the end of a day spent knee deep in cow and hog manure.

She forced Spencer to undress in the garage, then shower the minute he got home. Then she splashed him with expensive colognes. Spencer's arrival at any social gathering was predictably announced by the overwhelming scent of Armani or Calvin Klein. His friends gave him the same wide berth his wife did in the bedroom.

After three short years in Newbridge, where the biggest social event of the year was the summer art festival and the pork producers bar-b-que, a bored and sexually-frustrated Tammy Hawley suffered small town burnout. It didn't matter that the Newbridge Festival was rated a four star event by the Iowa Pork Producers, or that tradition dictated that the local veterinarian's wife act as co-chair. Tammy packed her suitcase, returned to Cedar Rapids, and promptly began screwing her mother's dentist.

It took three more harsh winters of treating livestock before Spencer himself burned out in Newbridge. By then, having sworn off cologne forever, he was tired of smelling like a hog who had just showered with Dial soap. He was also tired of dining at the local café with desperate farmers who sat in their overalls and feedcaps brooding over their steaming coffee. When his father died and left him the business, he didn't have the heart to continue nor the enthusiasm for another pork festival.

He simply said, "To Hell with it," and sold out to a practice in a nearby town. Then he packed Gidget in his Suburban and headed for this place in Florida where, according to family legend, his great grandfather had once settled to raise oranges. Winter Beach by name was an idyllic oxymoron where the natives had never seen snow nor suffered the pungent odor of hog shit.

Gidget had finished her chow and was now sniffing around Spencer's freezer. She had apparently forgiven him for locking her in his office all night. It had been so long since Spencer had mingled with real people that he felt energized despite the fact that Beebee had taken up residence in the freezer.

Spencer finished his eggs and placed his plate on the floor for Gidget to lick clean. After he showered and shaved, he spent the rest of the morning expending his new-found energy. He washed the dishes while he ran the laundry, then vacuumed and scrubbed the floors, putting off until last the mildew treatment of his shower. It was 1:00 before he sat down to read the paper.

His hangover had abated when the phone rang at 1:30. "Hello."

"Dr. Hawley?" It was a man's voice, familiar yet hesitant.

"Yes, speaking."

"This is Eldridge Stoval, O.J.'s owner."

"The sire of Gidget's new charges."

"So she is pregnant? I'm sorry about that."

"We're adjusting. Besides I should have kept the door shut. I assume O.J. will be forgoing his usual stud fee?"

A soft laugh at the other end. "Yes, I believe it could be waived, but I wonder if we might talk."

"Professionally or socially, Mr. Stoval."

"I'm afraid I'm not much good at social talk, but that's what I mean. I wondered if you might come over to my place at the grove." He paused. "For a drink." Mr. Stoval's proposal came with a certain degree of difficulty.

"Later today?"

"Would 3:00 be too soon?"

"I could work that into my schedule. Should I bring anything?" Spencer had no idea what he could offer to take to drink with a black widower and his dogs.

"No, Doctor, that won't be necessary. In fact I wouldn't even bring your dog. My bitches are pretty territorial."

"And I certainly couldn't leave her in the car in this heat."

"No, sir. I'll see you at 3:00 then."

The line went dead and Spencer hung up the phone. Between Lucinda's description of the Stoval legend and his brusque manner on the phone, Spencer felt a little uneasy about the upcoming cocktail hour. On the other hand, he certainly couldn't turn down a chance to meet with a local dog breeder and potential client.

Spencer changed into a clean pair of khakis and a fresh Polo shirt and scrounged through the closet until he found his loafers and slipped them onto his bare feet while Gidget watched expectantly. Spencer's routine meant they were about to go out. Gidget whined and looked toward the door. "Sorry, girl, I can't take you this trip."

Gidget looked from Spencer to the door again, then seemed resolved to her fate. She returned to the couch and curled up in the corner against the armrest giving Spencer one last sorrowful look before she emitted a soft snort of resignation. "I won't be long," protested Spencer, but it was too late. Gidget had already dismissed Spencer and closed her eyes.

"I can't believe it," muttered Spencer as he climbed into the steaming Suburban and rolled down the window. "Not only do I feel guilty about leaving a dog home alone, but I feel compelled to explain myself for Christ's sake."

Spencer drove over to the clinic and left the truck running while he went in to check his messages. He marveled briefly at how neat the reception area looked and made a mental note to mention it to Missy on Monday. He never admitted it but wondered what he would do without her. She could sure do better than working for him.

In his office he found a note stuck to the wall above his phone that he had missed earlier. In Missy's handwriting it simply said, "Mr. Stoval called, no message." It was signed M and was followed by a hastily scratched smiley face.

There being no other messages, Spencer returned to his truck and headed west on a blacktop that after a mile became a surface of white sand and dust that raised a cloud in the rearview mirror and seemed to erase civilization as Spencer knew it.

Spencer was soon surrounded by the groves. The manicured trees nestled against both sides of the road, their evenly spaced perpendicular rows reaching into infinity. Spencer had to slow to a crawl at each intersection since the foliage blocked any reasonable view of oncoming traffic.

Eventually he came to a break in the green wall where an arched white gate announced Stoval's Groves and a narrow lane split the greenery as crisply as a knife splits watermelon. Spencer slowed and turned south onto Stoval Lane and proceeded to the main house.

The house stood in the center of a cleared patch of ground. It was a white wood-framed structure with second story dormers, green shutters, and a green shingled roof. Except for a porch that surrounded it on three sides it had a distinct turn-of-the-century Midwestern look. The whitewashed outbuildings also presented a Midwestern familiarity, the only thing different being the citrus machinery and trucks parked nearby. The entire scene gave Spencer a shiver of déjà vu.

Spencer rolled to a stop next to a large flatbed truck, turned off the ignition and waited, half expecting Stoval to appear on the porch. Then he realized that this was a social call not a vet call where the farmer customarily materialized with a bucket of hot water the moment Spencer arrived.

Spencer climbed onto the porch and approached the door. As he reached up to knock, it opened suddenly and he stood looking up into Stoval's dark face. "Mr. Stoval."

"You're early but come in." His tone was brusque as he literally grabbed Spencer by the arm and dragged him over the threshold.

Spencer stumbled briefly but caught himself and shook Stoval's outstretched hand. He'd never been in a black person's home before. "I wasn't sure how long it would take to drive out here and I didn't want to be late."

"That's fine. Don't you worry about it. Come in and have a seat." Eldridge motioned toward the couch on the far side of the living room. Spencer noted a bottle of Jack Daniels and two glasses on the dining room table.

Spencer took a seat at one end of the couch and Eldridge took a seat opposite him in a worn overstuffed brown chair. They sat and looked at each other in awkward silence before Spencer finally spoke. "Do you keep your dogs here in the house, or are they kenneled?"

"They stay with me." With that he smiled and clapped his hands. There came a sound that resembled someone falling down the stairs and the room suddenly filled with a black-and-white blur of Boston terriers of all sizes.

Two bounded onto Eldridge's lap and licked his face while two more sniffed Spencer's feet, having surely picked up the scent of Gidget. A fifth dog sat in a far corner and barked at the white stranger while two young pups collided and rolled over each other in pursuit of a bright yellow tennis ball.

"Tangela, be quiet!" Eldridge turned his attention to the barking terrier in the corner. "She's the territorial one I told you about, and those little ones are her pups." Eldridge pointed to the two pups struggling in vain to wrap their jaws around the tennis ball.

At the sound of Eldridge's command the pups scurried for their mother and the rest of the pack, led presumably by O.J., and joined Tangela in her corner.

They sat at attention dangling seven pink tongues under seven pug noses awaiting their master's next command.

It came. "Lie down." And they did.

The room was quiet again and Spencer looked around. It wasn't quite what he expected from a widowed farmer. The room was immaculate even though the furnishings were dated and worn. Spencer speculated that while Eldridge kept the place up he hadn't changed anything since his wife died. Across the room sat an upright piano with a photo of a beautiful black woman in a wedding gown and two pictures of a young black girl. The first reminded Spencer of an old postcard with her as a child in a straw hat under an orange tree. She held a basket full of fruit and had her father's broad winning smile. In the second she was a young woman in a graduation-style portrait. Her childlike innocence had been replaced by the same look of wonderment and anticipation that Spencer had witnessed in young mares. In this photo she bore the smile of a girl approaching womanhood. It was her mother's smile.

Eldridge spoke as if he knew where Spencer's gaze had fixed. "That's my wife and Jasmine, our daughter. It wouldn't surprise me if you've heard the story." He rose from his chair and walked wearily toward the Jack Daniels.

"Some of it, yes."

"Where'd you hear it?" he asked over his shoulder as he poured two drinks and returned to his chair without offering ice or water.

"I had a drink with Lucinda Vickers last night and we were talking about my dog. Naturally the subject of O.J. came up."

Eldridge raised his eyebrows and passed a glass to Spencer. "You having drinks with Ms. Vickers already?"

Spencer squirmed uneasily. "I don't know her well. I just met her recently when she retrieved her grandmother's Jack Russell terrier."

"She'd sell her own grandmother if there was any profit in it."

"Gotta make a buck where you can these days."

"Always a wild one that girl. Be careful what you wish for, Doc."

"I'll keep that in mind."

"You do that. What'd she say about us?"

"She just said that you'd lost your daughter in a terrible accident and that people around here think your wife died of grief." Spencer immediately regretted mentioning the part about Eldridge's wife.

"She said all that did she?"

"That's about it. She wasn't disrespectful."

"I'm sure she was very careful. She tell you my daughter was aching to be her friend?"

"She didn't mention that."

"As you can see for yourself my daughter was a beautiful girl. She got that light complexion from her great grandmother, and foolishly thought that once they closed down the Gifford High School for the coloreds and integrated into Vero Beach that racism had ended. Poor fool."

"Were there riots?"

"No, it was all peaceful and civil-like but she was popular in her own school. She'd been a cheerleader and student council president and figured those white kids would just step aside and let her continue."

"I can't imagine making that kind of transition." Spencer couldn't since his upbringing didn't involve people of color. Eldridge had broken eye contact with Spencer and instead focused a bloodshot bitter gaze to the right as if he were speaking to someone sitting next to him.

"There's a lot of things you can't imagine, Doctor." Eldridge rose from his chair and with drink in hand approached the piano and absently struck at the keys with one finger. "I didn't need any vitamins when I came to see you a few weeks ago."

"I could take them back if you haven't opened them," Spencer offered.

"It's not that, thank you." Eldridge paused and drew a deep breath as he contemplated the ceiling. "I have some information and I'm not sure what to do or even how to deal with it myself."

"If it's about O.J. you can tell me." *Great*, thought Spencer. *O.J.'s got a genetic defect that he just passed on through Gidget and I'll be raising a litter of unsalable cripples.*

"It's much more complex than that. When you first arrived, I didn't think anything of it. Then word was that you were from up North or the Midwest. I didn't even think nothin' of that until I heard you were tellin' it around that your great granddaddy had settled here and tried to make a go of it."

"That's right. He moved down here with his family and tried to raise citrus."

"And he was a Hawley, too?"

"Yes, he died when I was very young. I never knew him."

"Robert Exum Hawley?"

"That's right. Did you find his name in the county records?"

"Not exactly." Eldridge hesitated. "You're sitting in the middle of your great granddaddy's groves."

Spencer smiled and looked around. "Incredible. He built this house didn't he?"

"Yes, but ..."

"I recognized the style. It's a Midwestern farm house."

"His name is in that family Bible over there on the table." Eldridge stared hard at Spencer. "Now, we can leave it at that or you can go over and look in that Bible."

Spencer was already on his feet and moving toward the Bible. "Where'd you find it? Was it hidden in the walls or buried under the floor boards?"

"I've always had it."

Spencer frowned. "I can't believe it. Here you are living on the same place and even raising Boston terriers like he did." He carefully opened the Bible's worn cover and turned gingerly to the family page that listed marriages, births, and deaths. It took him a minute to decipher the faded writing and comprehend its significance. He slowly turned and looked at Stoval and saw him for the very first time.

Eldridge spoke first his voice just above a whisper. "My grandmother was as white as you, and it says Robert Exum Hawley was her daddy. I think that makes us kin."

The walls closed in on Spencer as if all the air had suddenly been sucked out of the room.

"You don't look so good, Doctor. In fact, I didn't think it was possible for a white man to turn whiter. Maybe you should take a strong sip of that Jack Daniels." He handed the glass to Spencer.

"I'll be all right." Spencer looked down at his drink then toward the window. "In fact I'm fine."

"Fine or not, it is what it is."

"My uncle always snickered when Mother brought up great granddaddy's foray into Florida. I thought he snickered because she always used the word *foray*. She was into genealogy but never did find out what happened to Great Aunt Blanche."

"Your Aunt Blanche crossed the color line, and no one was goin' to look too hard for her."

"But we're not prejudiced."

"Not until your daughter runs off with one of us."

"Is that what happened?" Spencer leaned forward and rubbed his forehead.

"According to my grandmother, that's Aunt Blanche to you, Robert Exum came down here and worked hard to build these groves. Things were going along just fine until his daughter Blanche fell in love with my grandfather Moses. Fortunately, Robert's wife Primrose had had enough of the Florida snakes and mosquitoes, so rather than disown his daughter Robert gave the farm to Moses and her as a wedding present and returned North.

"But a mixed marriage couldn't have survived here. Not then," Spencer interrupted.

"Not easy now, but Moses and Blanche kept to themselves. While he quietly built this into one of the best groves in the county, she was content to raise her children and her Boston terriers, of which O.J. is actually a descendant."

"Then he and Gidget would also be … kin?"

"I don't think we need to go there. That's not going to be our problem."

"You and I must be something like third cousins." Spencer set his drink back down on the table.

"If you say so. Is that how it's done up North?"

"I don't get what you mean." Spencer looked up at Eldridge now.

"It's like saying we are distantly related, but down here kin's kin and that means family. There is no such thing as being distantly related."

"Okay, then we are kin and family. Whatever my great-grandfather was, I'm not prejudiced, Eldridge." Spencer smiled like he knew what he was talking about and Eldridge shook his head.

"It's not that simple, brother. Certain white folks down here, the crackers that live in trailers and drive the 4X4's with the gun racks, aren't going to get a warm fuzzy feeling about our kinship."

"Well, fuck them."

"I've been doing business here a long time. I didn't get where I am with that attitude. You won't either because you're not from around here."

"Times have changed."

"If it makes you feel better to think that, then go on. While you're at it tell the whole world about us. Then see how much business a Yankee outsider who's kin to Eldridge Stoval gets. You'll lose the coon hounds first then the poodles, while all the time my black brethren will be splitting their sides laughing behind our backs."

"So we just leave it be, like nothing ever happened?"

"Like you said, we are distantly related because of something that happened between two people a long time ago. Let's just leave it between you and me."

"It doesn't seem right."

"I'm black and have spent my whole life here. Believe me it's right, Dr. Hawley."

"Then at least call me Spencer." Spencer stood and looked Eldridge in the eye.

"All right, Spencer." Eldridge extended his hand and shook Spencer's. "I'm sorry if you thought the world had changed just because Bill Cosby got his own television show."

EIGHT

"Clayton, who's in that truck pullin' outa' Stoval's place?"

"How the fuck would I know, Delwood? But it kinda looks like the one we saw awhile back bein' chased by a jockaroondy." The Suburban disappeared as it became enveloped in a cloud of dust up ahead.

"I think it was a white guy."

"So what, Delwood? It's probably one of them 'secticide salesmen."

"On Saturday?"

"Sooooo? You sure have a hard on for Eldridge."

"I told you that bastard stole our grove. Ours started right here." Delwood rolled down his window and waved his bare arm toward the north.

Clayton began to cough. "Jesus, roll that window back up. You know I can't stand all this dust in my lungs."

"Sorry."

"I heard that your daddy was sick to damn death of oranges and got paid a fair price for that land."

"Like hell." Delwood changed the subject. "I wonder what that man's business was with Eldridge?"

"Like it's our fuckin' business. Let's just get the beer and cigarettes and get back to the trailer before the Marlins' game."

"I'm sick of the Marlins and that damn trailer. I'm sick of workin' odd jobs and diggin' graves for a living. And I'm sick of that uppity Stoval getting all the breaks livin' on land that was my birthright."

The truth was that Delwood's daddy, Delwood Sr. had gotten sick and tired of oranges. He sold out for a tidy sum to Eldridge's father and bought a condo on the ocean at the Moorings south of Vero Beach only to discover the old adage that money will buy property but not privilege. Since he didn't golf or have the slightest inclination toward tennis, Delwood's daddy took to drinking in the clubhouse and playing poker with another social outcast named Nicki, known as Nicki the Nose Gardino back in Jersey. Nicki had developed incurable acne rosacea at an early age which left him with a flame red proboscis that reminded Delwood of the backside of an orangutan.

Within a few months, Nicki cleaned Delwood out and forced him deeply into debt. The condo was mortgaged and Delwood was leveraged to the max, but Nicki still called at all hours of the night demanding his money. As the seams of the little family from the orange grove began to unravel, Delwood Jr.'s parents argued violently creating a perpetual storm cloud over little Delwood as he sat on the floor and played with his toy soldiers.

Eventually two of Nicki's associates showed up and encouraged Delwood's daddy to go fishing with them. The last time Delwood saw his father he was being escorted away wedged between two men whose backs were so broad their floral shirts looked like the wallpaper in the clubhouse lounge. They dragged him to a large blue Cadillac, his bare feet dangling a scant two inches above the asphalt. In the background Delwood could hear his mother pouring vodka into a tumbler as she shouted, "I told you this would happen, you bastard!"

Although never acknowledged by Delwood, the Stovals were the only family in Winter Beach that offered assistance to Delwood and his mother. They set up an old migrant's trailer on a corner of the grove near the irrigation ditch and let the two of them live there rent free until his mother's liver gave out.

"Look, there's that son-of-a-bitch now."

"What son-of-bitch?"

"The one from Stoval's. Jesus, Clayton, pay attention." With that Delwood cranked the wheel hard and followed the Suburban north until it pulled into the vet clinic parking lot.

"It must be that new vet, Delwood."

"I'll be damned. What's he doin' out at that peckerwood's place?"

"Maybe he's making a house call on those little black and white dogs Stoval raises."

"My ass. I'll twist those little dog's tails off and see what that vet does."

"I don't think they have tails, Delwood."

"Oh, shut the fuck up, Clayton."

NINE

Lucinda Vickers sensed the striking contrast she made against the surrounding landscape as she sped south on U.S. 1 toward Captain Hiram's. With the top down on her BMW and a Dodgers cap pulled down to her Ray-Bans, she slipped easily from lane to lane around the slower traffic. Her breasts strained against her white cotton T-shirt as she reached over and turned up the volume on Pat Benatar's *Heartbreaker*. A white hot sun pierced the cloudless sky like a laser and threatened to melt anything that didn't move. Even riding in a convertible required the full force of the air conditioner.

Her weekend had been fairly productive. She had succumbed to Ian's demand to work the Refuge and sold three lots with a good chance of closing the deal on another. Fortunately there had been a shift in the prevailing winds and the stench of the backed-up sewer systems in Phase One had drifted away from Phase Two toward the trailer park. Unfortunately the hot dog buns had wilted in the heat and humidity, but the coolers held enough ice to keep the soda a few degrees above tepid.

The rest of her stint had been uneventful until one of the musicians collapsed in the middle of *In the Mood*. Lucinda even managed to turn this to her benefit by pointing out the paramedic's quick response time to the silver seniors clinging to her surried golf cart. Before she swerved to avoid the small mob of slack-jawed onlookers, she managed to wave coyly at a young paramedic who looked up briefly from his resuscitation and at the sight of Lucinda lost all concentration.

"I sold his house when he and his wife divorced. Actually, they were married when they listed the house. The divorce came later. I don't think shift work is good for a marriage. Do you?"

The silver-haired couple smiled stiffly as Lucinda sped on to the next lot.

When she finished on Sunday, Lucinda grabbed her bag from the trunk and proceeded to the model home's master bath where she doffed her cowboy clothes, showered, and changed into her short shorts and her snug T-shirt. She had unfinished business at Hiram's and it was on the way home.

Enterprise Productions was a real estate development firm out of Miami. Lucinda gleaned that much from one phone call. They were a low-profile, cash-flush company, which was standard operation for the money laundering businesses of the Central America drug cartels.

It took a little longer to pin Tommy down, but she eventually tried the second number she had found at T. Pascoe Redstone's and got a Hispanic-sounding secretary who announced herself as the secretary to Tommy Canseco, Vice President of Acquisitions. Lucinda figured that anybody who'd use Tommy as a business name would come up one business ethic short of the Good Housekeeping Seal of Approval, but in Miami that wouldn't present a hindrance.

The lot at Hiram's was already half full when Lucinda rolled in but she couldn't help but notice the silver Porsche bearing Miami Dolphins plates parked near the front door. Lucinda's quarry was nearby. The vanity plate bore the letters TC-DVLPR.

Tommy was sitting at the end of the bamboo-lined bar talking to a local fishing guide when Lucinda entered and sat down six stools away. He looked up and smiled the smile of a boa constrictor as his leer took in every inch of her. Lucinda slid onto a bar stool, ordered a mojito, and started a slow count to one hundred. Tommy slithered to her side by twenty-three, not a record, but close enough to suggest that she would get what she wanted.

Tommy passed a five dollar bill across the counter. "Allow me, if I may."

"It's your money, Tommy."

Unfazed, Tommy looked deeply into her eyes. "So you already know my name; my reputation must precede me."

"I don't know jack about your reputation. I just heard that guy at the end of the bar call you Tommy."

"So you noticed me?"

"The bar's not that busy, Tommy, and I couldn't help but hear the rattle of your pretty gold chains. Are they real?"

"But of course, would you like to fondle them?" Tommy lifted up the chains and Lucinda reached for the small gold medallion in the middle. "It's an actual coin from a sunken pirate galleon. It's for luck."

Lucinda dropped the coin and turned to her drink. "Do you really think you should wear it? It didn't bring luck for its last owners."

Tommy smiled; his stark white teeth contrasted with his deep tan. He leaned closer, his musk cologne nearly but not quite overpowering. "You've got attitude. I like that."

"What brings you to these parts, Tommy?"

Tommy pulled back in mock surprise. "You don't think I'm a local?"

"Right, Tommy. You're a local, Hillary Clinton is a New Yorker, and my guess is that the little people are about to be screwed in both locations."

Tommy's smile faded. "You know all that? What are you some kind of social worker?"

"No, real estate." Lucinda put her straw to her mouth and sucked on her mojito as she awaited Tommy's response.

Tommy laughed. "Real estate is my game; you should work for me."

"Sorry, I've been to Miami, or wherever you're from, and the view is better here."

"But I'm working on something very big near here. It would keep you busy for years."

"Great. Another condo trailer park for snowbirds."

"You think I'm all looks and no brains but you're wrong." Tommy motioned to the bartender for another drink.

"Who said anything about your looks, but go ahead and impress me, Tommy."

"My company is working on a huge project which will include a very upscale community surrounding a championship golf course. I'm talking homes, luxury condos, and a commercial center."

"I'm surprised I haven't heard anything about it." Lucinda paused to suck on her straw. "You must not have the land."

"We've located the land but we need to get the zoning restrictions lifted before we move on it."

"So you don't have the land."

"In thirty days."

"You going to tell me where it is?"

Tommy smiled again and handed the bartender another five dollar bill. "Do you think I would spill that to some real estate agent I hardly know? You insist on underestimating me."

"Would you feel better if we went back to your place and fucked?"

Tommy visibly struggled to maintain his cool. "I know your life would never be the same, but you wouldn't be any wiser about real estate."

"Wanna bet your lucky medallion?"

"You're on, woman." Lucky Tommy waved away the bartender who had returned with his change.

"Oh, I'm on all right, Tommy." Lucinda smiled the same smile she had given earlier to the paramedic. "And I never lose when I'm on."

Three hours later Lucinda left an exhausted Tommy, his sweat-drenched body entangled in the bed sheets. She smiled as she walked down the hall toward the lobby. The Spanish medallion felt cool against the nape of her neck. Spencer Hawley wasn't the only one who could make trolling profitable.

TEN

Walker Braddock oversaw the minute details of his funeral home operation himself. Every employee who dealt directly with the public wore a dark suit and tie and spoke with a sympathetic honeyed Southern accent. After careful training by Walker himself, no one would discern that most of his assistants were former used car or vacuum cleaner salesmen.

For the less glamorous behind-the-scenes work, like cleaning the morgue and hauling supplies, not to mention applying the armadillo repellent, Walker hired any derelict he could find for minimum wage. Of late he retained the services of Delwood and Clayton, two local crackers who owned a back hoe and contracted with the county to dig the graves at the cemetery.

Delwood claimed that he went to high school with Walker, that is until he dropped out to support his mother. The association apparently gave Delwood the impression that he and Walker were equals and he addressed him as such. Walker, who couldn't fathom ever being in any class or organization with someone like Delwood, bore the indignity of Delwood's familiarity simply because entry level help was so hard to find.

"Walker, we're running out of this here bug repellent you've had us spraying on the cryptics." Delwood shook a near-empty plastic container of Rid-a-Bug to emphasize his point.

"It's *crypts* not *cryptics*, Delwood."

"Oh, yeah. I forgot. You want I should get some over at the hardware store?"

"Let me look around and see if we can't find that in bulk somewhere. We've been selling a lot of that protection lately." Walker pulled out his Palm Pilot and entered a reminder note.

"Can't for the life of me figure why people are suddenly so scared of armadillos." Delwood had resumed his application of the protective film.

"It's a cultural thing, Delwood."

"You mean the spooks and the spics."

"I'd prefer you'd not use those words, Delwood. Our Black and Hispanic brethren have certain cultural values which, while different than our own, are no less sacred to them. As a funeral director providing their last resting place I must be sensitive to their needs, folklore though it may be."

"So you spray bug repellent on their cryptics and tell them it will keep the armadillos from devouring their innards?"

"For a nominal fee I provide that perception which, I might add, is a great relief for their families in their time of grief." Walker slipped his Palm Pilot back into his coat pocket.

"Armadillos have flat little teeth. Their ain't no armadillo here or in the hereafter that could chew through one of these concrete cryptics, Walker. I just thought I'd tell ya."

"Thank you for sharing that, Delwood, and I'm sure you have a valid point. But the spraying of the crypt is something of a ritual. Our brethren expect it."

"Like holy water."

"Exactly. Excellent analogy."

"Would it hurt this holy bug juice any if I diluted it with water?" Delwood turned and held up the container again as if Walker would want to inspect it. "It could cut your cost in half."

Walker smiled and tapped the jug with his forefinger. "Delwood, your perception is remarkable. From now on you're in charge of the ritual armadillo formula."

Lucinda paced Walker's office impatiently. She had chosen to meet him here to discuss her proposal rather than some local bistro where there were too many ears. One wall of his expansive office contained a large oak bookshelf, but close inspection revealed the leather-bound classics to be fakes. The other walls were adorned with art reprints of fox hounds and their red-coated masters mounted on imposing steeds. Behind his matching oak desk with its massive flat surface hung various diplomas and awards all in color coordinated triple mats and frames.

Lucinda was reading the fine print on Walker's national innovation award when he entered the room.

"Lucinda, what a pleasure to see you again, but I'm sure this is business. Am I correct?"

"Always business before pleasure, Walker." She ignored his outstretched hand and made herself comfortable in a peach leather wingback chair facing his desk.

"I'm sorry to have kept you waiting, but I had some details to attend to with one of my employees."

"Another award-winning innovation, Walker?" She was purposely flippant now and waited until he was sitting across from her before she crossed her legs and smoothed her skirt.

Walker licked his lips nervously and smiled. "I've got to keep one step ahead of the competition."

"Walker, you crushed the competition years ago; you must be richer than God."

Walker smiled and appeared to relax at the mention of his financial security. "I have done well, haven't I?"

"I think your daddy would be proud, but I can make you even richer."

"Why would I need more money? I have all I need."

Lucinda smiled. "You know you'll never have enough money. Besides, money is power." Her argument was inconsequential. Walker Braddock, like the moth to the flame, had been hopelessly drawn to her since high school and could deny her nothing.

"So I've heard, but something tells me I should send you packing right now."

"There's no rush. We're about to enter the citrus business, dear."

"Citrus? There's no money in that." Walker leaned back in his chair and smugly clasped his hands behind his head. "I'm surprised at you, Lucinda."

"You're half right, Walker, but there's a developer out of Miami with even more money than you who's about to plop a mega-retirement complex right in our back yard."

"Really?" Walker leaned forward on his desk. She had his attention now.

"You'll have to double the size of your loading dock just to handle the flow of corpses northward when the new owners begin to kick off."

"I'd have to double the size of this whole place just to handle the volume."

"There you go." She had him now. "That's going to take some planning."

"And you would help me how?"

Lucinda leaned forward in her chair. "I know whose land they want and the fact that they haven't approached the owner yet."

"Let me guess. We approach the owners first and buy the land for a song before the developers arrive."

"That's pretty much it. We'll be in the citrus business for less than three months with a down payment of merely fifty thousand."

"Then we sell big to the boys from Miami."

"And plunge our huge profits into the surrounding property before word gets out. We'll sell it off in pieces for the inevitable strip malls, convenience marts, and fast food sites."

"Fast food is good for my business. It steps up the whole dying process." Walker paused but Lucinda didn't laugh. "So, we'd be partners?"

"That's right, Walker. You put up the down payment and I'll do all the paperwork and manage the transactions."

"Fifty-fifty split?"

"Of course. I figure you deserve at least fifty percent."

"Since we'll be using my money."

"And my brains." Lucinda shifted in her chair and casually recrossed her legs. She noticed Walker notice and smiled. Men were all suckers for the old-fashioned nylons with garters. She wondered if it had something to do with their mothers.

ELEVEN

When Spencer awakened to a scratching noise his first reaction was that the termites had followed him home from his office and had infested the walls of his house. Could they latch onto his clothes or Gidget's coat and do that? He obsessed on the thought of those parasites destroying his clinic from the inside out. Actually, he didn't own a clinic; he owned a cancer.

He pulled his sweat-dampened pillow over his ears to drown out the noise until he heard Gidget whimper and realized she had climbed out of bed and was pawing at the door. He rolled over and looked at the clock. It read 3:00 a.m. In her late stage of pregnancy, Gidget could no longer sleep through the night without going out to pee.

Spencer propped himself up on one elbow, relieved that it was Gidget's scratches not termites that had awakened him. Once again he pulled on a pair of jogging shorts and proceeded to the kitchen where he opened the door and let her out. He flicked on the porch light, and as Gidget disappeared around the corner of the house he marveled at the variety of insect life that instantly materialized around the dirty yellow bulb.

Florida's night air was damp and heavy. It was a phenomenon this born-and-raised Iowan hadn't gotten used to and prompted surprise every time he stepped out into the darkness.

His thoughts returned to the termites that until now he couldn't afford to exterminate. Eldridge Stoval had paid him a visit at the clinic the previous morning. Spencer hadn't seen him since their talk at the groves and greeted him with the genuine Midwestern enthusiasm that a Southerner might reserve for kin. Eldridge glanced over at a perplexed Missy and asked Spencer if they could talk in his office.

"Sure, Eldridge, come on back." Spencer motioned eagerly toward the hallway as an expressionless Eldridge followed.

"Do you treat all your clients this way?" Eldridge asked when they were behind the closed office door.

"Just clients who are cousins. Sit down, Eldridge." Spencer reached over and swept his vet magazines from the chair.

Eldridge frowned. "Like I said before, you don't want to draw attention to that. The girl out front looked at you like you were some kind of Democrat about to drive me to the polling place."

"I'm sorry, Eldridge, but the fact that you're black doesn't bother me. I think you're ashamed to be related to me."

"I'm not ashamed of anything. Embarrassed might be a better word."

"Embarrassed?"

"Listen, Doc, I've spent a long time getting to where I am. I provide a good product, but I'm not in the Rotary or the Citrus League. I don't draw attention to myself ; I make out just fine."

"And you're all alone out there."

"Like I said, I make out fine. I don't need the embarrassment brought by a bunch of rednecks speculating on our ancestry. Believe me, you don't need it either."

"Fine, if that's the way you want it. We'll keep this conversation on a professional level."

"It's the way it has to be." His speech finished, Eldridge eased himself into a chair.

"Then what brings you here, Eldridge?"

"Termites."

Spencer raised an eyebrow. "I am a vet but I don't do termites."

Eldridge forced a smile. "They're about to do you. In less than six months you'll be practicing on the roof if it doesn't kill you first when it collapses."

"How do you know?"

"Everyone knows. The kid that inspected this place is the nephew of the guy three places down. He's afraid this whole street will become a termite buffet if they aren't stopped here."

"So what's your role in this?"

"I've worked with your bank and I suspect you're maxed out or you would have taken care of this already."

"You suspect right I'm afraid. There's not much I can do about it right now."

The room became silent. Eldridge looked down at the floor then over at the diplomas on the wall. Eventually he cleared his throat. "What if I were to loan you that money?"

"You?"

"You think I can't afford it? Like I'm some share cropper."

"Why? What if it got out?"

"It'd be just between you and me."

Spencer sat still, momentarily stunned. Then a broad smile spread across his face. "You can't do it can you?"

"What are you talking about?"

"You can't turn your back on kin even if they do embarrass you. Am I right?"

"I don't know what you're talking about. This is a business proposition and I got the papers right here." He quickly reached into his pocket and pulled out a wrinkled promissory note and slapped it on the desk. "Sign it."

Spencer picked up the note and laughed out loud. "One year at three percent. You could do better depositing this money at any bank in the county."

"You want to save the building or not? I got a money order right here with me."

"I can't take this. I'm a pretty big risk right now."

"Consider it hush money. Sooner or later everyone down here gets some. Besides you're a decent man. You could have made a big fuss after what my dog did to yours, but you didn't."

Spencer looked at the note again then picked up a pen. "I wouldn't let you do this if there was any other way for me." He scratched his name across the note and handed it back to Eldridge.

"I wouldn't do this if I didn't believe you'd do everything in your power to pay me back." Eldridge extended his hand and Spencer shook it.

"Thanks, Eldridge. I really appreciate your help."

"It's all right."

"Can I ask you another favor?"

"Depends."

"You know my dog's almost certainly going to need a cesarean when she delivers those pups."

"She probably will. You're going to want some help."

"I've only got Missy, the girl out front, but I need one more pair of hands."

"Just give me a call any time. I'll come." Eldridge stood up to leave.

"Thanks."

"You know, Doc, you don't look so good. Like you need a nap or something. That dog keeping you up at night?" Eldridge smiled broadly and winked as Spencer shrugged. "We're just two dog breeders who have to look out for each other, Doc. That's all."

Gidget worked her way back toward the kitchen as she carefully sniffed each shrub bordering the house. Spencer gave an involuntary shiver despite the heat and whispered, "Come on, girl, let's get some sleep."

Ten days later the exterminators arrived. Spencer and Missy had spent the prior evening packing up the drugs, dry dog food, and chew toys and stashed them in his living room. The project took on a circus-like atmosphere when a team of men engulfed the entire clinic in a monstrous tent before the fumigation commenced.

School children wearing multicolored backpacks halted on their ten speeds to watch. Joggers slowed to walk and the entire men's breakfast club from the Unitarian Universalist Fellowship poured out of the nearby diner to observe and offer their moral support with such comments as, *I hope you didn't leave the dog food in there.* (That comment itself engendered an earnest discussion amongst the membership concerning the merits of organic Fair Trade dog food versus the cheapest brand on the shelf.)

Spencer's neighbors also stepped out to the curb to witness the purge, their arms folded and their brows furrowed. They spoke in low tones and occasionally pointed at Spencer's clinic in a manner that suggested they knew all there was to know about drywood termites and the deterioration of property values once they entered a neighborhood.

It didn't matter that they had neglected to keep up their own buildings for years to the point that they couldn't even attract the Harley Davidson crowd on their way to Daytona Beach, or that the two chains whose names ended in *Mart* were building their own super stores to the north and south. If business dropped off or didn't improve in the next twelve months, Dr. Spencer Hawley and his termites would bear the blame.

TWELVE

"Explain to me again about Beebee, Dr. Hawley." Missy sipped an Orange Crush in a chair next to the antiquated autoclave in the small lab that doubled as a break room. She and Dr. Hawley had just finished neutering a small shih Tzu.

"As I said, I sort of sublet her to another clinic down in Vero Beach. A month is a long time to care for a dog of Beebee's caliber, and we don't have that much space in the event we get more inpatients. It's a tactical maneuver. We'll retrieve Beebee before her owner returns, do the billing, and keep twenty-five percent."

"But I was taking good care of her and you could have kept all the money."

"Yes, but it's just business."

"Do you love animals, Dr. Hawley?"

Hawley turned his back to Missy and poured himself another cup of coffee as he contemplated Beebee, her lifeless form wedged between the ice cream and the T.V. dinners in his freezer. "I suppose I do. Why?"

"I've always loved animals since I was a little girl. I'd bring home stray cats and dogs to feed or play animal hospital with the neighbor's pets. I've been a member of Save the Manatees since I was twelve, and that was before I ever saw one."

"I've never seen one in person."

Missy pulled what must have been the day's seventh strip of Big Red chewing gum from her smock pocket and began to thoughtfully strip off its paper sheath. "Just wait until winter when it gets cold."

"Cold?"

"I mean less than sixty-five." She carefully peeled back the foil as if she expected something other than chewing gum. "That's considered cold here and that's when the manatees gather around the power plants to stay warm. You can see them in Vero Beach at the plant by the Seventeenth Street Bridge." Satisfied that the wrapper did indeed contain gum she tore the strip in half and popped one half then the other into her mouth. "I always go there when the temperature drops. I saw more than forty once."

"I guess that does make you a serious animal lover."

"I am, Dr. Hawley. I tried to get into vet school you know but I didn't have the grades." As she worked her jaws the scent of cinnamon filled the room.

"I didn't know that. Have you always worked in animal clinics?"

"Ever since I flunked out.... . I mean left Auburn."

"I thought you were some sort of princess or beauty queen."

Missy flushed. "That was before. I was the Alabama Peanut Princess. That's how I got my scholarship to Auburn."

"Really?" Dr. Hawley studied the bottom of his coffee cup. He couldn't stand to watch a pretty girl chew gum.

"I sang a Jimmy Buffett song. He's the one who's trying to save the manatees, you know."

"How about you, Dr. Hawley?" A loud cracking noise emanated from the gum somewhere in Missy's mouth. Spencer fought an uncontrollable urge to shove his hand down her throat and retrieve the gum.

"Me? I was never in a beauty pageant. Can't even carry a tune."

"Dr. Hawley, don't make fun. What made you become a veterinarian?"

"It might surprise you but I never thought much about whether I loved animals or not. Animals, mostly livestock that is, have always been there. It was the family business."

"Didn't your father love animals?"

"He never said, but it didn't seem important. His practice was mostly large animal. Farming is a business and livestock are investments not pets or endangered species. I think he loved the business part—working the stockyards, discussing corn prices or dairy herd management. He loved agriculture not animals."

Missy furrowed her brow. "But you don't do that here. The only agriculture is oranges and grapefruit."

"I know. I enjoyed the diagnostic and surgery part, but nine months a year we lived in a deep freezer and it took the other three months to thaw out." Spencer's thoughts returned briefly to Beebee as he contemplated how long he should allow for her to thaw.

"But you worked with your father." The gum snapped again and Spencer flinched.

"His partner retired, and I did what was expected and came home to join the practice. Unfortunately, my wife left me and then my father died."

"So you left?"

"Obviously. In the thirty years I lived there the blizzards never missed us, the farmers remained poor, and the herds all looked alike. I decided I didn't want to die there like he did." Spencer spoke softly into his coffee cup.

"So why'd you come here?"

"My family …" He started then stopped. "I decided to find a place without blizzards or hogs."

"Oh."

"I guess I danced around your question, about loving animals."

"Do you know the answer?" Missy reached for a strand of her long blonde hair and began to twist it around her fingers impassively.

"I'm not sure."

After a thoughtful pause Missy said, "You know, Dr. Hawley, I've worked in clinics for several doctors now, and I think that the business part seems to interfere with the caring part."

"I think you've learned a lot already."

"I've learned that maybe I'm glad I didn't make it into vet school." Then before she could stop herself she blurted, "I don't think I could love a man who didn't love animals."

Spencer looked up at Missy and studied her face for the first time since he'd hired her. "You could have worse motives, like my wife. She couldn't love a man who didn't love spending money."

Missy slammed her empty Orange Crush can on the counter. "That's so lame, Dr. Hawley. I feel sorry for her. And you, too," she quickly added.

"Thanks." Spencer paused. She would be a beauty queen if she lost the gum he thought. "Did I ever mention that chewing gum in a vet clinic can be hazardous?"

"No way!" Missy gasped.

"Oh yeah. I read it somewhere. It has to do with all those anesthesia and antiseptic molecules floating around. They get stuck to your gum then go right into your system. It can even affect fertility."

"Oh my gosh, Doctor." Missy sat astonished her mouth wide open revealing the large pink wad of poison lurking behind her left lower canine tooth. She quickly spit the gum into her hand and onto the top of her soda can. "No one ever said anything about my chewing gum at work before."

"I can't imagine why not," Spencer added.

Lucinda decided to drive out to Eldridge Stoval's and make her pitch. Like her new dog-killer vet friend, she needed a lucky break soon. T. Pascoe Redstone was about to pull her listing on his house because she couldn't find anyone damn fool enough to sink four hundred thousand dollars into a sprawling ranch at the end of a dirt road in the most isolated section of the county. It didn't matter that the septic system plugged up more often than a senior citizen on cheese curds, or that the kitchen had twenty-five year old harvest gold appliances. T. Pascoe wanted action.

In the meantime his county board had initiated an investigation of the septic systems in The Refuge to the north. Dubbing the development The Refuse, the neighbors in the adjacent trailer park claimed the odor intolerable and presented a signed petition to the board demanding action. The board, who generally considered the rights of trailer owners to be just above those of squatters, migrant workers, and Sierra Club members, actually listened. Under the leadership of T. Pascoe, they launched an investigation after issuing a ninety day building moratorium. It was no coincidence that the moratorium coincided with the dates of T. Pascoe's own realty contract and would significantly reduce home sales competition in his neighborhood.

Lucinda's speculative plan to purchase the citrus groves was proceeding smoothly. Eldridge Stoval, the owner of the groves in question, could be stubborn, but she had poured over the data provided by the Citrus League for hours and come up with an offer just under ninety percent of what the land was worth as an agricultural property. However, it was a lot of money, and she was nearly certain he would jump at the chance to sell. He'd be one of the richest black men in the county.

She had followed the dirt road to Eldridge Stoval's to meet with him face to face and make her case. As she drove up the long gravel drive, she looked for the funny looking black and white dogs Spencer called Boston terriers. Even though their pug-ugly faces suggested they were the canine world's version of the manatee, she fully planned to extol Eldridge on their virtues. She had even read about the breed at the library and could speak about such things as brindle coats, white blazes, and shawls. To her disappointment they did not materialize.

Eldridge stood in the open door of his shed and shielded his eyes to get a better look at his guest. Lucinda stopped short of Eldridge and got out of the car. "Hello, Mr. Stoval. How are you today?"

"Hello, miss, what can I do for you?" His query was cautious, like he suspected she was selling something.

"Where's the dogs?"

His face brightened at Lucinda's inquiry. "I've got them up at the house. I never let them out this time of day; it's too hot." Eldridge put down his wrench and wiped his hands on a dirty red bandanna he'd retrieved from his pocket. "I've got three pups left, but only two are show quality. Are you looking to show or do you just want a dog for the kids? I can make you a good deal on the mismarked one. He'd be great with children."

"Sorry, Mr. Stoval, I'm a career girl with no time to show and no kids in tow, if you know what I mean."

The wall went back up as Eldridge's face resumed its suspicious look. "What can I do for you?"

"My name is Lucinda Vickers and I'm a realtor." She handed Eldridge her card. He glanced at it and handed it back.

"Keep it, Mr. Stoval."

"No need. I don't plan on buying or selling today."

"Don't be too quick to reject a notion, Mr. Stoval, especially one that could make you rich."

"Since I didn't see no Prize Patrol sign on your car, and you're not carrying any balloons I suspect there are significant strings attached to me becoming rich today, Ms. Vickers."

"Mr. Stoval, I represent an individual who is very interested in your groves and willing to pay a fair price for them."

"That's nice." Eldridge picked up his wrench and went back to his machinery.

"It's worth considering; I assure you. Think of the direction fruit prices have taken the past few years."

"I've managed."

"It's got to be tough worrying about citrus canker and citrus greening disease. Why not sell now ahead of their invasion?"

"Invasion?" Eldridge shook his head and smiled.

"It's serious. Once those pests entrench themselves in the county your property values will plummet."

"That's what they said when my grandfather took over this place. The value's seemed to hold up just fine." Eldridge reached for his sweat-stained ball cap and placed it squarely on his head. "If you'll excuse me I've got to check on the dogs up at the house."

He started for the house and Lucinda followed. "What about your heirs and estate planning? Have you thought about that?"

Eldridge stopped and turned. "My heirs? Honey, you might say that's all I think about, but then I don't have any."

"I'm sorry. I forgot, Mr. Stoval."

"Forgot?"

"Your daughter. We were in the same class. Such a tragedy."

"Yes, I remember." Eldridge's face froze.

Lucinda wished she hadn't used the heir ploy but she was getting desperate. "All the more reason to plan, Mr. Stoval." She had no idea what she meant.

"For the dogs then?"

"Of course!" Lucinda replied, but Eldridge had already turned his back and broken into a long stride. Lucinda raced across the lawn after him but her progress was slowed as her high heels sunk into the sandy soil. She slipped them off and followed in her bare feet.

Eldridge stopped at the porch and turned. "I'm not interested in what you're trying to buy or sell, miss. There's no need to go on."

"Did I mention the migrant worker shortage? It will run your costs sky high."

"I always pay a fair wage and treat my workers right. But then why do I need to tell you that?"

"Mr. Stoval I must insist that you consider this generous offer. It's the chance of a lifetime."

"Miss Vickers, I just want to ask you one question."

"Shoot, Mr. Stoval." Lucinda sensed she had begun to make progress.

"Is there any chance you have a severe allergy to fire ants? I need to know that for a fact."

Lucinda was suddenly perplexed. "What does that have to do with anything?"

"Since they're beginning to swarm over your bare feet, I need to know if I'll be needing to call an ambulance."

Lucinda looked down at her tingling feet in horror. It appeared as if she was wearing reddish brown socks with a delicate yet shifting pattern. Before she could react, she experienced the sensation of charcoal briquettes dosed with lighter fluid and set aflame.

"I have a supply of Rid-a-Bug but I'm afraid it's too late for that, Lucinda, darling."

Lucinda lifted one foot then the other out of the ice water basin in Walker's office and began to cry.

"Maybe you should get some of that cortisone cream over at the Quickstop."

"It burns so bad, Walker. Can't you do something?"

"Maybe you should see a doctor. You're going to get some really nasty pus spots all over those feet by tomorrow. I'll bet you won't even be able to walk."

"You think this is just a big joke, you bastard. It's all you can do to keep a straight face."

"Lucinda, you know that isn't true. I could never stand to see you suffer." Walker smiled a broad glib smile.

"I'll sue that bastard Stoval."

"I don't think you can sue for fire ants, darling. I could have told you that you wouldn't have any luck with Eldridge Stoval. He doesn't own those groves; he *is* those groves. Besides I've thought it over, and I don't think it's wise for you and me to be dealing with him."

"Christ, Walker, would you get over his daughter. He didn't even recognize me."

"He won't sell to you or anybody else." Walker leaned forward and peeked over his desk at Lucinda's crimson feet.

"Everyone has a price."

"Ah yes, another real estate platitude. I don't think money matters to Eldridge."

"What are we going to do then?" Lucinda lifted her feet and stomped into the ice water causing Walker to scurry for the nearest towel. "I can't lose this deal."

"I'm not sure there is anything we can do." Walker dropped to his knees and feverishly mopped the water off the Persian rug. "But wait a minute ..."

Walker paused and looked over at the door as if he expected someone. "I'm waiting, Walker."

"I overheard two men who work for me part time. It seems that Eldridge and that new vet, Dr. Hawley, are spending a lot of time together."

"Of course, they both own those matching dog things. What good is that?"

"Maybe that vet knows something or could help us somehow?" Walker stood up and wiped his hands on the towel.

"What's he going to know?"

"That's for you to find out, darling.'"

"But you said I won't even be able to stand up tomorrow."

"Darling, you do your best work in the horizontal not the vertical."

"Up yours, Walker Braddock." Lucinda caught the lip of the basin with her toe and flipped it over on the floor. She laughed as Walker scrambled to protect his precious rug.

After a fitful night's sleep, Lucinda awakened from a dream that Eldridge Stoval and Walker Braddock were dipping her in an oversized fondue pot. She shrieked at the sight of her own feet. Her toes looked like Vienna sausages, while her ankles resembled those of the ladies in the *before* pictures of the Weight Watchers ads. Little white pustules had erupted and engulfed her inflamed appendages.

Gingerly she eased herself out of bed and onto the floor. She screamed again at the sensation of walking on hot coals and dropped to her knees. Beads of perspiration formed on her forehead as she crawled to the bathroom. Ten minutes later she had managed to both relieve herself and smear half a tube of cortisone cream over her feet. Then she wrapped them in Walgreens gauze and crawled back into bed.

She thought about calling her grandmother but had second thoughts. She didn't need her lectures. Then she remembered what Walker had said about Spencer Hawley. The man was an enigma. At times he struck her as honest to the point of being naïve, but then there was the matter of the poodle in his freezer. She decided to call him.

There was no answer at the clinic yet, so she tried his house. Spencer answered on the third ring. "Hello."

"Dr. Hawley, good morning. This is Lucinda Vickers. I'm glad I caught you at home."

"Lucinda, how are you?" His voice was hesitant.

"Not so hot. In fact, I was wondering if you made house calls."

"Is your grandmother's dog sick?"

"No, I am. I was attacked by fire ants yesterday and my feet are swollen up like sausages. I'm afraid I might die."

"If you haven't died by now I don't think you will. But you should soak them and try some cortisone cream."

"You didn't answer my question, Doctor. Do you make house calls or have you found another bitch you have to drag through the neighborhood?"

"I've been known to make them when pets are involved. And the other night was an accident."

"Why don't you stop by this evening and see how I'm doing. I know you'd never forgive yourself if I ended up in surgery."

"I could do that. I certainly don't need to add to my list of *never forgive myself* but I think it would be wiser to see your own doctor."

"He's ancient and has the bedside manner of a constipated telemarketer. Why don't you stop by after work and have supper with me."

"But you can't …"

"Don't worry about your food. There's a deli over on the beach that makes wonderful meals, and they deliver."

"Well, all right. Can I bring you anything?"

"What a sweet man. I knew I could count on you for another interesting evening. Do you know any good Pinot grigios for fire ant bites?"

Lucinda's invitation perplexed Spencer. She had information on people. Not the good kind, and she already had plenty she could use on him. But how?

He quickly finished shaving and called for Gidget, who had just finished backing a large spider into the corner of the living room. She looked up at Spencer with anticipation as she held the spider on point while he grabbed a tangerine-colored flip-flop from his closet and brought it down swiftly on the cornered prey.

Gidget yipped a short victory bark.

"Gooood dohhhg." Spencer patted her on the head and she awkwardly rolled to her back for a tummy rub. Spencer avoided her nipples and rubbed her under the chin. From her size he guessed she was carrying four pups, which was average for a Boston terrier. "Let's go to work, girl."

Gidget rolled to her feet and trotted toward the back door stopping briefly to look over her shoulder at Spencer as if to say, *Move it, bug killer.*

Once outside, she stopped briefly to sniff the front tire of the truck before squatting to relieve herself. Then she plopped herself next to the passenger side door and shivered with anticipation as she waited for Spencer to lift her onto the front seat.

"Up you go. There was a time you could do this without my help. That's before you let O.J. knock you up." Spencer paused and looked out to the East where a large cloud bank was building. It used to mean something to him when he worked for farmers.

In Florida he had quit listening to the weather report because it was always the same: hot, humid, and a thirty-percent chance of showers. In the short time he'd lived here, Spencer had grown to appreciate the monotony of the weather and the fact that no one seemed to care about it. In his former life the soil frost depth, wind chill, and winter road conditions had become as tedious as an Iowa presidential caucus.

His spirits lifted again as he climbed behind the wheel and the engine roared to life. "We've been invited out to dinner, Gidget."

Gidget looked up at the mention of her name then plopped her head back down on her forepaws.

"I forgot to tell her you were coming, but that won't matter."

Gidget snorted softly and closed her eyes.

Missy's car was in the lot when Spencer arrived at the clinic and she was already stationed at the phone when Spencer unlocked the front door and entered. "Good morning, Missy. Any calls?"

"No," she replied. She sounded unusually distracted which irritated Spencer. He didn't often arrive in the same 'chipper let's get to work and save the animal kingdom' mood that Missy exuded every day. Now he had it and she didn't.

"Something the matter?" Spencer asked as Gidget trotted around the counter and began to sniff Missy's shoes.

"Didn't you hear the weather report?"

"You mean the ninety-five degrees, humid, with a thirty-percent chance of showers that nitwit on Channel Five spits out three times a day?"

"This is hurricane season, Doctor."

"And?" It irritated Spencer that someone was out to spoil his day. He'd beaten the termites and met payroll for the first time in a month, his dog was about to whelp a pure bred litter, and a beautiful woman had invited him to dinner on the pretext of a house call. Now Missy wanted to bring up that old hemorrhoid the weather.

"There's a hurricane building off the coast. It could strike here."

"Don't they calculate the paths of those things? It's not like a tornado that just materializes and smacks a trailer park in the middle of the night."

"They do, but the path can change and you have to be ready." Missy reached over and scratched Gidget behind her ears. Gidget promptly rolled onto her back for an obligatory tummy rub.

"I see." Spencer didn't see. Some idiot weatherman with a hard on for some real weather was ruining his day. In Iowa he had never paid much attention to hurricanes. He'd never heard of Hurricanes Frances and Jeanne striking Vero Beach. Other than Katrina flooding New Orleans, they usually struck exotic places like French Kiss, Louisiana. He couldn't identify with CNN footage of rednecks as they rowed down Main Street waving to their neighbors perched on their roofs like crows on a power line.

He did recall his mother boxing up some old clothes and blankets and hauling them down to the Methodist Church, but that was when Hurricane Andrew tried to take out Miami. His mother loved Miami because his father took her there for the National Swine Conference when Miami was still an exotic destination, before Disney put Orlando on the map.

"This is serious, Doctor." Missy straightened up as Gidget stared back at her with a look that said, *Is that all there is?*

"It's not time to line up for bottled water and plywood yet is it? I've got a full schedule today and a dinner date tonight."

"It's still too early to tell, but I'll keep the radio on."

"Missy, I'll count on you to keep me posted." Spencer sensed clouds of doom forming again as he started for his office. He wondered when he'd last gone a whole week without a crisis.

"Yes, sir. I've already checked the storage room and found some old battery lamps and sheets of plywood left over from a previous scare. I'll get some batteries on my lunch hour."

"Take it out of petty cash."

"But we don't have any, sir."

"Oh, that's right. Well then just charge it to the clinic."

"Yes, sir."

"While you're at it, Missy, pick up some Pinot grigio if they have it."

"Sir?"

"It's for my dinner date."

Missy smiled and Spencer found himself trying to read its significance. "Do I know the lady?"

"I think you've met her. It's Lucinda Vickers."

Missy wrinkled her nose and made a face. "The Jack Russell lady."

"It's her grandmother's dog, but you don't approve?"

Missy shook her head. "It's none of my business but she seems sort of, I don't know, superior like."

"Superior how?"

"Like we used to say at the sorority, she's a sizer."

"Excuse me?"

"The way she looks at people, it's like she's sizing them up as to whether they'll be a main portion or a side dish."

"Really? I didn't notice." Spencer had noticed, but since he'd been invited for dinner he let Missy's analogy pass.

"It's not an attribute that men usually notice for what it is, but I'm sure you'll have fun."

Spencer didn't care for the emphasis Missy put on the word *fun*. "Gidget will chaperone. I can't leave her alone now that she's almost due."

"You'll call me when she goes into labor? I'll come right down and assist you." Missy picked up Gidget and cradled her in her arms.

"Thanks, and I will." Gidget sniffed Missy's perfume then promptly licked her face as if to give her a kiss. Grateful for Missy's devotion, Spencer sensed a brief desire to nuzzle her himself.

The rain began by late afternoon. It started as a tropical downpour, the innocent warm kind that dances off tin roofs with a steady sonorous rhythm. Outside work stopped, appointments called to cancel, and the world in general resolved that nothing more than a good nap would be accomplished today. Gidget curled up next to Spencer on the office couch and snored softly.

Spencer had relinquished his radio to Missy, who listened intently to the hourly news updates on what had now officially been named Hurricane Buzz. As Spencer read and Gidget slept, Buzz had organized itself into a Category 3 monster bent on the Florida coast. The plywood vendors in Nassau had already witnessed a brisk upturn in business.

THIRTEEN

Lucinda gingerly straightened herself as she stood naked in front of her vanity. Each attempt engendered searing jabs of pain from somewhere deep beneath the gauze that enveloped her feet. When she was twelve, before her breasts started to develop, her gym teacher said that since Lucinda was right handed the right half of her body would always be larger than her left. The thought that the right breast would be larger than the left horrified her. In fact, the breast bud on the right indeed erupted two months before the left and confirmed her worst fear.

To this day Lucinda had the habit of standing in front of the mirror to examine her breasts. Unlike most women who took their doctor's clinical approach to look for dimpling or asymmetry, she studied her soft contours searching for subtle changes in size and gently cupped each breast in her hands as she attempted to ascertain one's weight against the other. Reassured she'd step back and admire the perfect uplifting symmetry topped off with small but now erect nipples. *Perky* is how the romance writers would describe her. She liked that word. It gave her breasts character with just the right amount of attitude.

As the doorbell rang, she slipped her peach-colored dressing gown over her head savoring the sensation on her bare skin as it drifted over her body. She took a quick survey of her face and hair in the mirror, and with a brush of her hand made a minor adjustment to the blush on her left cheek.

She turned and started for the door only to stop and wince with the sharp reminder of her peripheral imperfection enveloped in bandages. "Dammit!" she whispered as she braced herself against the door frame before resuming her hobbled trek to greet her dinner guest.

As she approached the foyer she became cognizant of the pounding rain and flung the door open to face a dripping Spencer Hawley. He stood there like a rain-saturated adolescent waiting for the school bus.

"Please come in, Spencer. I'm sorry but I don't get around very well."

"That's all right." He stepped into the tiled foyer and slammed the door as small puddles began to form immediately on the mosaic tile. "This is really some rain. The streets are already underwater."

"Don't you own an umbrella?"

"I should consider it." With one hand he clutched the front of his shirt and began to wring out the water.

"Let me take this." Lucinda reached for the wilting paper bag which she assumed contained a bottle of wine. "There's a linen closet just down the hall across from the powder room; help yourself to a towel. I'd get it myself but you'd have pneumonia before I could get there and back on these wheels." She pointed to the gauze appendages poking out from under her hem.

"You weren't kidding about those bites." Spencer hopped on one foot then the other as he struggled to remove his soggy loafers. He started down the hall and returned shortly his head engulfed in a large bath towel.

"I have a hair dryer if you'd like to use it."

"That's all right. But I almost forgot." He paused as his head popped out of the towel—a turtle with a bad hair day. "I left Gidget in the truck."

"Gidget?"

"Yes, she could go into labor any time and I can't leave her alone."

"Your dog, right?"

"Yes." Spencer beamed like a new grandmother with baby photos. "I'll be right back." Without another word, he shoved his feet back into his shoes and bounded out the front door only to return moments later with his pug-faced pooch wrapped in Lucinda's best bath towel.

"Well, here she is," Lucinda pronounced of her evening's rival.

"Isn't she cute in this towel?" Spencer asked as he rubbed down his disinterested dog. "Phone home, E.T., phone home," he mimicked as he extended the entoweled creature. Gidget held her E.T. expression as if this Abbott and Costello routine was not unfamiliar to her.

Lucinda managed a polite laugh and Spencer, apparently disappointed that their impression hadn't brought the house down, turned Gidget loose. Gidget trotted off and began to check the place for new interesting odors while Spencer resumed toweling down his head.

"I could get you a different towel if you like."

"Don't bother. This one's fine."

"Then I'll just take this wine into the kitchen and put it on ice." Lucinda began to limp toward the kitchen.

"Let me help you with that." Spencer retrieved the wine. "I'm sorry but Pinot grigio hasn't reached Winter Beach yet. If you want red they hand you Merlot and white gets you Chardonnay. I hope this Chardonnay is okay."

"Fine," Lucinda muttered as she limped toward the couch. "There's an ice bucket and two wine glasses on the counter and ice in the freezer."

"I see them." Spencer was already in the kitchen.

"I'm afraid I forgot to put out the corkscrew."

"Don't need one." There was a short delay before the scr-a-aa-ck sound of the seal breaking on the Chardonnay's screw cap.

Lucinda stretched out on the couch and smoothed her gown. Gidget trotted to her side and sniffed at her dressings before she selected a nearby chair for a nap. She jumped awkwardly onto the chair, circled four times, then curled into a tight ball emitting soft snorts of abdication and closed her eyes.

Spencer returned with two glasses of wine and handed one to Lucinda. "I see Gidget made herself at home. I can get her down if you'd rather."

"That's okay, leave her be. It won't be long and she'll have her hands full rais-ing puppies."

"With an absent father to boot."

"I assume Mr. Stoval is providing child support."

"He has been very conciliatory." Spencer took a seat opposite the couch.

"Word has it he's a very enigmatic man."

"No doubt," Spencer replied. "But I think that's just a front to hold people at bay."

"Why's that?" Lucinda sipped her wine and waited for a response.

"In the first place, he's a black man in the white business world, and secondly, there are his devastating losses. He's vulnerable but can't admit it, so he builds this protective shield around himself to keep everyone out."

Lucinda shifted and tried to casually cross her feet but was rewarded with a searing pain that radiated to her knees. She winced. "I'm sorry, I thought my feet would feel much better tonight." She managed to force a tear which rolled slowly down her cheek.

Predictably, Spencer stood up and started for her. "It's all right. Gidget and I can leave if you like."

Lucinda reached for his hand. "Please don't go. I've been alone in this house all day, and the storm is getting so bad. I think I'm feeling a bit vulnerable myself right now."

Spencer squeezed her hand and smiled. We'll stay if you want us to, but only if you trust me to take care of the kitchen."

"Thank you. You're a bit of an enigma yourself, Doc."

Spencer withdrew his hand. "How so?"

"One moment you're full of guileless compassion and the next ..."

"I'm an avaricious dognapper."

"Avaricious might be a bit strong, but that sums it up."

"Until the other night, it seemed like a relatively harmless way to keep my practice afloat. I have this aversion to financial failure."

"Most do."

"Financial failure is relative. For some it has to do with the loss of millions and its corresponding power and status. For me it has to do with paying the help and feeding my dog."

"Avarice versus survival."

"Succinct but well put."

"So what about Beebee?"

"Beebee is in cold storage. I'm afraid if my practice doesn't turn around this month, she's next month's meal ticket."

"That's sad." Lucinda forced another tear down her cheek.

Spencer squatted and softly brushed away Lucinda's tear with the back of his hand. "That's life." Lucinda closed her eyes resigned to receive the kiss she'd earned.

"Where's the food?"

Lucinda jerked as if awakened from a dream. "The food? Yes, the food. Of course." Regaining her composure she continued, "I put some appetizers on a tray in the refrigerator and two covered dishes on the shelf above."

"I'll find them." Spencer rose to leave and Gidget looked up briefly then returned to her nap.

"You'll have to preheat the oven to 350 degrees," Lucinda called out as Spencer disappeared once again into the kitchen.

"What are we having?"

"Oh, I forgot to ask. Veterinarians aren't vegetarians are they?"

"If they are, I haven't met one. Why?"

"Because we're having beef Bourguignon."

"Looks like you slaved over the stove all day." Spencer's voice echoed from inside the refrigerator.

"Slaving over the telephone is more like it. Hurry up with those hors d'oeuvres, and don't forget the wine."

Dinner proceeded just as Lucinda had planned. Since Walker Braddock was the only man she knew who could set a table properly she had set her own during the afternoon. She also had the foresight to add candles to the setting which became more mandatory than romantic when the power failed during the beef Bourguignon, itself savory yet not sedating. As she finished the last bite of her crème brulee and gingerly pushed back her chair, Lucinda sighed with self satisfaction. "This was nice. I'm glad we lost the power."

"Excellent dinner, although I must say I drank a bit too much wine." Spencer took Lucinda's hand in his as the corners of his mouth turned upward in an intoxicated grin.

"Shall we retire to the drawing room?" Lucinda asked with mock sophistication. "I may need some assistance."

"Absolutely, my lady." Spencer rose and managed an awkward over swept bow before taking Lucinda's arm.

As she rose, Lucinda feigned a buckling of her knees. "Whew! I guess I had a bit too much to drink myself. I think I'd better lie down for a minute."

"I'll help you to the couch."

"If you don't mind I think you'd better help me to my bed."

Spencer flushed and Lucinda felt his grip tighten briefly then relax. "Point the way then."

As they approached the bed Lucinda freed herself momentarily. "Is it me or is it hot in here?" With that she turned to Spencer and slowly pulled the single cord that held her gown in place. As it drifted slowly past her shoulders and her newly acquired antique Spanish coin pendant and over her pelvis, she watched Spencer's eyes widen in surprise then focus on her perfectly matched perky breasts.

He did not surprise her with the speed in which he took her into his arms pulling her against his damp cotton shirt. What did surprise her was the gentle care he took in lifting her onto the bed. First he kissed her softly on her closed eyelids, then her neck, and finally her breasts before he spoke.

"Are you sure you'll be all right if we do this?"

"I can't think of anything that would make me feel better. You're just what the doctor ordered."

As Spencer stood and Lucinda watched him undress she tried to recall the last time she'd had gentle sex but couldn't. In the future she would bandage her feet more often.

He eased himself onto the bed and began to gently kiss her again as his hand found her breast with its now firm nipple. As Lucinda responded to his touch, the enigma of Dr. Hawley returned and his soft compassion gave way to a famished passion that bordered on avarice.

Lucinda suddenly felt as small and powerless as her own perky breasts. She bit her lip hard as he penetrated her. This time the tears that rolled down her cheeks were real.

FOURTEEN

"Good morning, Walker."

"Lucinda, how nice to hear from you. I've been so worried. Are you feeling better?"

"Don't try to blow sunshine up my ass, Walker. I'm not in the mood."

"I'm sorry; I can barely hear you, dear."

"What's that damn pounding noise? Are you remodeling again?"

"In case you haven't heard, dear, there's a hurricane headed our way. My boys are putting up the plywood as we speak."

"I thought you put hurricane shutters on that mortuary of yours."

"You misunderstood. I put them on my house."

"That sounds like you, Walker."

"Seriously, are your feet better?"

"Much. I can now walk from my bed to the bathroom and the tile no longer feels like a bed of burning coals."

"That's progress I suspect. Did you see a doctor?"

"Yes and no. I didn't go see my doctor, but I did have Dr. Hawley and his slut puppy over for dinner last night."

"Oh my, how did you manage?"

"Unlike you I'm not opposed to spending a little money to make big money. I had dinner catered."

"And the bedroom, how did you manage to cater that?" A lurid chuckle at the other end of the line.

"Bite me, corpse jockey. Sometimes you just have to play with pain. Isn't that what you sports freaks always say?"

"I wouldn't know, dear. Sports aren't my thing, and I avoid pain at all costs. You don't need to get huffy."

"Sorry, but the fire ants have taken a little of the lilt out of my step."

"I understand, dear, but did you find out anything?"

"That's why I called. You're not going to believe this, but our new veterinarian and farmer Stoval are related."

A pause. "By blood? You must be kidding."

"Their reunion is a long touching story I'll have to share with you later, but you can believe it, Walker."

"I can't imagine what would happen if people found out."

"Depending on which people, it could become very uncomfortable for those two to continue living around here."

Another pause.

"Walker, are you there?"

"I'm thinking."

"It's about time you put some mental energy into this project."

"I have a man in my employ. In fact, he's installing the plywood as we speak. His father was duped, or so he believes, out of his grove by Mr. Stoval, thus denying my employee his birthright. There's no telling what he'd do with information like this."

"I like where you're going."

"The problem is we have no control once the information is out. It might be better to approach Mr. Stoval with the information ourselves and see if he will bow out gracefully."

"It would take a fire to move him out of that house."

"That may happen or it may not if we leak this out. It's like Hurricane Buzz. You just don't know what sort of damage it's capable of inflicting."

"I say let the big dogs run, Walker."

"The rumor could get traced back to you."

"I own this vet. Leave him to me."

"All right, Lucinda, if you're convinced. I've never denied you a thing have I?"

"No, Walker, and I've never let you down."

"I guess I'm forever in your debt, Lucinda."

"Maybe we're finally even after we clinch this deal." Lucinda smiled as she hung up the phone. "You'll always owe me, Walker Braddock."

*   *   *   *

Once again Missy's white Paseo was already parked in the lot when Spencer pulled in. She consistently beat him to work and he needed to set a better example. Last night he had been awakened in Lucinda's bed at 3:00 a.m. by a rather desperate Gidget. The rain had stopped briefly and the dark night was silent except for the steady drip of rain from the live oak trees. He put Gidget back in the truck and returned to Lucinda's bed to kiss her good-bye and to apologize for having to leave. She murmured something unintelligible and rolled over.

After sex he had cradled Lucinda in his arms and struggled to remain awake as she insisted he recount his life story. He remembered telling her about Eldridge and their relationship as well as her response, *"Holy shit!"* That was just before he slipped off into a post-coital coma.

It seemed like the right thing to tell her at the time, but now Spencer wasn't so sure. "What the night summons, the breaking day rejects," he muttered. It sounded Biblical and foreboding.

Evidently the night had also summoned Hurricane Buzz because Missy, dressed in faded jeans and a T-shirt that read *Dothan Alabama, Peanut Capital of the World*, rounded the corner struggling with a large sheet of plywood. She looked grimly at Spencer as he exited his truck.

"Buzz has been upgraded to a Category 3 and is headed for the Treasure Coast. No doubt about it, Doctor, we'd better get this place boarded up."

"What about your own place? Shouldn't you be home?"

"Yeah, right." Missy set down the plywood and wiped her brow. "I live in an apartment complex. Their idea of hurricane preparedness is to go door to door and hand out maps of evacuation routes and disclaimers for anyone who elects to stay."

"Don't they try to board them up?"

"Are you kidding? The way those building are constructed I'd be safer in a tent. At least I wouldn't get impaled on flying glass."

Missy's sudden resolve and energy intrigued Spencer. "Shouldn't you be on your way to Orlando to a motel or something?"

Missy brushed back her hair and widened her stance. "We can talk about this all day, Doctor, but the fact is that Buzz is heading for us, my family is all in northern Alabama, and based on what you pay me I couldn't afford a couch in a hotel lobby."

Spencer felt a pang of guilt and shoved his hands into his pockets. "I'm sorry about your pay. I could loan you my credit card. It's not maxed out yet."

"That's real sweet, Doctor Spencer, but you forget one thing."

"That would be?"

"That would be Gidget is about to have pups and I promised to be here. You certainly wouldn't be able to do that c-section without me."

"You're right." A sudden gust of wind caught the plywood and tore it from Missy's hands. Spencer rushed over and helped her pick it up.

"Get the hammer and wood screws, Doctor. They're lying on the counter inside."

As they picked up the board Spencer looked into Missy's eyes. What had struck him before as bimbo blue now took on the appearance of hardened steel. As if she could read his mind she said, "My great-great-grandmother was all fluff and petticoats when she sent her husband off to fight the Yankees. Then she tore up the petticoats for bandages and marched out to the fields and picked cotton with her Negroes. She managed just fine until Sherman's army stormed through and burned it to the ground. I imagine I have it in me to fight a hurricane."

Spencer smiled. "I'm impressed."

"Thanks, but that won't cover the windows."

"Let's get this place boarded up; then we'll go back and check on my house." He guessed he'd never tell Missy his great-great-grandfather rode with General Sherman.

Walker rummaged through the refrigerator and came up with two bottles of Killian's Red. "This should do it," he said as he walked around the perimeter of his building in search of Delwood and Clayton. He found them sitting in Delwood's pickup on their second cigarette break in an hour.

"You boys have been working pretty hard. How about a beer?"

Delwood beamed and reached out with a dirty nicotine-stained hand for the two bottles. "That's right thoughtful, Walker."

"It's the least I can do for you boys." Delwood and Clayton, whose combined oral cavities didn't contain enough teeth to strip an ear of sweet corn, would look better laid out as corpses than they did alive. "Have you got things taken care of over at your place, Delwood?"

Delwood twisted off the top of his beer and stared off into the distance, apparently in deep thought. "I been thinking on that, Mr. Braddock. Clayton and I can't think of any human way to prepare a trailer for a hurricane. No amount of cable, board, or duct tape is gonna keep that piece of shit I live in from becoming a flying turd when this hits the fan."

"Well, if you two are intent on riding this one out, you can stay here in the mortuary. It's going to be as safe as anything else around especially with this fine work you're doing."

Delwood turned to Clayton, who took a long draw from his beer before contemplating Walker's offer. "It's as good as any place I guess. Me and Clayton would be much obliged. At lunch time we'll go back to my place to get the cooler and load my big screen T.V. onto the truck."

"You live out there by that Stoval fella, right?"

"Damn, Walker, what'd you have to go and mention him for? You're about to ruin a perfectly good beer."

"I just heard some talk. That's all. It's probably just a rumor."

Delwood tucked his chin, then released a long slow belch. "Pardon my French, but when my home goes airborne I hope it fuckin' lands on his house. That's how close I live to him and his dogs."

"That's right I forgot; he and that vet raise the same funny looking dogs."

"Yeah, go figure. Me and Clayton we got our eyes on them two; they're up to something." Clayton nodded in agreement. He had finished his beer and was now using the empty bottle as an ash tray.

"Well, I hear they hang together like homeys because they're related."

At this both Delwood and Clayton sat up straight in their seats and looked hard at Walker. "You don't mean kin?"

"I do. It must be why that Yankee vet moved down here."

"Goddamn, he must be one them there octamorons Clayton and I been reading about."

"It's not the vet. Stoval's got white blood."

Delwood gripped the steering wheel of his truck hard and stared straight ahead as he appeared to be computing what he just heard. Finally he spoke. "Him being part white; that explains it, Clayton."

"Explains what?"

"Don't you fuckin' see? It explains how he tricked my daddy out of his land and stole my birthright. I never understood how a colored got the better of Daddy, but now I clearly see it was that white Yankee blood in him what's caused it."

Walker leaned against the truck. "As they say in the vernacular, Delwood, you are one insightful mother fucker."

Delwood didn't smile. "You got that right, Walker. Something's got to be done to protect Winter Beach from the likes of those two. You get my drift?"

"I hope you aren't suggesting something illegal."

Delwood shook his head then spit out the window just missing Walker. "I ain't sayin' nothin' yet. Me and Clayton have some powerful figurin' to do before this hurricane is over."

FIFTEEN

Spencer and Missy finished boarding up the clinic and drove over to his house in the Suburban. Resigned to her position in the back seat, Gidget curled up on an old towel and took a nap. The drive down Spencer's road felt like a tequila-laced ride on a mechanical bull as the truck rocked and lurched over the deep ruts created by the storm. Missy braced herself with one hand on the dash. Spencer had never seen her look this intense, except maybe when she was reading her Save the Manatee newsletter.

"I've called all over the county and there's no more plywood to be had," Missy offered.

"It doesn't matter. I couldn't afford those pirates' prices anyway."

"We could load your valuables into the truck and haul them back to the clinic."

"The good news is we can do it in one trip. My important papers are already in the file cabinet at the office."

"We should take some canned goods, too, if you've got any."

"Are you kidding? My entire larder is canned goods. I've got enough Dinty Moore and Chef Boyardee to last a month." Spencer swerved to miss a flying garbage can.

"SpaghettiOs?"

"Tons."

"I brought some Ramen Noodles and a gas cook stove. Ever have SpaghettiOs over Ramen Noodles?"

"No, can you make that?" Spencer looked over at Missy trying to get her to loosen up.

"Make fun and you'll be eating yours cold from the can."

"Sorry." Spencer fell silent. She was sullen now like her cooking was a big deal. He felt uncomfortable because he was her boss, yet right now she might as well be in charge for all he knew about hurricane preparedness. "I really do appreciate your bringing those noodles and that stove."

"And my time. You'll still owe me for my work you know. Some day."

"And somehow I'll pay up."

"Going to college made you smart about some things but it doesn't mean you know everything."

"You're right. From now on I'm going to listen to you and do what you say."

"Like I'm the boss?" She looked at him but she wasn't smiling.

"Yes, only I'm paying you not the other way around."

"Think of me as a professional storm consultant."

"If I do something dumb will you just remind me and maybe smile? I work better in a nurturing environment." Spencer smiled, but he wasn't kidding.

"I'll try to keep that in mind, but this is serious business. People do dumb things and die in hurricanes. Did you know that if you leave just one small window unboarded the wind will blast through, and it's worse than not boarding up at all."

"I must have slept through that lesson."

"It's true. That wind whips in and turns your whole place into a giant blender. It'll pick your T.V. up and throw it right through the living room wall. No place is safe once that happens."

"Might as well kiss your ass good-bye," Spencer said.

"You're getting the picture. I'm just trying to save yours." The corners of her mouth turned up briefly, almost in a smile.

"My ass thanks you. I thank you."

"I'm just saving you and your firm butt so I get paid."

"Excuse me, Missy, but that remark could be interpreted as sexual harassment."

"So sue me, Dr. Spencer. That's if there's one lawyer left within a hundred miles of here. They don't do hurricanes. They do aftermaths."

"Aftermaths?"

"Within twenty-four hours of this storm they'll have their experts climbing over what remains of the rooftops to study the trusses and note the missing hurricane straps. Within days they'll file suits against the very contractors they represented at the zoning commission when they promised their clients would follow code."

"That sounds a bit cynical for a former peanut princess," Spencer said.

"It's the truth; my brother's a lawyer."

"I'm sorry."

"That's okay. He's my parents' pride and joy."

"Do I detect a bit of bitterness?" Spencer added.

"Probably. My family values professional achievement for the males and beauty titles for the females."

"They must certainly be proud of you, too."

"They were when I won, but as you already know, parental acceptance comes at a price. But this is boring."

"No it's not." She was bordering on self indulgence but Spencer found himself surprisingly interested.

"Let's talk about something more interesting than hurricanes." Missy turned away and stared out the rain-streaked window.

Delwood strained against his large screen T.V. "Come on, Clayton, slide that cardboard under there." It had been his idea to bring along the cardboard container from one of Mr. Braddock's coffins.

"I'm tryin' to git it. Move your damn foot."

Delwood struggled to balance on one foot as Clayton worked the cardboard. "Push it under as far as you can. Then we can slide the whole thing over to the door."

"It's gonna be too heavy."

"That's what you know, possum dick. How do you think they got it in here in the first place?"

"It's not gonna fit through the door, Delwood."

"It will when we take it off the hinges. Now get up here and push."

They had pushed away the trailer's portable rusted metal steps and backed Delwood's pickup against the door. It was almost even with the floor of the trailer. "Come on, Clayton, push. You're not trying."

"I am trying, Delwood." The Phillips big screen began to slide slowly across the pond-scum green shag carpet. The scent of mildew filled the air as the tiny spores escaped their carpet home.

"It's startin' to move. Keep pushing, numb nuts."

Clayton groaned and the T.V. moved a few more inches. "If we get it out there it's just gonna get all wet."

"We'll take the tarp off the bass boat and wrap it around with bungee cords."

"I gotta rest, Delwood." Sweat poured off Clayton's face like rain off a tin roof.

"All right, we'll stop and rest when we get to that hole in the paneling."

"Where you put your fist when the Packers beat Tampa Bay?"

Delwood groaned as he strained against the simulated oak cabinet. "No, I covered that one with Mother's portrait of Elvis." He nodded toward the black velvet rendition of Elvis his mother had tried to copy from the *Blue Hawaii* album. She had made Elvis' head too big and compensated by shrinking his body to include all of him in the frame. He looked like Charlie Brown with sideburns.

Delwood eased up as they reached the gaping hole. "This is the hole I made when they fucking lost the first playoffs." Delwood looked solemnly at the splintered paneling. "They got to get a quarterback before I tear this whole damn place apart." Then he sighed. "You want a beer, Clayton?"

"You got any Killian's Red like Mr. Braddock?"

"No, and I don't have any fuckin' Grey Poupons either. It's just domesticated beer."

"That's fine, Delwood. You don't have to get all agitatored like. I was just asking."

Delwood went over to the refrigerator and retrieved two cans of Glades beer and sat down at the kitchen table. He popped the top on his and slid the other across to Clayton, who had already lit up a cigarette. Clayton inhaled deeply and flipped the match into a Skippy Peanut Butter lid which served as an ashtray. He picked at the beer's pop-top with a blackened fingernail as if he wanted to say something but was holding back. Sort of unsure like.

"What's eatin' at you, Clayton? My brand of beer offend your sensitivities?"

"I was just thinking."

Delwood smiled. "Well, don't strain your brain, pardner."

"Do you think Braddock was tellin' the truth about Stoval having white blood?"

"Don't know why he'd lie about it."

"Then why would Stoval keep it a secret all these years?"

"I been thinkin' on that, too. But then I says to myself, it's obvious what he's been doing."

"What's that, Delwood?"

Delwood pointed a finger at Clayton. "He figures he can shuffle around playin' this old Uncle Tom trick on everyone. Saying, 'You all must be right cause you're white. I'll go about my business.' Meanwhile, he's plottin' to take over all the honest white folks' groves like my daddy's."

"You mean he looks dumb because he's black but smart because he's got that white blood?"

"Xactly, Clayton! It's like he's a wolf in sheep's clothing."

"Only it's a black sheep."

"That's about to be sheared, Clayton."

"What are you going to do about it, Delwood?"

"I been thinkin' on it. I say we ride out this storm at the mortuary until the eye comes over. You know, the quiet part in the middle of a hurricane. And when it does we slip out and go set ourselves a little fire."

"Burn down his house?"

Delwood lifted his can and tipped it toward Clayton and grinned. "Everyone will think it was lightning."

SIXTEEN

Hurricane Buzz had charted a course for land. The National Hurricane Center predicted the eye would come ashore somewhere between the Ocean Grill in Vero Beach and Dell's Ice Cream in Melbourne. Winter Beach lay just south of center like a plucky heroine tied to the Florida Coast train tracks. If Buzz didn't decide to take out Dell's to the north, her fate was sealed.

Spencer felt like one of those poor schmuck reporters that the Weather Channel sent to cover the disasters. He stood in the muddy street and surveyed his house one last time as the rain poured down in torrents. Plastic garbage cans paired with the occasional lawn chair rolled past him heading west after the tourists. Most of the locals had weighted down their cars and left hours earlier.

What the hell am I doing here? he thought. The clinic was headed down the toilet, Gidget was about to deliver, he had another one on ice, and he had put his life in the hands of a blonde beauty queen with a learning disorder. *I'd be better off if Buzz leveled both the clinic and the house so I could collect the insurance money and head back to Iowa. If Gidget weren't due any time, I would leave.*

Gidget squirmed in the back seat of the Suburban. She was getting another cramp just like a few minutes earlier. It was almost as if these things that had been growing and kicking inside her wanted to get out. The pain emanated from that area. She was at once both excited and anxious. Something told her that nothing was ever going to be the same again. Gidget raised her head and saw her master standing alone in the rain. She wished he were nearby patting her on the head and scratching her behind the ears saying that everything was going to be all right.

Just then the front passenger side door opened and quickly closed again. It was that girl called Missy. Gidget raised her head in greeting but was quickly seized by another cramp and whined softly as she lay her head back down.

The girl Missy looked back at her and spoke. "Oh dear, it looks like your time has come, Gidget."

She rolled down the window and shouted something Gidget couldn't understand to her master, and within moments he was at Gidget's side speaking in that soft voice she loved to hear. "It's all right, girl. Everything is going to be fine."

Gidget felt her muscles relax as she stretched her neck forward so he could get better access to that spot behind her ears. She wished she felt well enough to roll onto her back for a tummy rub.

"We'd better get her over to the clinic," Spencer said to Missy. "I'll call Stoval from there. He said he would help us deliver the puppies."

Puppies, thought Gidget. *They're always talking about puppies. He used to call me puppy. Is that what's trying to get out of me?*

"We'll be lucky if the phones aren't out."

"Damn, I never thought of that," Spencer said.

When they arrived at the clinic Spencer was surprised to see Eldridge's pickup parked next to Missy's Paseo. At the sight of Spencer, Eldridge bounded from the truck. He wore an oversized yellow slicker with a matching rain hat and, despite the practicality of the outfit, Eldridge reminded Spencer of Big Bird as he lunged across the lot and rapped on the window.

"I lost my phone about an hour ago so I thought I best pack up the dogs and drive over here. She in labor yet?" As Eldridge stuck his head through the open window to assess Gidget's status, the water rolled off his hat into Spencer's lap.

"She just started a bit ago. Let's get her inside." Spencer handed his keys to Missy. "You go ahead and unlock the door while I carry Gidget."

With all the speed and agility of a box turtle on the interstate, Eldridge retracted his head and lumbered back to his truck to retrieve O.J., Tangela, and their brood.

A few moments and a large thunderclap later they all stood in the lobby of the clinic. As Spencer clung to Gidget, Missy and Eldridge shed their slickers while O.J. and his family all shook themselves hard, the cast off water forming a small lake on the waiting room floor.

Missy efficiently collected the coats and offered to get the mop as Spencer trudged straight back to his office and placed Gidget on the couch. "Bring some towels for Gidget first."

Spencer shed his coat and as soon as Missy returned he began to towel off Gidget. Eldridge along with O.J. and Tangela stood motionless in the doorway like a family portrait in black and white. "It looks like the early stages," Eldridge commented.

"I believe so. We didn't leave her alone that long. It's definitely too early to tell if she'll be able to have them on her own."

"We can only hope she will. This is no kind of storm to be operating in, Doctor."

"Just in case I'll get the operating suite ready and figure out the light situation in case we lose power."

"Hello?"

"Lucinda, darling. It's Walker. I'm glad I caught you at home, dear."

"You thought I might be showing some prime beach property before it washed into the Atlantic?"

"No, I thought you may have already driven your grandmamma inland." A thunderclap shook the house and Walker instinctively moved under a door jam.

"I'm staying this time. I'm not taking my eye off that Stoval property. Grandmamma and her bingo buddies commandeered a Disney tour bus up at the Vacation Club and are riding out the storm at the Polynesian Resort in Orlando. She says she's too damn old to spend the weekend on the toilet with her flashlight, praying the roof doesn't cave in."

"She always ride out a storm on the commode?"

"Not always, but she had a friend once who was sitting on the commode when his house got converted into kindling. The only thing left on that foundation was him, the commode, and his *Reader's Digest*. The blast even blew the pants off his ankles. Anyway, it made grandmamma a believer. That's where she's sat out every storm since."

"I was wondering, if you weren't too attached to your commode, if you'd consider helping me out and weather the storm at my place. It's closer to your groves and I've got CBS construction with automatic hurricane shutters."

"You mean the shutters you supposedly purchased for the mortuary so you could write them off as a business expense?"

"Turns out it was a good idea."

"Why do you need me, Walker?"

"I'm frantically packing up my Grecian collection and I could use some help."

"You've had a morbid fear of drowning since high school and want someone to hold your hand."

"And you're the first person I called."

"You got lamps, batteries, water, and some good food?"

"Let me see: a case of Perrier, a honey glazed ham, English biscuits in a tin, Swiss chocolate, Greek olives …"

"Enough said, pardner. Just let me throw a few things in a bag and I'm on my way."

"What about your place?"

"Forget about it. I rent and my personal stuff is insured."

"Clayton, let's roll Braddock's big screen T.V. over in front of those two caskets there and plug it in. My set will be safer in the storage room. Then we'll run this cable to the outlet in Braddock's office." Delwood took a deep breath and pointed to the Silver Cloud model which sat adjacent to the one labeled Bronze Redemption. Both were equipped with the optional heaven's simulated gold handles and angel's hair satin lining.

"I'm not too comfortable with the notion of sleeping in a coffin, Delwood."

"Safest thing there is in a hurricane, Clayton. Plus, these models have the adjustable head raises for the viewings. Sets up the dearly departed so's if you stand at the end of the casket you can look him right in the eye, like you were at a family bar-b-que. It makes it perfect for watching the big screen while you're tossin' back a brewski."

"We'll probably lose the power anyway."

"Until we do I plan to see how the other half lives."

"You mean the other half dies."

"Whatever, Clayton. You're always so negative. Let's get this set up and get the cooler out of the truck."

"Do you remember your father's funeral, Delwood?" Clayton began to uncoil the roll of cable they'd liberated from the Time Warner truck.

"Hell, yes. I was the oldest and had to help Mother with all the arrangements. The problem was we didn't have a body so we didn't know what to do at first."

"I didn't know you never found him."

"Never will I suspect. Hand me that cable cutter. They took him fishing in the Atlantic Ocean and deep sixed him. Probably weighted him down with concrete or chains like them Sopranos."

Clayton shook his head and started down the hall toward Braddock's office. "Nasty way to go."

"I suspect they were quick about it. A couple of pops to the head, then weighted him down and tossed him over the side. That's how they did Big Pussy on the Sopranos, not like that sick shit you see in the movies now where the Russian Mafia cut off fingers or their you-know-what and send them to the family in little boxes. The hookup is over in the corner, Clayton. They had more class when they hit people in my daddy's day."

"That must have provided your family with some comfort." Clayton knelt and unscrewed Braddock's cable and replaced it with their own.

"Yeah, but it woulda' been nice to have the body. It might have given my mother what the shrinks call closure. In the back of her mind she never could shake the idea that he might have run off to Vegas with some cocktail waitress. Let's go see if this hookup works."

"I hadn't thought of that."

"The mortician did and that was probably good. He said he could help her get closure by selling her a casket for the funeral. He would have rented her one but he said it's against the law. Anyway, she spent five grand from his life insurance on a casket and the whole shot. We even bought a plot and buried the fuckin' thing. Ten years later we planted Mother next to it. I think the only closure mother found was in the bottle if you get where I'm comin' from."

"Sorry to hear it, Delwood. My mother has just about paid off my daddy's bill. It's been about six years now since he passed on."

"I remember that. See if this cord will reach that outlet."

"He got crushed by a forklift full of Ruby Reds at the packing house."

"Hard to imagine someone getting kilt by grapefruit."

"The brakes gave out and he got pinned to the back wall of an empty semi they was loading. But the funeral parlor got him fixed up real nice so's you could hardly smell the citrus. Mom was pleased, and like I say she's almost got it paid off. She even took out one of them policies on herself where she pays each month toward her own funeral so's she won't be a burden to her children. Try turning on the T.V. now."

"That's a thoughtful idea on her part. We left the remote in the office. I think my mother had the notion she could save us from funeral expenses by pickling herself with Jim Beam. Bless her soul."

"That man Stoval pretty much shambled your family, Delwood."

Delwood sighed, "That he did, Clayton. It's what my parole officer once called dysfunctional. We never functioned right after Daddy sold Stoval that land. I think this is the power button here."

"It's only right he should pay for what he did to your family, Delwood."

"Abso-fucking-lutely, Clayton. He's about to get smited for his sins."

"That's a good word—*smited*. It makes me feel more like we're doin' the Lord's work."

"'Let there be light'! sayeth the Lord. We got power to the set, Clayton, and here comes a perfect picture."

"Do you suppose he gets the *Playboy* channel, Delwood?"

"The radio says the hurricane is still a Category 3, but it seems to be veering north." Missy brought the news and made the announcement to the room as Eldridge and Spencer stood over Gidget.

"She's been strainin' for awhile now, Doc. I don't see nothin' happening."

"Her perineum is bulging; we could wait a bit longer." Spencer bent over and examined the area expectantly. He sure as hell wished he wouldn't have to operate.

"It's up to you, but she's gonna' need an operation to have those pups."

"The surgical suite is ready to go so we'll give her a little more time," Spencer snapped.

As he reached down to stroke Gidget on the forehead he felt a hand on his own shoulder. It was Missy. "This is hard for you but I've seen you work, Dr. Hawley, and Gidget couldn't be in better hands."

"Thanks, Missy. I appreciate that." Beebee had been in good hands, too, before he ran her to death behind his truck.

Gidget strained hard again but nothing happened, then she let out a pitiful whimper. "That's enough; let's take her back and get this done," Spencer said.

While Spencer picked up Gidget, Missy and Eldridge headed for the door. Tangela and O.J. scattered down the tiled hallway ahead of the procession as if they knew full well what was about to happen. Missy donned a surgical gown and took her position at the head of the table. She methodically checked the dials on the anesthesia machine.

"Eldridge, you take that spot over there near the extra oxygen tank. Use those warm towels to dry off the pups, and there's an oxygen mask if they need it." Spencer laid Gidget on the table and stroked her head again. She was too tired to resist as he stretched out her four legs and tied them down.

Just then a clap of thunder shook the building. "Damn, that's it for the power. Let's get the lamps lit, folks."

As Missy and Eldridge lit and arranged the lights, Spencer found and prepped Gidget's abdomen. Gidget lay listlessly on the table, apparently oblivious to the storm and her imminent cesarean. Under the soft glow of the kerosene lamps, Spencer carefully surveyed his instruments one more time to make sure he had what he needed.

You can't put this off any longer he thought as he took a deep breath and nodded to Missy. "Put her under." Missy solemnly reached for the small mask as Spencer took up a scalpel and poised it over Gidget's abdomen.

Missy placed the mask over Gidget's face and turned up the gas as she slowly counted to ten. "Go," she said, and Spencer made a quick vertical incision between Gidget's nipples. He blotted the incision briefly with a sponge to clear the blood and exposed the shiny thin peritoneum that separated the abdominal muscles from the abdominal contents.

With a pair of forceps he lifted the membrane off the bowel and cut through it. "We're in. Now I've just got to tuck back the bowel." He reached for a cloth sponge about the size of a handkerchief and began to tuck it against the bowel. "That should hold it."

Spencer looked down at Gidget's bulging uterus. As opposed to the human uterus which is a single pouch, the dog's uterus is bicornate, which means there are two horns that come together at the base to form a V. The puppies develop in both horns. "I'm still guessing four pups, Eldridge. My guess is there are two in each horn."

"I'm ready for them," Eldridge shouted as the storm reached a deafening pitch.

Spencer's instrument tray quivered like Jello as the instruments migrated precariously close to the edge. The roof creaked and there followed a sound like repeating rifle shots. Missy looked upward and emitted an involuntary shriek. "It's awright, Missy, we just lost some shingles. That's all." Eldridge reached over and patted Missy's arm and she resumed her rhythmic squeezing of the ambu bag that breathed for Gidget.

Spencer bent over what was now a moving target and tried to steady the right horn of the uterus with his forceps as he made his incision. Momentarily he exposed the small wet head of a puppy that when gently extracted was no bigger than a hamster. "Here you go, Eldridge." Spencer passed the wet squirming pup to Eldridge's outstretched towel. "Keep him under the warm lamp as much as possible."

As Spencer gently massaged the second puppy down toward its incision, Eldridge dried the first puppy, which gave out a small cry inaudible above the storm. "This one won't need oxygen, Doc. Keep 'em coming."

Spencer handed Eldridge the second pup and proceeded immediately to the other horn. Carefully he extracted the third and fourth and passed them carefully to Eldridge. "How's the mother doing, Missy?"

"Respirations are good, but I can't check a pulse with the table shaking like this."

Spencer reached for his suture. "I'm going to oversew the uterus right now then close the abdomen." Despite the conditions Spencer made quick progress on his incision using one hand to maintain the tension on the suture while he worked the curved needle with the other. He began to sense that everything would be all right if the building didn't blow down around them before he closed the abdominal wall.

If only his father were alive, what a story this would be—delivering his own dog in a hurricane. They had delivered calves in icy stream beds together and cesareaned four-hundred pound sows by employing old doors between straw bales to make operating tables, but nothing topped the rush of performing surgery in a hurricane with a peanut princess as anesthesiologist and his black cousin as first assistant. But his father was gone and he'd just have to save that story.

"I'm about to close the skin, Missy. Shut off the gas and just run the oxygen. She should be coming to just as I finish."

Missy reached for the valve. "Only fifteen minutes under anesthesia and the patient is doing fine, Doctor."

"Puppies are also fine. Going to have some exquisite markings, too."

"Thanks, Eldridge." Spencer controlled his enthusiasm for the puppies until he was sure Gidget was all right. "We'd better set up recovery in the hallway where we can all hunker down and ride out the storm." The building's trusses groaned again as another gross of shingles popped loose and disappeared.

SEVENTEEN

"Jesus, Delwood, the whole building is shaking. We shoulda' gone to Orlando."

"That's why these caskets was such a good idea, Clayton. We're safe and sound as Ft. Knox lyin' in these."

"I felt better when the television was still working."

"We shoulda' thought of one of those gas-motored generators."

"It feels closer than a family reunion photo in here, Delwood." Clayton struggled to free his left arm from the confines of the casket and scratched the tip of his nose.

"It's fine. We're snug as a bug in a rug."

"Maybe I'm getting that closetophobia they talk about. My Aunt Irene had that. She had to leave the Catholic Church because she sweat so bad in the confessional."

"You're fine, Clayton. And it's claustrophobia not closetophobia for Christ's sake!"

"Still, I hope we don't have to bring the lids down." Clayton wriggled free and sat upright.

"You got your flashlight, don't you?"

"Yes, but I'm afraid if I pull the lid down I won't be able to get it back open."

"Bullshit, Clayton, we tested yours five times. As long as the roof don't collapse on it you can open it any time."

"The roof fallin' in?" Clayton looked up at the ceiling in horror. "You never said nothin' about no roof fallin' in. Dammit to hell, Delwood."

"The point is, Clayton, if the roof does fall in you'll be protected. Someone will find us and get us out. Why don't you get some sleep?"

"Awright." Clayton slid back down into his casket. "Delwood?"

"Yes, Clayton."

"How long do you think it would take for them to find us?"

"Would you forget about it, Clayton? It's just one of those worst case scenarios I'm talking about. Let's talk about something else, okay?"

"Okay, the roof's creakin' and I'll bet we're short of shingles. I just hope they put the hurricane straps on right."

"Clayton, I didn't mean let's talk about the roof. I meant something other than this damn storm."

Clayton paused for what seemed like an eternity and Delwood began to think he had fallen asleep. Delwood dreaded that since he wasn't too secure himself lying there in the dark waiting for the roof to blow in.

"Clayton?"

"Yes."

"You're awake aren't you?"

"Yes."

"Are you pondering something else?"

"Yes, I am."

"Would you care to share that thought with the group here?"

"Well, I was just wondering if Eldridge Stoval had a generator. We could look for it and load it on the truck before burning him out. Then we could watch T.V."

"Now that's a worthwhile contemplation, Clayton. Very worthwhile. See how much more creative we can be if we just quit sweating the little things and focus on the positive."

"Well, I'm positive I'd rather be watching T.V., Delwood. It would take one of those monster truck shows to get my mind off this mess."

"You want me to climb out and get you another beer, Clayton?"

"It might help."

"You'll have to pee."

"I reckon I'll have to risk it. I don't know how long this empty gallon jug I got situated between my legs here will last."

"You're good for at least a six pack, Clayton."

"How do you know that?"

"Because it works for me at the Tampa Bay games, that's how."

*   *   *   *

Walker paced his foyer and scanned the driveway for Lucinda. He could just make out a pair of headlights at the end of the drive. Yes, it was dear Lucinda.

Since the power was out, he ran into the garage to raise the door himself only to be drenched by a wall of horizontal rain. He stumbled backwards as Lucinda rolled quickly into the garage and squealed to a stop.

As she extracted herself from the car Walker exclaimed, "My God, Lucinda, you look dreadful!"

"The amount of praying I did to get here and as soaked as I am, I guess I'm sufficiently baptized in His Holy Name, Walker."

"I've never seen such rain, dear. The roads must be treacherous. Come inside and let's dry ourselves off."

"Get me a towel and a big terry cloth robe. I gotta get out of these wet clothes."

Lucinda stepped into the laundry room to the greeting of Ajax, the wonder dog. The storm had turned him into a Rin-Tin-Tin on Ecstasy. He drove his nose straight into Lucinda's crotch and his eyes rolled up to meet hers.

"Whoa, big fella.' Have the Indians got Rusty?" As if on dramatic cue, a thunderclap shook the house. Ajax retrieved his nose and raced straight for the bedroom. "I guess they got Rusty tied up under the bed, Walker. Should we save his ass?"

"Screw Rusty. Let's get dried off." Walker handed Lucinda a large soft towel as she proceeded to nonchalantly disrobe. When she got down to her bra and panties she motioned to Walker to turn his back and she continued to strip.

"Sorry about Ajax, Lucinda. He has a mind of his own."

"And the manners of a frat boy at a toga party. Where's the robe?"

"Right over here." Walker fumbled with the robe and held it open in front of his face as he advanced toward Lucinda.

"Close your eyes and lower the robe, big boy. I can't reach the armholes up there."

"Sorry." Walker squeezed his eyes shut and lowered the robe as ordered. Lucinda thanked him and turned to slide her arms into the garment giving Walker a chance for a quick glimpse of the top of her rounded buttocks and a partial side view of her right breast.

Lucinda pulled the robe tightly around herself and turned to face Walker. "Nice butt, huh?"

"What?" Walker protested as the blood rushed to his face.

"It's okay, Walker. I know you peeked. I'd be crushed if you didn't. Unless you're gay that is."

"Gay! Now there's a laugh," Walker scoffed. "How about a hot toddy in front of the fireplace?"

"Sounds delightful." Then she began to sing, "Since the weather outside is frightful."

"Unfortunately, I had to turn off the gas so the fire is nonexistent."

"Then let's pretend."

After they had eaten and opened the second bottle of wine, Lucinda and Walker lay comfortably head to head on Walker's L-shaped white leather couches as they watched the candle's flickering pattern on the ceiling. "I'm amazed at how insulated we are from the storm, Walker. This place is like a fortress."

"The hurricane shutters, which I appropriated from the business for the house, make all the difference."

"It would be pitch dark in here without the lamp or a flashlight."

"Absolutely; they don't allow anything through."

"Unfortunately we can't see what's going on."

Walker rolled on his side to face Lucinda. "Do you want me to turn on the radio to get some weather news?"

"No, I'll let my imagination run. I can't believe how safe I feel here." With that she stretched and yawned like a cat on a sunny window sill. Her robe started to slip away at the maneuver and she slowly pulled it back into place as she straightened out on the couch. "Are you worried about your artifacts? Should we begin packing?" She smoothed the front of her robe over her thighs.

"I'm not worried." He motioned toward the antiquities encased on the far wall. "In fact I never was."

"No kidding?"

"I just didn't want to ride this one out alone." He paused. "Thanks for coming over, Lucinda. I hope it wasn't too much trouble."

"That's all right, Walker. This is the safest place around, the food is great, and I'll be the first real estate agent on the scene to assess the opportunities after the storm. I can't think of anyone I'd rather ride this one out with."

"Not your grandmother?"

"God no! She'd try to make me sit the whole thing out in the shower stall next to her commode. You are kidding aren't you?"

"Yes, I'm sorry. Just making sure you meant what you said."

"About being with you?"

"Yes."

"I did mean it. You're my best friend, Walker."

"We've been friends a long time. Why do you think we were never more than friends, Lucinda?"

Walker stared at Lucinda with an alcohol-induced gaze and paused. Lucinda instinctively reached for the neck of her robe. She focused on the candle's pattern on the ceiling.

"Did you hear me, Lucinda?"

"I'm thinking, Walker. Give me a minute."

"You didn't find me attractive?" He had begun to slur his words.

"Don't be silly, of course I do." She didn't and never had. "It's just that we're so much alike in how we think and act that anything more than friends would ruin what we have." What she didn't add is that they would be in constant competition as lovers even to the point that they both desired the same thing in other women. "Does that make sense?"

"No more now than the thousand times I've heard it from women over the years." He rolled onto his back in resignation. "Sometimes I've just wanted to scream, 'Screw the friendship and let's just screw!' More than once the so-called friendship turned to shit anyway so we might as well have consummated it."

"I'm sorry, Walker, but our friendship means more than that to me. I hope it does to you and it would hurt me deeply if you thought otherwise." She mostly meant what she said but at the same time shuddered to think of his sweating bulk on top of her. Sex with men took the form of a workout for her and for that she preferred top of the line equipment: dark eyes, defined abs and pecs, and the ability to go the distance.

"Have you ever truly been in love, Lucinda?" Walker directed his question toward the flickering shadows on the ceiling.

Lucinda laughed. "Thousands of times, Walker, thousands."

"No, I mean truly in love."

"Let me think." She pretended to ponder counting on her fingers as if about to go through all the men she had known. She didn't need to count because his question, like the question of what's your very first memory, instantly brought forth the image of Eldridge's ebony-skinned daughter Jasmine. She remembered the first day she saw her walking into her newly integrated high school. She neither marched nor held back but was purposeful. Although her skin was black her nose and lips were almost Grecian.

. The look in her eye suggested an optimistic confidence and determination, and that separated her from the rest of the interlopers, who masked their fear with a mix of defiance and disinterest. Jasmine appeared open to the new possibilities, and for that reason was destined to lead both white and black. It was love at first sight—as instantaneous and unsettling as the light switch at a surprise party.

"Lucinda?"

"I'm thinking, Walker. Let me be." Silence. "No, Walker, when I really think about it I don't think there was anyone. In the Biblical sense that is, but what about you?"

"I guess in that way we are alike. I can't honestly recall anyone."

"Not even high school?"

He paused. "If you insist on going back that far, dear, I could include Jasmine."

"Oh yes. You were quite smitten with her." Lucinda forced a laugh.

"She was beautiful," Walker sighed.

"And your daddy would've whupped your ass if you had brought her home."

"It didn't matter. She never gave me the time of day. I would have given anything if she would."

"She was pretty in her own way, Walker." They both fell silent. *She was perfection,* thought Lucinda, *and if I couldn't have her no one else would.*

EIGHTEEN

At 5:00 the wind had noticeably died. Gidget lay in a box on a beach towel as she nursed her brood. Eldridge rose from a reclined position on Spencer's couch and wandered down the hall to the surgery suite where he found Melissa and Spencer restoring order, as if they would be performing another operation today.

"What's the word on the radio?" Eldridge asked.

"The brunt of Buzz hit Melbourne smack in the center at the south causeway. Lots of damage."

"Damn. You ever been to Dell's, Spencer?"

"No."

"Well, I don't expect you ever will now. The man made fine ice cream."

"No doubt about it," Missy responded solemnly.

"So you know the place?" Eldridge asked.

"Until this morning I lived just a few blocks away. Dell's soft serve machine probably blew through my kitchen an hour ago."

"The wind's died down now that we're in the eye of the storm. I best be getting back to my place and check the damage. If it's okay with you, Doc, I'll leave the dogs here."

"Eldridge, I don't think it's such a good idea to go out in this downpour. There's nothing you can do now."

"I'll be all right. I've been out in worse than this; besides I've got a generator I can load on the truck and bring back for the second half. It would be nice to get some real light in here and put a heat lamp on those pups of yours."

"That's not necessary, Eldridge, but be careful."

"Don't worry, Doc."

"I really appreciate your help, cousin." Spencer extended his hand.

Eldridge took it as he looked over at a perplexed Missy and just shook his head. "You're every bit the surgeon I thought you'd be, Doc. I'm proud to have been your assistant."

"Thanks, Eldridge. That means a lot coming from you."

"I'll be back shortly, Doc."

Delwood gripped the steering wheel as his truck bounced over the storm-rutted road leading west toward his trailer and Eldridge Stoval's home place. "Redstone and his county board should have had this road surfaced three years ago, Clayton."

"Winter Beach sucks the hind teat when it comes to county funding. Everyone else gets their milk before we do."

"That's a fact, Clayton."

"There's a tree down up ahead."

"I see it, Clayton. I can get around it on the left."

"The shoulder looks pretty soft."

"Jesus, Clayton, you worry too much. It's four-fuckin'-wheel drive." Delwood wrenched the wheel left and accelerated. The truck hit the soft sand and for a moment appeared to stall. But before Clayton could say *I told you so* the front tires dug in and the truck lurched forward. Delwood let out a whoop. "Nothing can stop us now, Clayton. We're gonna get that son-of-a-bitch."

"You mean set fire to his place. That's all."

"Whatever it takes. That chicken shit probably fled west with the tourists."

Clayton lit up another cigarette. "But what if he's still there?"

"We'll just have to deal with that situation if need be."

"Have you got any kind of plan, Delwood?"

"Sure I got a plan. We splash the gas all around the house where the electric meter is fixed. It'll look like it got hit by lightning and took the whole house. No one will figure it any different."

"You sure about that?" Clayton's hand had begun to tremble and gray ash floated down onto his lap.

"I saw it on one of them soap oprys. Some guy's father was doin' his own son's woman and knocked her up. So the son waits until she and his ol' man were in the sack at his place and burns it down using the same plan."

"And he never got caught?" Clayton sounded skeptical.

"He wouldn't have except them two had already tied up his mother in the kitchen and run off to Vegas."

"So he killed his own mother?"

"Nah, she worked her way over to the Veg-a-matic and cut the ropes before she passed out on the lawn from smoke inhalation."

"So she lived?"

Delwood grimaced. "Yeah, her son gave her mouth to mouth."

"What happened to his father and the woman?"

"Hard to say. This all happened a year ago and just last week this guy's woman drops the bastard kid off on the son's doorstep."

"The baby?"

"Yeah, 'cept now he's twelve already."

Clayton slapped the dash. "I hate when soap operas do that."

"Me too," Delwood replied. "Here we are. These are Stoval's trees."

Clayton let out a low whistle. "Looks pretty bad, Delwood. He's lost a lot of them."

"The soil is getting pretty waterlogged from all this rain, Clayton. The second half of this hurricane could lift the rest of them right out of the ground. He's gonna be piss outta luck if this don't let up some."

"That's his lane right up ahead."

"I know that." Delwood eased up on the gas. "Did you put the gas can in the back like I told you?"

"You never said anything about gas."

"Shit, Clayton, I did so."

"You did not, and where was I supposed to find a gas can?"

Delwood sighed. "I should have done it myself before you found those damn *Playboy* magazines in Braddock's office. You get a hard on and your brain loses its entire blood supply."

Clayton bit his lower lip and turned away. "I musta been lookin' at them pictures of that *Survivor* show girl."

"Jesus, Clayton, couldn't you think of us for once. Hurricane Buzz is trying to drown our asses. If we don't start thinking as one, he's gonna' douse both our torches. 'Delwood and Clayton, the tribe has spoken.'"

"Sorry, Delwood, but I bet we can find some gas in his shed."

"That's your fuckin' job."

Delwood turned into the lane and inched his way forward. "The house should be right up there, but I can't see shit through all this rain."

"His power must be out; I can't see any lights."

"Of course his power's out. It's out everywhere."

"Then what do you suppose those lights are over there?" Clayton pointed toward the shed.

"Oh shit. It must be his truck backed up to the shed."

"Turn off your lights." Clayton instinctively reached for the switch but Delwood slapped him away.

"I can't see. Besides he's seen us by now."

"What are we gonna' do?" Clayton began to panic and looked back over his shoulder half expecting to see the sheriff.

Delwood bit his lip and furrowed his brow like he always did when he was figuring. "Just act natural like we're making a social call."

"In a fuckin' hurricane?"

"It's the eye of the fuckin' hurricane. I'll think of something—like we're just trying to help our neighbor." Delwood smiled like he'd just been relieved of a terrible strain. "Sure, that's it."

"Why don't you say, 'Hey, Eldridge, we're just two crazy mother fuckers riskin' our pickup and rednecks to help out our neighbor.' I'm sure he'll buy that."

"Shut up, Clayton, unless you got a better idea."

Delwood pulled alongside Eldridge's pickup and rolled down his window. "Need any help, Eldridge?"

Eldridge smiled and waved, the rain not seeming to bother him. "I never thought I'd see you two again. Your trailer is scattered all over my west grove."

"We been holed up over at the mortuary," Clayton blurted.

Delwood glared at Clayton then turned back to Eldridge. "We work for Mr. Braddock, and he suggested we ride out the storm there. I didn't spec that trailer would last. Not like that fine house of yours."

"It made it so far. Just lost some shingles but still dry inside."

"Looks like you got yourself a generator there. You takin' it up to the house?"

"No, I'm running it over to Doc Hawley's clinic. They just had pups."

"Awe, isn't that something." Delwood grinned like he cared. "Smashed nosed pups just like yours I'll bet. And real cute, too."

Eldridge's smile faded. "Yes, Boston terriers like the ones I breed."

Delwood turned to Clayton. "Well, come on, Clayton, let's help the man get the generator onto his truck. Those little puppies are waiting."

Clayton gave Delwood a perplexed look which Delwood returned with a *Don't worry I've got everything under control* smile. "Let's go, Clayton."

"It's not really necessary, boys. I've got some skids."

Delwood laughed. "You hear that, Clayton? He called you *boy*." Delwood paused and Clayton stared straight ahead his teeth clenched. "Get out of the truck Clayton. Don't leave me do this all alone." Clayton reluctantly climbed out of the truck.

Now Eldridge looked perplexed.

"Clayton hates to be called *boy*, don't you Clayton?" They were all in the shed now out of the rain.

"It ain't no big thing, Delwood."

Delwood turned slowly on Clayton. "Shut the fuck up, Clayton."

"I don't know where you're going with this, Delwood, but you know I didn't mean anything by it. Why don't you two move along and I'll handle this myself."

"Man, you are uppity. Clayton and me come out here to help you out, but first you insult Clayton then you try to run us off like you did my daddy."

"I'm sorry if I insulted you, Clayton, and I'm not trying to run anyone off. If you two want to help me lift this generator onto the truck I'd be obliged. But I've got to get back to the clinic." Eldridge turned his attention to the generator sitting on the floor.

Suddenly Delwood raised his right hand which now gripped a ball peen hammer. He drove it down at the base of Eldridge's skull with the sudden force of a lightning strike. Eldridge sank to his knees then slowly pitched forward over the generator as Delwood raced to his side and struck him again. "That's for Daddy."

"Jesus, Delwood!" screamed Clayton. "You kilt him. What the fuck?"

Delwood looked up, his eyes filled with hatred. "Control yourself, Clayton. He got what he deserved." Delwood's arms slumped to his sides, as spent and lifeless as the corpse before him.

Clayton waved his arms frantically. "But we were just goin' to burn him out not snuff him." Clayton clutched his groin. "Oh, Delwood, I gotta pee and I think I'm gonna be sick."

"Help me move him to the house."

"Oh, no. I'm not touchin' no dead man." Clayton ran to the far corner of the shed and unzipped his pants. "I can't believe you did this, Delwood," he said over his shoulder. "We are so screwed."

"I said I had a plan. Just piss and listen. We'll burn down the house like I said, and make it look like lightning. The only difference is Eldridge will be inside, another victim of the storm. Now shake your dick off and get over here."

"I can't do this, Delwood, it's murder. Oh God, I'm going to throw up." With that Clayton began to wretch fitfully onto the dirt floor.

Delwood marched over and grabbed him by the shoulder. "Jesus, Clayton, I don't believe you. Look at this fuckin' hammer." Clayton was still retching and didn't look up. "Look at it dammit."

Clayton, still bent forward with his hands on his knees, slowly looked back over his shoulder. When the recognition came he let out a low moan. "Jesus, Mary, and Joseph," he rasped.

"Yes, Clayton, it's your goddamn hammer."

"Awe, Delwood."

"Your hammer, both of our fingerprints, and we're both here. Now pull yourself together and help me make this look right."

Clayton straightened up and looked over at the body on the ground. "We're gonna die, Delwood. They're gonna send us to the pen for killing a black man and when the coloreds are done using us as their punks they'll cut our nuts off with a shank."

"Where in the hell do you get this stuff?"

"I saw it in a movie." Clayton wiped his mouth with his shirtsleeve.

"In the first place, nobody is going to find out. Secondly, look at the bright side; we found that generator we needed."

NINETEEN

"That wind is picking up again." Spencer looked over at Gidget and her pups, who slept peacefully on the couch under the warmth of the kerosene lamp. "I wish Eldridge would get back here with the generator." At the mention of Eldridge's name O.J. and Tangela looked up toward the door in anticipation then lay their heads back down on their forepaws, seemingly unconcerned with the storm.

"It's the back half of Buzz. We've lost the radio reception again, Doctor."

"I figured that much, but I guess it doesn't matter."

"Fortunately we're not in the middle. The worst of it hit north of us."

"I wonder how your apartment building is, Missy."

"Considering its construction it's probably somewhere over Orlando about now."

"I'm sorry. Maybe you shouldn't have stayed."

Missy shrugged. "It wouldn't have mattered. Besides it was my mother's cast-offs and thrift shop furniture. My father made me buy contents insurance, so I'll probably come out ahead."

"I'm glad you stayed. I needed you in that operating room; you did well. I'm surprised you didn't get into vet school."

"You're a better judge of animals than people, Doc. I'm just another dumb blonde like the ones men joke about."

"I don't believe that." Spencer shifted his weight and looked straight at Missy.

"Do you know how to drive a blonde crazy?"

"Stop."

"Give her a bag of M&M's and ask her to alphabetize them. Good one, huh?"

"Somehow you telling it is not that funny. You run this office well and you're as good with people as you are with their pets. Don't put yourself down."

"Is that an order?" Missy looked away before he could answer. When she looked back at Spencer tears were streaming down her face. "I took some psychological tests at school. They said I'm a visual learner."

"What's that mean?"

"It means I can't remember a damn thing I read in the textbook, but if you show me how to do something, like assisting, I retain it just fine. And being blonde I'm doubly cursed. I'll bet you even hired me because I was blonde."

Spencer flushed. "Actually, I almost didn't hire you because you were blonde … and too pretty."

"So why did you?"

"You were the only one who'd work for what I was offering."

Missy shook her head. "Sounds like another dumb blonde joke."

"And you were the only pretty sight in Winter Beach."

Now Missy flushed. "When this storm is over there's going to be a lot of scared stray pets needing attention. Can I stay here in the clinic and help?"

"No."

"But I can put up a cot in the storage room."

"You can stay at my place and help with the dogs. I'll sleep on the couch."

Missy smiled. "I'll stay at your place on one condition, Doctor."

"What's that?"

"That you still have a place tomorrow."

"Delwood, how long is this going to last?"

"Clayton, I can't fuckin' hear a word you're sayin' with that coffin lid down. Jesus, you'd think you were the one kilt not Stoval."

The lid on Clayton's coffin cracked open. "I might as well stay in here; we're going to die anyway, Delwood."

"It must be a freakin' oven in there."

"Get used to it. We're going to hell."

"I don't believe in no hell. Now open that up. We got beer, the generator is cranked up, and you're missing the *Playboy* channel, Clayton."

"I don't care. I'm not comin' out."

"Clayton, nobody is going to figure this out, especially Deputy Dawg, our county sheriff. We dragged the body inside and burned the place to the ground. The rain will wash away any sign of us being there."

"We should have left the generator."

"What the hell for? Eldridge was stone cold dead. He didn't need it any more."

"They might trace it."

"Clayton, do you know how many Honda generators there are in this county right now?"

"No. How many?"

"A lot. And they're all running full bore. No one's going to even think twice about us having this generator. Now pull your head out of your ass and open that coffin lid."

"Awright."

Delwood reached for a beer and handed it to Clayton. "Here. Christ Almighty you smell bad. Don't you use deodorant?"

"It's been a bad day, Delwood. It must have slipped my mind." Clayton popped the top on his beer.

"We'll find you some when this is over. Drink up. Those two girls who show the naked amateur videos are about to come on."

"Delwood?"

"Yeah."

"Aren't you worried about where you're going to live? Stoval said your trailer was blown to bits."

"I've been thinkin' about that very thing, Clayton, while you hunkered down in that coffin like some damn turtle." Delwood paused to take a long draw on his can of Glades before he reached for another handful of Cheetos. "Now that Eldridge Stoval is finally out of my way I'm going to buy his land and get into citrus just like my daddy."

"That'll cost a lot of money."

"Maybe not so much." Delwood popped a Cheeto into his mouth and pointed the remote at the naked housewife who lay on the kitchen floor smearing her writhing body with corn oil. "My God, Clayton, these housewives must be more bored than a coon in a cage."

"It kinda turns me on."

"Husbands filming their naked wives' beavers for pay T.V. What kind of family values is that?"

"I still don't see where you're gonna get the money. If you had a wife, you could film her and enter the T.V. contest."

"My trailer is gone, Clayton, but I figure Indian River County will be declared a disaster area, and I'll get a FEMA check for my trailer and maybe even a low interest loan. Besides, Eldridge's orchards look pretty beat up. I'll bet I can buy them pretty cheap."

"Who you gonna buy it from? He don't have no family."

"It will probably go through some kinda probates, and when nobody steps forward they'll sell it."

"Isn't that vet kin? What if he steps forward?"

"Aw shit, Clayton, I didn't think of that."

Lucinda shed her robe and slid into the tepid bath water. Reliable Walker had the foresight not only to buy bottled water but to fill his tubs and sinks before Buzz hit. It wasn't the hot shower she craved, but after two days of living in what felt like a dark hot cave this felt like heaven. The wind and rain had let up for the past hour, and the radio weather station said the worst was over.

Lucinda scattered lit candles, creating a scene of flickering light and shadows. Who could guess when the power would be restored? Until then they would need the candles and the bottled water since Walker's supply depended on his well and its electric pump. Still, it seemed silly to be conserving water and candles now that the storm had passed.

What really pulled Lucinda was the call of damaged and undamaged real estate. Hopefully T. Pascoe Redstone's place was blown to hell and she could be rid of that albatross. Eldridge Stoval's place was her main concern, however. If it was damaged enough, maybe he would sell for a lot lower price now. The Miami developers wouldn't care what state the orchards were in. They were just going to plow them under.

There was a knock at the door. "What do you want, Walker?"

"You aren't bathing in that precious water are you, hon?"

"The storm's over, and I've got to freshen up and get to work."

"But what about me?"

"The radio said no one died in Indian River County, so unless you plan to drive up into Brevard County and haul back the bodies from that trailer park, I don't think you have any work to do. Sorry, Walker, these advanced storm warning systems have really ruined your business."

"That's why I need to develop the pet crematorium and cemetery. I'll bet the little critters didn't fare nearly as well as their masters in this."

At the one hundredth mention of the pet cemetery since she had moved in two days ago, Lucinda slid completely under the water. When she surfaced she added shampoo to her wet hair. "Walker, sometimes your ability for small thinking amazes me."

"Lucinda, you really hurt me, but I know the business. The only place there is more chance for markup than on a widow's deceased husband is her poor departed poodle."

"But it takes time and all that effusion would wear me out. One quick killing in real estate and you're set for life. You never have to kiss anyone's ass again." Lucinda slid back under the water and shook her head free of soap. She surfaced and reached for her towel. "Why don't you men ever keep any conditioner around?"

"Sit tight. I'll run in to Vero and get some since I don't have any real work to do."

"Bite me, Walker."

TWENTY

Spencer awakened to the sound of multiple dogs scratching at the front door. His first thought was Gidget, but when he looked over at the couch she was still lying there with her pups and looked up sadly as if to say, *What have you done to me? How am I supposed to eat or pee?*

Spencer realized it must be the other dogs. He stood up and stretched his aching back. The sound of the wind and rain was gone. Padding past the exam room where Missy had chosen to drag a mattress, he noticed the door ajar and her bed empty.

O.J. howled. "I'm coming. I'm coming," Spencer replied.

He reached for a handful of leashes off the sale rack and looked down at the anxious faces. O.J. and Tangela had soft brown eyes and matching white blazes on their foreheads with white shawls that surrounded their shoulders and met the chest areas. They had show dog markings. Two of their remaining pups had the same show quality and while the third shared the same sad eyes and facial expression of the rest, he lacked the proper blaze and shawl. He was mismarked since one half his face was white while the other half was black. He lacked the brown markings around both eyes that the judges required and was destined to be neutered and become just some kid's dog. He didn't know how lucky he was.

Spencer leashed O.J., Tangela, and the three pups. "Ok, kids, let's see what God hath wrought." With that Spencer opened the door and was immediately jerked into the parking lot by the pull of the dogs. The perfection of the bright sun in a cloudless blue sky contrasted with the destruction that surrounded him, left Spencer speechless.

"I think we got off pretty easy." Missy rounded the corner of the clinic, hammer in hand. Her blonde hair was piled on top of her head and held in place by a large butterfly clip. She wore off-white short shorts and a hot pink Mr. Manatee's T-shirt which sported the familiar logo, a smiling manatee in a pith helmet.

"I'd hate to see Melbourne if you call this easy." Spencer looked around. Most of the signage had blown off the buildings or their curb posts. Palm fronds lay everywhere and every uncovered window was broken. To the south he could see an FPL truck parked near downed power lines.

"We lost some roofs and power lines, but all the buildings are still standing. It could be a lot worse, and I guarantee it is in Melbourne."

The dogs strained at their leashes as each tried to go a different direction. The mismarked pup had wrapped himself around Spencer's right leg. "Here, you take O.J. and Tangela while I try to sort out these pups." Spencer handed two leashes to Missy as he untangled his leg.

As Missy moved effortlessly across the debris-strewn parking lot she shouted back over her shoulder, "What about Gidget?"

"I think she already misses her days of liberated womanhood. I'll get her out next for a little break."

Two of the pups crawled under a Dr. Pepper sign and squatted to relieve themselves while Mismark sat down next to Spencer and cocked his head to one side as if the process was entirely unfamiliar to him. "Come on, pup, you might as well join them. You know you gotta go." As if waiting for the invitation Mismark slowly crept under the sign and joined his siblings.

Missy returned shortly with O.J. and Tangela. "Why don't you give me the pups and I'll take them all inside. It's too hot for them out here."

"Fine, I'll take the hammer and start peeling off the plywood. Would you take Gidget out, too?"

"No problem. The ladder is around back. I thought we'd start in the shade." Missy turned and started off with the dogs. She looked as if nothing had happened. Her clothes were fresh, and except for the small beads of perspiration that had formed on her upper lip, she looked like she had just jogged, showered, and was off to get the paper before breakfast.

Spencer, on the other hand, looked like he had slept in his clothes, which he had. He needed a shave and the inside of his mouth tasted like a three-day-old box of kitty litter. Despite how he felt, he couldn't help but admire Missy's retreating behind, but reminded himself he didn't need a sexual harassment suit on top of everything else.

Two hours later they had pulled the last of the nails and had stored the still damp plywood inside. "We'd better not leave this stuff unattended. I imagine it's worth its weight in gold to those who've lost their roofs."

Missy smiled. "Spoken like a native, Doctor."

Spencer thought of suggesting she call him by his first name but thought better of it. "We'd better load the dogs into the Suburban and drive out to Eldridge's. I'll run the air conditioning on low. It will be good for Gidget to cool down a bit; she's not used to the heat."

"I'll get my stuff and ride along."

"But what about your place?"

"The National Guard has blocked the roads in Melbourne. My stuff isn't worth the hassle right now. Like I said, I don't have anything worth digging out of the rubble."

"I appreciate the help, but whenever you think you need to go …"

"You'll be the first to know. Now I'll load up the dogs while you change your shirt and use some of that soap and water by the sink in the lab."

Spencer looked down at his sweat-stained shirt. "I guess I am a sight. I'll just change my shirt and …"

"Shave."

"Yes, and shave."

"Take your time. I'll cool down the truck for the dogs."

The trek to Eldridge Stoval's was slow and tedious, but the clean shirt and shave felt good. It also felt good to get out of the stifling midday heat and the boarded clinic. As they picked their way around debris and fallen branches, Spencer looked out over the groves. In some areas the trees were completely defoliated, yet still standing. Other areas reminded Spencer of the aftermath of an Iowa tornado. Large swaths had been cut through some of the groves where trees were upended, their bare roots exposed like a compound fracture. Sections of the road were strewn with mobile home siding and cheap paneling, but occasionally they'd pass something personal like a smudged doll or a deserted bicycle, its frame twisted beyond repair.

"I think that's his driveway up ahead. It's hard to tell with all the damage."

O.J. began to whine. "Somebody recognizes the place even if his doctor doesn't," Missy said.

Spencer slowed and turned into the lane. "Yeah, this is it; I recognize the shed over there." O.J. barked and scratched at the window.

"Oh my God, look at the house."

Spencer felt a knot tighten in his stomach. He stopped the truck as close as he dared to the house and got out, but before he could close the door O.J. slipped out after him and ran toward the charred rubble. He stopped short of the house and cocked his head momentarily. Then he began to trail the perimeter, his nose to the ground as if searching for a clue to the catastrophe.

"Spencer, do you think Eldridge was … is?"

"His truck is over there but he couldn't be. What the hell happened?"

"Maybe lightning?"

"Or the generator. It runs on gasoline."

"But why haven't we heard from Eldridge? Oh, this is so awful." Missy suddenly turned and ran for the car. O.J. returned from his investigation and sat at Spencer's feet as they both contemplated the ruins.

"I have my cell phone." Missy rummaged through her bag. "I'm calling 911."

"Cell phone? How can you afford that on what I pay you?"

"It's from my father. He insists his daughter have one for security purposes." She pulled out the phone and punched in the numbers. "Darn, 911 is busy."

"It can't be." Spencer looked over at the truck. Now all of Eldridge's dogs were barking and pawing the windows of the Suburban. "Might as well let them out, too." He opened the door and was almost knocked over by the bounding dogs. "Try 911 again."

"Hello? Yes, this is an emergency. There's been a fire. No, it's just smoldering now. We don't know if anyone's inside; we just got here."

"Tell them it's Eldridge Stoval's place."

Missy waved at Spencer to be quiet. "It's Eldridge Stoval's house just west of Winter Beach. I don't know, maybe five miles on Orange Blossom." Missy looked up at Spencer for confirmation and he nodded. "No, there doesn't appear to be any danger to the surrounding buildings, but he might be in there." Missy gestured toward the rubble with a free hand as if to clarify the situation to the voice at the other end. "No, no one answers when I shout. I know you're busy, but can't you send someone?" Missy scowled and shifted her weight to her right hip. "All right, we'll wait."

"What's the deal?"

"She says they're really backed up and all their firefighters have been dispatched. She'll try to catch a deputy and send him out. We're supposed to wait here."

"Great," Spencer moaned. "I've got a new mother and her pups in the car. I'll have to leave it running so she doesn't overheat."

"Maybe they won't be too long." Missy bit her lower lip and looked toward the shed and Eldridge's car.

"Let's check the shed." Spencer didn't wait for a response but instead approached the outbuilding and stopped at Eldridge's truck. He waited for Missy to catch up then said, "His truck is empty and the keys are in the ignition. He also left the door to the shed open during the storm. Why would he do that?"

Missy walked past Spencer and cautiously entered the shed which was the size of a three-car garage. "I don't see a generator." Her voice echoed off the tin walls. "He said he was going to bring one. Do you think he had it in the house?"

"It's not in the truck." Just then the white cruiser of the Indian River County Sheriff's Department rolled into the drive. Missy joined Spencer and they walked over to the young deputy. "That didn't take you long," Spencer said as the officer rolled down his window.

"I was just south of here at T. Pascoe Redstone's. You'd think he was the only one in the county who lost a roof. I don't know what he thought I was going to do about it, but when the county supervisor calls ... You know how it is." The deputy opened his door and climbed out. "Where'd all these dogs come from?"

"They belong to Mr. Stoval."

The dogs had now surrounded the deputy and took keen interest in his boots and the tires of the cruiser. Mismark balanced awkwardly on three legs and christened the left rear tire. "Were they here when you arrived?"

"No, Mr. Stoval had left them with us and we were just returning them." Spencer didn't know why but he felt compelled to refer to his cousin as *Mr.*

The deputy motioned toward the house. "Not much left of his place I'm afraid. I hope we don't find him inside."

"His truck's over there and there's no sign of the generator," Missy blurted.

The deputy turned to Missy and his face immediately brightened. "Miss." He tipped the brim of his hat as he took in every square inch of Missy.

"Yes, his truck is over there by the shed. We couldn't find the generator," Spencer interjected sensing he was about to be left out of the ensuing dialogue. He was caught off guard by this unexpected feeling of possessiveness toward his attractive assistant.

The deputy began to follow Missy back toward the truck. "You looked in the shed for a generator?"

"Yes, it wasn't in the truck or inside."

"You didn't touch anything did you?"

"No." Missy paused and looked at the deputy. "You don't think a crime was committed here do you?"

The deputy pulled himself to his full authoritative height and hooked his thumbs on his belt. "We've got to consider all possibilities until we can fully assess the situation. You brought up the alleged missing generator yourself."

Spencer spoke now. "He and his dogs were staying with my assistant and me at the clinic. He left during a lull in the storm to get his generator and never returned."

The deputy turned to Spencer. "You don't talk like you're from around here. Are you a doctor?"

"I'm a veterinarian and I have a clinic in Winter Beach. Mr. Stoval is a client. We both raise Boston terriers, and he helped my assistant and me deliver my dog's pups." Spencer spoke rapidly offering more information than necessary, but he suddenly felt compelled to establish his innocence.

"He could have had the generator already set up in the house with the storm coming in and all," Missy interjected.

"That's a very good point, miss," the deputy continued in an official mono-tone. "It shouldn't be too hard to establish. In any case there's not much we can do here now. I'll get you two some routine name-and-address forms to fill out while I seal off the area. We need to get the fire chief out here. In the meantime we'll list Mr. Stoval among the missing. Do either of you know if he has any fam-ily in the area?" The question was for both of them but obviously directed at Missy.

"He doesn't have anyone that we know. His wife and daughter died years ago."

Spencer swallowed hard and nodded. He didn't feel compelled to share his relationship to Eldridge with anyone at the moment.

The deputy returned to his car and spoke to someone on the radio before he returned with two clipboards and a large roll of yellow crime scene tape. "If you two would just fill out the top half of these I'll start with the tape." He handed one board to Spencer without taking his eyes off Missy, then carefully instructed her regarding each required section.

"I think my assistant and I can manage, officer, thank you."

"Yes, I'm certain you can. Let me know if you have any questions." The dep-uty marched off tape in hand.

As she began to work on her form Missy spoke. "I don't think our deputy liked being called on his flirtation."

"Like he was surprised I noticed. If he spent half as much time looking around this place as he did at you we might know something." Missy just smiled one of those girl smiles and looked down at her clipboard. Spencer didn't know her well enough to ask what she was thinking, but he wondered. They wrote in silence for several minutes. "I'm finished. I'd better round up the dogs and we'll go check my place," Spencer said.

"I'm done, too." Missy reached for Spencer's clipboard. "I'll take these over to the deputy."

"I'm sure he'd like that," Spencer grumbled. He waited until Missy reached the deputy then yelled, "We'll be in touch!"

The deputy looked back at Spencer quizzically as if he wasn't sure if he was being put on or not. Missy smiled then shook his hand and walked back to the truck. Spencer thought that if it were possible the deputy would have stared a hole in her butt.

O.J., Tangela, and the pups looked back toward home and whined in resignation before they curled up on the seat to sleep. Spencer turned east at the end of the drive and began to work his way back toward town. He drove in silence, unsure if he was more uncomfortable with his new found possessiveness toward Missy or the disappearance of Eldridge.

Missy finally broke the silence. "Do you think Eldridge was in that house?"

"He wouldn't break a promise."

"And he wouldn't just leave the dogs."

"I hope we're both wrong."

"He liked you."

Spencer smiled. "We might have become good friends. Lord knows I could use some."

"We're both starting to talk like he's gone."

"Yeah, let's not do that." Spencer tried to focus on the road ahead. "Maybe your deputy friend will find him."

Missy turned and looked out across the ravaged groves. "He doesn't know me enough to be my friend. He just thinks he wants what he sees. I get so tired of that."

"I'm sorry I said that."

"That's okay. Let's go check out your place."

TWENTY ONE

As she picked her way home along U.S. 1 Lucinda couldn't help but notice the patrol car entering the highway from the vicinity of Tip Redstone's albatross. She turned where the deputy pulled out and followed the road back toward the Redstone place. Her best case scenario was that the place had been demolished. Whether Tip and his wife were buried under the rubble was of no consequence.

An upturned live oak blocked the driveway, but just beyond the wilted foliage she could see the remains of the home. The stucco and concrete block walls still stood, but shutters and broken glass were strewn everywhere. There was no sign of the roof. It was as if the hand of God had reached down and twisted it off like the top of an Oreo cookie.

Tip stood on the front porch, head and arms thrust skyward, and Lucinda suspected his conversation with his Creator was getting ugly. He turned and stared for a moment as Lucinda rolled to a stop and got out of her car. When he finally recognized her he scowled and ran off the porch to greet her. "I suppose you're here to tell me I have a fucking showing today. Just give me a moment to freshen the place up. Sorry, but I won't have time to get a loaf of bread in the oven to give the place that homey aroma."

Lucinda suppressed a sudden urge to rip Redstone's Magoo glasses off his face and punch him in the nose. "I saw the deputy and stopped to see if you and Mrs. Redstone were safe. Obviously, you're no worse for the wear. Is she all right?"

"She packed up and bolted for her sister's place in Winter Haven before the first storm cloud appeared. I wouldn't leave this place just to have it violated by the damn looters or some nosey reporter."

Lucinda stifled a smile as she thought of the contents of Tip's bedside drawers and wondered how many other secrets dwelled in that shell of a house. "I'm sure you also felt the need to be near your constituents in their time of need."

"Constituents? I could give a rat's ass. They can fuckin' fend for themselves." The Magoo glasses bobbed up and down on the tip of his nose. "I've got this house and the new one on the beach to worry about."

"Speaking of someone who apparently doesn't give a damn about his constituents, I couldn't help but notice you were having a little conversation with God about your roof as I drove up."

"He couldn't just level the whole house, could He? No, He had to just maim it so my insurance company wouldn't call it a total loss. Now I'll have to pull it off the market while I get the roof repaired and water damage corrected. In the meantime we close on the new place in less than a month."

"I'm sure the roofers will give your place top priority."

Tip had already tuned Lucinda out. Instead he'd climbed back up on his porch and began to kick at the walls like a spoiled little kid. He'd apparently lost his golf cap in the storm because his exposed bald head emitted a medium rare hue. Lucinda felt certain he would be blistered by evening. "What am I going to do to protect all my papers and shit?" Tip asked.

"How about you gather them up and lock them in your pool shed out back, if it's still in one piece?"

"Good idea, Vickers. Come on." Redstone leapt off the porch and started around the house at a trot. Lucinda pushed back branches and straddled splintered trusses as she struggled to keep up. Thankfully she had donned shorts and a cotton shirt when she left Walker's instead of work clothes. Tip stopped and pointed at the shed. "Ah ha! That aluminum piece of shit made it. Thank you, Jesus."

"Well, there you go, Mr. Redstone. The Lord acts in mysterious ways. It's not much, but it's a place to start."

Without answering Redstone opened the gate and ran toward his shed like a child leaving day care for his mother. His feet made a clickety-click sound on the cement as he ran, and that's when Lucinda noticed that he was wearing golf shoes. "If you want I can stay and help."

Tip unlocked the shed and stuck his head inside. "And how much does your agency charge for that?"

"It's no charge at all, Mr. Redstone. You make some room in there and I'll start emptying the drawers in your bedroom." Lucinda turned and started for what remained of the patio doors.

Her offer had the exact desired effect on Redstone. He almost tripped and fell into the pool as he raced past Lucinda to bar her entrance. "That won't be necessary, Ms. Vickers," he puffed. "I appreciate your offer but it's just a few things."

"But I thought you said …"

"No, no problem at all. I can manage. You run along and de-list the place."

"You're sure?"

"I'll be fine." With a trembling hand Redstone pushed his glasses back up on the bridge of his nose.

"I'll be on my way then. Call if I can be of any assistance." Lucinda turned and walked toward the gate. It had been worth the trip and the lost commission just to watch Tip Redstone squirm.

Walker knew Delwood and Clayton had sequestered themselves in the mortuary during the storm, but was totally unprepared for what he found upon his return. He gasped at the sight of the two men sound asleep in two of his top-of-the-line caskets amidst a pile of beer cans, candy wrappers, and empty Cheetos bags. Nearly every visible square inch of satin lining that surrounded the two men bore the trademark fluorescent orange stains. The engine of an unfamiliar Honda generator hummed nearby, barely audible above the sonorous snoring of his two employees.

"What in the name of God is going on here?"

Delwood stirred then pushed himself upward to free his arms. "Good morning, boss." He stretched his arms and rubbed his eyes with Cheeto stained fists and left two orange rings around his eyes. He looked like a psychedelic raccoon.

"I can't believe this mess. And my caskets!"

Delwood reached over and shook Clayton. "Wake up, Clayton. We survived Hurricane Buzz."

Clayton jerked awake with a start and Delwood pointed in the direction of Walker. "Good morning, Mr. Braddock. We didn't expect you this early." Clayton struggled to free himself from his steel sleeping bag and stood beside it in his underwear like Luke Skywalker reporting for duty with his X-wing fighter.

"It's 11:00 a.m.; the storm ended hours ago." Walker ran to his caskets and gingerly fingered the lining. The entire receptacle smelled like a giant sweat sock. "They're ruined!" he exclaimed as he turned his head and gagged.

"Don't worry, Walker. Clayton and I can clean 'em up and air 'em out just like new." Delwood climbed down out of his chamber and adjusted his sagging underwear. He scratched his butt and walked over to Walker's television. "We'll put this back, too, sir."

"My television? From my office?"

"Yes, sir, but we'll have it back quicker than a two dollar whore. You'll see."

Walker ran over to the big screen and dropped to his knees. "My imported marble floors! You gouged them with my television."

Delwood walked over and put a hand on Walker's shoulder. Walker looked up to face Delwood's crotch and gagged again. "A little Johnson's wax and this floor will shine like one of them new Weber Grills. Don't you worry none."

Meanwhile Clayton pulled on his pants and scampered around the room retrieving armfuls of beer cans and wrappers. "It's looking better already, sir. That sure was some storm."

Walker slumped against his entertainment center and held both hands tightly against his stomach. "Get ooout!"

"I spec Clayton and I should get out and check around the building for damage."

Walker pulled himself to a stand. "You can return later for your belongings because you're not staying here another night."

"Since my trailer was demolished I thought we might stay another night or two until we can get resituated."

"Your trailer?"

"We was out once during that lull." Delwood glanced at Clayton who suddenly blanched. "Clayton and I went back to get my generator. Trailer was gone, but the generator was right there in the shed so we brought it back. Right, Clayton? That's how it was?"

"I gotta pee, Delwood." With that announcement Clayton rushed from the room.

"What's wrong with him?"

"Got weak kidneys. Had them since we were kids."

"Look, I'm sorry about your trailer, but this is a business not a homeless shelter. You two will have to work out something else."

"Yes, sir." Delwood smiled. "We'll be out of your *business* tonight."

TWENTY TWO

Delwood and Clayton bounced along the rutted back roads of Winter Beach in Delwood's pickup. Fortunately they had secured their precious Honda generator with bungee cords. At Clayton's insistence they had also covered it with a tarp. "I don't know why we're drivin' around like this, Delwood. I got an aunt up in Tallahassee we could stay with until this blows over."

"I got an aunt in Tallahassee," Delwood mimicked in falsetto. "Tallahassee rhymes with sissy. I didn't run from no hurricane and I'm not runnin' from my birthright. We're stayin' right here until I find us a place." Delwood reached over and turned up the volume on the radio and began to sing along with Bobby Bare's *Drop-kick me, Jesus, through the Goalpost of Life*. "I love this oldies channel, Clayton. They don't write songs like this anymore."

Clayton shrugged and stared out the window in silence.

"What's your problem, peckerwood?"

"I've got a headache and a crick in my neck from sleeping in that coffin."

"It's not like you ain't been hung over before."

"I can't lose the picture of you dragging that poor man's body from the shed to the house and setting it on fire."

"Would you just let it go, numb nuts? We covered our tracks and poured gasoline around the outside electric meter before we set the fire. Nobody's gonna figure us out."

"But we should have left the generator, Delwood. Someone might remember that generator."

"Just leave the fuckin' generator to me."

Clayton turned away and began to bite his fingernail.

"Lookie yonder, Clayton. Isn't that Tip Redstone's place?"

Clayton looked in the direction of Delwood's pointed finger and shrugged. "I reckon it is."

"I think that's ol' Tipper himself packing up his car. Let's see what he's up to." Delwood turned the truck sharply into the drive and came to a stop behind Tip's red Lincoln.

Tip slammed the trunk quickly and turned to face his unexpected guests. He squinted at them through his pop-bottle lenses. "What can I do for you fellas?"

"Howdy, Mr. Redstone. Clayton and I were out surveying the damage and seen you working over here like some citrus picker and thought you could use a hand."

"Is that you, Delwood? I thought that was you." Redstone relaxed and walked toward the truck.

"It's me, Mr. Redstone. This is my partner Clayton."

"Hey, Mr. Clayton." Tip reached into the truck cab over Delwood and shook hands with Clayton.

"It's been a long time, Delwood." Then speaking to Clayton he said, "My wife and I used to run with Delwood's parents, until all the tragedy that is." Tip's announcement was followed by a few moments of reverent silence for the departed couple.

"No, we haven't seen much of you and the missis, Tip. Not since we moved back into the trailer." Tip hung his head and scuffed at the gravel with his golf shoe.

"It was a real tragedy about your mom. Is your place damaged?"

"Scattered like shit through a fan."

"Aw, I'm sorry."

"Lost every bit of Mom's art work, too."

"Not the Elvis tribute?"

"I expect he's somewhere over Orlando as we speak, Mr. Redstone."

"Damn shame, her havin' such a fine talent and all."

"You've got some serious roof damage there, Mr. Redstone. Are you pulling out?"

"I'm afraid so." They all focused on the damaged home.

Delwood finally spoke. "Clayton and I saved my generator but got no place to stay. What if we moved in and watched over the place for you? We'll keep the looters out."

"Looters?"

"Oh yeah, Mr. Redstone, you'd be amazed at the criminal activity that goes on during one of these disasters." Delwood turned and winked at Clayton who looked away.

"I've got my important stuff locked in the shed, but …"

"It's the first place they'd look. Guaran-fuckin'-teed." Delwood opened the door and stepped down as Redstone backpedaled out of his way. Delwood taking charge now. He walked over to the house and looked at it real serious like he was an insurance inspector. Then he turned back to Redstone. "It ain't the Ritz, Tip, but I reckon Clayton and I can make do and save you a lot of trouble."

Redstone looked at Delwood, adjusted his glasses, then looked down at his golf shoes for a moment before he looked back at Delwood and Clayton and smiled. "Why not? We'd both be doin' each other a good turn. Take over, Delwood. I'll be in touch." Redstone scrambled for his car and drove off as if he were just minutes ahead of the thieving hordes.

Delwood walked back to the truck and shook his head. "Fuckin' politicians are all alike, Clayton. They scatter like hens at the first sign of trouble."

"I thought you were old family friends, Delwood."

"Yeah right," Delwood sniffed. "After Daddy died old Tipper used to sneak around to our trailer behind his wife's back and try to play grab ass with my mother."

"What a mess!" Spencer stepped out of his truck and stood paralyzed as he gazed at his uprooted shrubs and the debris that had collected in his lawn.

Missy ran ahead nonplussed by the apparent damage. "Amazing! Only part of your roof is gone, not even a quarter of it. You lost your living room window though." She stuck her head through the opening and after a few moments hollered back. "Nothing's missing but it's good you've got tile floors or you'd have a mildew problem by tonight."

Spencer picked up the remains of a rhododendron and looked up at the hole in his roof. "It's a mess. What are we going to do?"

"You sound lost. Don't worry, Doc, we'll haul some of that plywood back here from the clinic and cover this window. We can use the rest to patch that hole on the roof. It will hold until the insurance adjusters arrive. You're lucky."

"Lucky?"

"Oh, yeah." Missy had followed the foundation of the house around to the back door. "Come on. Let's check inside."

Spencer fumbled for his keys as Missy peered through the window. "I forgot you had a freezer. Is it full?"

Spencer pushed open the door. "Not very, just some hamburger, chicken, and a couple of frozen dinners."

"It doesn't sound like you lost much." Missy marched over and studied the door.

"Lost?"

"The power's been out almost twenty-four hours. Everything in there has thawed by now."

"Damn!" Beebee's lifeless carcass suddenly flashed before his eyes.

"It's all right; we might be able to save the chicken if we cook it right away." Missy reached for the handle.

"No, that's okay. I'm sure it's not safe. I'll throw it out later."

"We might as well check."

"Spencer reached over and slammed the partially opened door. "Salmonella. I worry about that."

"Salmonella?"

"Yeah, it could kill you."

"Then we'd better get it out of there right now and scrub this freezer down."

Before Spencer could think of anything else to say, Missy opened the door and stuck her head inside. "Oh my God, Doctor. There's a dog. I think it's Beebee!"

Spencer's knees weakened and beads of perspiration began to form on his forehead. "Oh that. I can explain."

"My God, he's dead. You weren't going to eat him were you?" she whispered. "I think I'm going to be sick."

"No, of course not! He's in there because …"

"I thought you farmed her out to a place in Vero Beach."

"I couldn't tell you."

"Tell me what?"

"That she's dead and I …"

"And you stuffed her into your freezer next to your chicken, as if that's more sanitary than salmonella?"

"I didn't know what else to do. I was just exercising her."

"And she dropped dead?"

"That's it."

"What were you going to tell Beebee's owner?"

"I wasn't sure, but I didn't want to ruin her cruise, plus I figured she'd want to make proper funeral arrangements herself." Spencer was beginning to believe himself. This was easy and Missy was leading him right through it.

"Like a pet cemetery?"

"Right again. I thought she might want to know the cause of Beebee's demise and have me post her. I mean perform an autopsy."

"Why didn't you tell me?" Beebee's head and neck, which had been folded back and frozen into position to fit her into the compartment had now thawed sufficiently, and as if she were alive, her head flopped forward and she unceremoniously slid out onto the floor. Missy squealed and jumped back.

Spencer quickly rushed to Beebee and knelt to straighten out her carcass as if this would make it all better. Small pools of water began to form beneath the pompon on her tail and under her little paws. "This is just such a shock. I'm sorry." Spencer looked up at Missy with his best *I'm sorry your pet didn't survive the operation* face.

Then he reached for her hand. "I couldn't bear to tell you. I did all I could to revive her but to no avail. She was gone and I blamed myself."

"But it wasn't your fault. Was it?"

"I took her for a routine workout. I had no idea."

"You should have told me." Missy reached over and touched Spencer on the shoulder.

"You once said you couldn't work for someone who didn't love animals. What would this look like?"

"An accident, that's all." Her face softened and she knelt beside Spencer and Beebee. "You poor man, you shouldn't have shouldered the burden yourself."

Spencer sighed and to the patron saint of veterinarians whispered, *Thank you.* Then he took Missy in his arms. "I'm so sorry. I should have trusted you; forgive me."

Spencer awakened from his nap to the sound and smell of sizzling meat he couldn't quite place. He rolled over on the couch and looked toward the kitchen where Missy had set up her camp stove. "Where did you get that fresh meat?"

"Who said it was fresh? It's Spam." Missy stood over the fry pan with the determined look of a terrier at a gopher hole. In one hand she gripped a spatula and with the other she brushed back a lock of hair.

"I think my grandmother used to make it, but I can't recall for the life of me why. Grandfather raised cattle, chickens and hogs," Spencer said.

"I was raised on it. Mother knew a hundred recipes."

"Sounds intriguing."

"You're out of luck, mister. Mother's not here, and I just fry it."

Spencer smiled at her use of *mister*. She was loosening up. When he reopened the clinic their roles would revert to doctor and assistant and *mister* would be inappropriate. But it had been a long time since he had lain on his couch while a woman cooked for him in the kitchen. It felt comfortable even if it was just Spam.

They were just finishing their meal of canned corn and fried Spam when there was a knock at the door. They looked at each other and shrugged. "Maybe they had to send the telemarketers out on foot," Spencer suggested.

Missy looked at him quizzically then smiled as she caught the joke ... "I'll get it." She got up from the table and bounded for the door like a teen queen about to greet her *dork du jour*.

As the door opened Spencer strained to catch a glimpse of the intruder. "Hello, Bob. What brings you out this way so late?"

Spencer leaned out of his chair to see who it was. The voice sounded familiar but he didn't know any of Missy's friends.

"Can I come in a minute, Missy? I'm sorry to interrupt, but it's business I'm afraid."

"Certainly, I was just about to pour some coffee. With no electricity or ice I'm afraid it's all we have."

By now Spencer was standing. The arrival of the deputy wasn't as surprising as the fact that Deputy Bob and Missy were already on a first name basis.

"Sorry to disturb you, Doctor."

"No problem," Spencer managed through clenched teeth. "Have a seat."

"I can't stay. I just came by to tell you that we did find Mr. Stoval."

"Thank God. Is he all right?"

"No, I'm sorry to report that he died in the fire."

Spencer felt like he had been slapped in the face even though he had expected the inevitable all afternoon. Missy let out a soft whimper and began to cry, but Deputy Bob, who had evidently slept through the sensitivity sessions at the academy, stood as mute as a wooden soldier.

"What happened?" Spencer managed.

"We don't know yet. There'll be an autopsy, and the fire chief will investigate." Deputy Bob looked over at Missy as he spoke and it appeared as if he would approach her, but his feet were apparently nailed to the floor. "The sheriff sent me out here to see about his dogs."

"His dogs?"

"We can't pay you to kennel them during the investigation. Our contract is with the Humane Society. They'll keep them for us for a week and if no family claims them then they'll try to find them a home."

"Or destroy them," Missy ventured.

"Only if they can't be placed."

Now Missy was angry. "If it's all the same to you, Bob, the doctor and I will take responsibility for the dogs. There won't be any charge to the county."

"I'm sorry, but I can't do that. Regulations state that the dogs must be impounded until claimed by family."

"That's bullshit, Bob." Missy said *Bob* like a dirty name.

Spencer intervened. "Missy, there's no need to get upset. Bob, I'm Eldridge's cousin and I believe his only living family so there'll be no need to remove the dogs from our care."

O.J. trotted into the room and sat next to Missy. They both cocked their heads to the right not sure they believed what they just heard. Deputy Bob sneered. "Like we're going to believe that."

"I'll tell you what. I'll keep these dogs while I prove we're related. If I don't you can arrest me, fine me, or whatever your book dictates. But until then the dogs stay with me."

Deputy Bob looked over at Missy, who stood dumbstruck, then down at O.J. who growled softly. "Fine, you got forty-eight hours to come up with something. And if anybody of his persuasion shows up before then and claims to be a relative, I'll come for the dogs."

"It's a deal, Deputy. Sorry you came all the way out here for nothing."

"No problem, Doctor. Missy, I'll have to take you up on that coffee some other time."

"Sure, Bob, thanks," Missy whispered. "Good night."

The deputy turned back to Spencer. "You got forty-eight hours, Doc."

"Good night, Deputy." The door closed and the room was silent except for the sound of Deputy Bob's boots. Spencer turned to Missy. "I didn't know you and Deputy Bob were on a first name basis. When did that happen?"

"He read it off my form then told me his, and quit calling him Deputy Bob. You two sounded like two high school boys about to square off." Missy was angry now. "And where the hell do you get off? Why did you tell him you were related to Eldridge?"

"Because it's true."

"That's a cruel thing to say. Eldridge just died for goodness sake."

"My great aunt married his granddaddy. I just found out myself a couple of months ago. That grove of his was started by my great grandfather in the early nineteen hundreds."

"You're kidding!" Missy gasped.

"It's not a good thing to kid about down here."

"You're just full of surprises today. Why didn't you say something?"

"Eldridge didn't want me to. I think he was more upset about his white blood than I was about finding a long lost black cousin."

"It's a good thing you know how to prove it."

"It's all in the family Bible over at his house."

"The one that burned down?"

"Oh shit."

Walker sat at his desk reviewing the plans for his new pet cemetery when his cell phone rang.

"Walker, this is Lucinda."

"Oh."

"You sound disappointed."

"I thought it was Big Town Appliance Center returning my call asking for someone to come out and return my entertainment center to my office."

"You'll never guess what I saw today."

"A terminal geezer who wants to be buried in Cheetos."

"What?"

Walker sighed and rubbed his forehead. "Never mind. Just wishful thinking."

"Lord, you're weird."

"So tell me what you saw today."

"I drove out to our property and it seems Mr. Stoval's house didn't weather the storm well at all. In fact, it burned down."

"Was he in it? I handled the arrangements and interment of his parents some years ago."

"I don't know for sure, but there's enough yellow tape around the property to stripe the highway from here to Ft. Pierce."

"No kidding? He must have gone on to meet his creator in the fire."

"Walker, would you get out of your funeral director mode. I'm not the god-damn next of kin here. We've got bigger fish to fry."

"You mean the land."

"Yes, and I don't mean his funeral plot either."

"I see." Walker twirled his pen aimlessly on the desk top. "My specialty is burn victims you know."

"Do you remember if any brothers or sisters attended the funerals of his parents?"

"I'm not sure. It's been awhile. And three out of five of my burn victims have open casket funerals."

"Well, think dammit. Don't you keep records on that sort of thing?"

"They're on my computer, but that would require electricity wouldn't it?"

"Damn, I forgot. But we can't just sit on this. We've got about forty-eight hours before the boys from Miami are on this like a dog with a boner."

"You're right but it's *on a bone.*"

"What?"

"It's *like a dog on a bone.*"

"Walker, are you with me on this or not?"

"I am, Lucinda, but I'm not comfortable rushing in before the body is even cold. That's if Stoval is even dead."

"I think one of us should talk with Dr. Hawley, his cousin. Why don't you go out there and talk to him about your precious pet cemetery idea, and in the process find out what he knows. I'll try to get some records at the court house."

"Won't he think it odd if I approach him immediately after this storm?"

"Walker, everyone thinks you're odd. Never mind. I'll do it myself."

TWENTY THREE

The next morning Missy reluctantly drove to Melbourne to assess the damages. She had called her parents to assure them she was okay and they insisted she make the trip. As Missy suspected it had been a waste of time. The Florida National Guard surrounded her entire block, and the rubble that was once her apartment had been declared unstable. Her duty finished, she smiled at the young guardsmen and turned the car around. She was back in Winter Beach in less than an hour.

Spencer looked up from his newspaper when she entered the clinic. "That was fast."

Missy shrugged. "I hope you're all happy. It's just like I said—all in ruins and nothing to salvage."

"You don't seem too upset."

"You're right. I thought about it on the way back and realized the only thing I'd worried about was this crummy building and your practice, and I decided I need to get a life." Missy reached for her green smock with the little animals embroidered on it. "Anything going on here?"

"In case you haven't noticed we've got the power back, and the air conditioner still works." He started to read his paper again.

"Water?"

"They say later this afternoon, but we have to boil it for another forty-eight hours."

Missy wrapped her arms around herself and turned slowly in the cool office. "I don't want to drink it. I just want a long hot shower."

"Sounds like a wonderful afternoon work break." Spencer turned the page. "The Vero Beach Dodgers were rained out."

"Where's the dogs?"

"They're in back. I put Gidget and the pups in the large post-op cage with some old towels. The others seem content to lie on the cool tile for now, but we'll have to exercise them later."

"After I shower," Missy sighed. "Then I'll shower again."

"I got a call from the Humane Society. They've got volunteers out looking for lost pets."

"I'll go help them." Missy started to pull her smock back over her head.

"Leave it on, Florence Nightingale. They're bringing over a golden retriever with a broken leg. I need you to help get the surgery suite ready."

Missy smiled. "This is good. I mean being needed and all."

"You're right. In this cynical world it's a rare occurrence we should savor."

"If we get time we'll do that, but I better get the surgery ready."

Spencer put down the paper. "Check on the pups first. I'll answer the phones."

Missy turned and started for her tasks. Spencer had to admire her youthful enthusiasm and dedication, and he wondered when he'd lost his. Her smock almost completely covered her shorts which enhanced her sculpted long legs. At times they seemed almost too long for her to manage as she reflected the awkward grace of a palomino colt.

Spencer heard a car door slam and approaching footsteps. The clinic door stuck briefly then opened. It was Lucinda. "Good morning, Spencer. I was worried about you when you didn't call."

Spencer felt his face flush with obvious rebuke. Since the storm, Gidget's delivery, Eldridge's death, and the acquisition of a new platonic roommate, he hadn't given his dinner and dessert with Lucinda a second thought. "Sorry, but it's been a little crazy."

"You weren't even worried about me?"

"I should have called, but with the storm, Gidget's cesarean, and then Eldridge Stoval dying in his house fire …"

"Eldridge Stoval is dead? Oh, Spencer, I'm sorry I didn't know." Lucinda bit her lower lip then reached over the counter and embraced Spencer in an awkward hug just as Missy returned from surgery.

"Excuse me. I didn't know we had company, Doctor." Her demeanor was proper but her tone could have frosted the balls on a snowbird.

Spencer struggled to disentangle himself. "Missy, you remember Ms. Vickers from the realty company."

"Yes, I believe you brought your grandmother's dog in some time back. A Rottweiler I believe."

"A Jack Russell terrier actually."

"Of course."

Spencer remained mute. Missy never forgot a dog or its owner.

"Dr. Hawley just informed me of the tragic death of Mr. Stoval. It will be such a loss to the community both black and white." Lucinda ran her hands down the front of her blouse as if to smooth the fabric. The maneuver accentuated her upturned breasts, but Spencer wasn't sure for whose benefit she performed. Lucinda's eyes never left Missy's.

Missy didn't appear to notice. "Mr. Stoval was a good client and friend. None of his dogs died under our care. We will certainly miss him here." She turned to Spencer. "If you'll excuse me, Doctor, I have the instruments to prepare." Without waiting for a reply Missy turned and left the room.

Lucinda followed Missy's legs down the hall with her eyes. When she was out of earshot she said to no one in particular, "Lovely girl."

"I don't know what I'd do without her."

Lucinda turned back to Spencer as if she'd just noticed his presence. "But, Spencer, what are you going to do about Eldridge? Surely you'll come forward now that he's gone. There's nothing to be gained by your silence. Consider the funeral arrangements and the will, not to mention the dogs."

"I already have the dogs. I had to tell the deputy we were related to get them, but I didn't think about the funeral arrangements."

"Did you say Deputy Bob?"

"No, I didn't, but it was him. Don't tell me you know him too?"

"He helped me with some speeding tickets once, but that's another story. You should talk to Walker Braddock; he'd know what to do. He may have handled the arrangements for Eldridge's parents."

"It couldn't be any worse than talking to Deputy Bob." Apparently Deputy Bob attracted all the ladies. Spencer was beginning to dislike him intensely.

"What about the land?"

"What about it?"

"If you're the only living heir you could claim it." Lucinda leaned forward with both hands on the counter. She was all business now.

"I couldn't do that."

"Of course you could and you should. Your family owned it originally."

"That's more than I can handle right now." He stepped back intimidated by Lucinda's encroachment.

"When you change your mind I know some excellent estate attorneys that can help you."

"Thanks. I'll let you know if I need anything." Lucinda's aggression disconcerted Spencer, although she'd made a good point about the funeral arrangements. He'd have to look into the matter.

Lucinda studied Spencer for a moment. Then she backed off and began to fumble through her purse for her keys. "I'd better run. I promised Mudge I'd check on her house and give her a call. Plus I don't want to wear out my welcome with your girl Misty."

"Missy. Her name is Missy."

"Whatever. She seems a bit possessive of you."

"I wouldn't go that far. The past few days have been stressful, plus Buzz leveled her apartment in Melbourne."

"And she's staying with? …"

"Me. Up at the house."

"Really, Spencer?" Lucinda raised one eyebrow and touched her ignition key to her lips.

"That's right. It's purely platonic." Her accusatory Joan Crawford look irritated Spencer.

Lucinda pointed the key at him. "I'm sure this is all platonic on your part. She's certainly not your type, but if you, as her employer, want to avoid a sexual harassment charge you might want to send her to stay at my place."

"Thanks for the offer, Lucinda, but I think we can manage our platonic relationship just fine."

"Just a suggestion, dear. I've got to run." Lucinda headed for the door and stopped. "I hope you'll pass my offer on to Missy."

"Good-bye, Lucinda."

When she had gone Missy returned to the waiting room. "The surgery suite is ready if you'd like to check it."

"Thanks, Missy. I'm sure it's fine. That dog should be here any minute."

Missy looked beyond Spencer to the car as Lucinda squealed out of the parking lot. "She seemed to take the death of Mr. Stoval pretty hard."

"She felt badly for me. Lucinda knows Eldridge and I were related."

"You told her?" Her tone was more incredulous than inquisitive.

"Before Hurricane Buzz in a weak moment," he replied.

"That's more information than I need. Do you think that was a good idea?"

Spencer and Missy stood side by side at the window staring down the now empty road. "I wish I knew, Missy."

Delwood lay in Redstone's king-sized bed staring up at what used to be the ceiling but was now open sky. The high pitched whine of the mosquitoes could be heard above the generator and, while guarding T. Pascoe Redstone's provided some perks, this rated just a notch above sleeping in the truck. Since they couldn't get the television to work, they entertained themselves with Redstone's police scanner.

"Do you copy, thirty eight? Over."

"I copy. Over."

"We have a woman who claims her husband left during the night to relieve himself in the drainage canal and never returned. Over."

"I copy. I'm just finishing at US 1 and SR 520. We've pushed the stalled golf cart out of the intersection."

"Copy."

"What's your 20 on the missing urinater? Over."

"1520 Gator Lane. Over."

"I'm on my way. Over."

Delwood climbed out of bed. He'd smeared his entire body with a jar of Mrs. Redstone's pea-green beauty cream, but the mosquitoes had still managed to keep him awake. Lying there contemplating Eldridge Stoval's citrus groves had given him a headache. He padded across the damp shag carpet to the bathroom. After he relieved himself and poured a bucket of pool water into the toilet tank, he flushed and grabbed a clean towel and a bar of soap and headed for Tip's pool to bathe.

Clayton, his face puffed as a ripe honeydew melon, stood at the side of the pool wrapped in a lemon yellow printed sheet. A cigarette dangled from his lips. "I never seen so many fuckin' mosquitoes in my life. I must be bled dry by now." With that pronouncement he dropped the sheet revealing his boney white nakedness and jumped into the pool.

He surfaced and rubbed his eyes. "Delwood, what's on your face? It looks like you've been dipped in guacamole, man."

"It's some of Tip's ol' lady's beauty cream. I thought it might repel the little blood suckers but it draws 'em like flies to horse shit."

"You don't smell so good either."

"I'm gonna wash it off and go see Walker Braddock about buyin' that land."

"What's he got to do with it?" Clayton eased into a back float and began to paddle tight circles.

"He's an educated businessman; that's what." Delwood was about to cannonball Clayton, but he thought better of it and eased himself into the pool. "He'll tell me how to go about getting a loan." Delwood took the hand soap and tried to lather his hair. "Did you stay awake last night and listen to the scanner?"

"I sat up for a spell. The bugs wouldn't let me sleep."

"Anything on Stoval?"

"Nope."

"Anything on the missing urinater?"

"Frickin' awesome, Delwood. They found a twelve-foot gator and some body parts a hundred yards down the ditch from the house. You could still hear the deputy retchin' when he called it in."

Delwood scrubbed his head hard. "Jesus, I wonder what my last thoughts would be as I stood there fending off a ravenous gator with my dick."

Clayton just stared at Delwood's shampoo progress. "Your hair turned green from that beauty cream, Delwood."

TWENTY FOUR

Spencer's afternoon looked free. They had fixed the retriever's leg with a small pin and the patient was resting comfortably. The volunteers from the Humane Society had also brought in two kittens and a duck, none of which really needed medical attention, but then at 10:00 business dropped off when the volunteers joined the protesters at Gator Lane. Apparently Fish and Wildlife had condemned an alligator for dining on a gentleman who'd decided to pee-pee *al fresco*.

The break gave Spencer time to call his local insurance agent. After twenty minutes on hold he spoke to a Minnie Mouse voice who referred him to their 800 number in Orlando. Half an hour later a Truman Capote voice greeted him, took his policy information, and assured him someone would stop by in the next ten days to assess the damage to his roof. All of their available agents were tied up in Melbourne.

Having accomplished that, Spencer decided to leave Missy with the phone and the contaminated surgical suite and drive over to Walker Braddock's mortuary to see what could be done about Eldridge. Braddock's building looked undamaged but two men, one of whom wore a Marlins cap over pea-green hair, busied themselves with the downed tree limbs and damaged shrubs.

A young man in a black suit and narrow black tie, who looked more like a poster boy for *Reservoir Dogs* than a mortician's assistant, greeted Spencer at the door and escorted him to Mr. Braddock's office. Walker, preoccupied with two movers as they inched a large-screen television over an expensive marble floor, didn't notice Spencer's arrival. He startled when the young man announced his guest.

His look of alarm turned to one of elation when he recognized Spencer. "Dr. Hawley, how good to see you again. I see you weathered the storm without a scratch or scrape." He extended his soft puffy hand.

"Yes, nothing a shave and shower won't cure. I hope you're not too disappointed."

"Disappointed?" It took a few moments for Braddock to get the joke. "Oh yes, disappointed. Ha, ha. I get it. These advance warning systems dramatically reduce casualties. Very bad for business I'm afraid. Ha, ha."

"How did Ajax do?"

"Six years in PTSD counseling and he'll be fine, but nice of you to ask." Walker motioned to a chair. "Sit down. What can I do for you? I'm still looking for a professional partner in the pet cemetery business you know."

"Thanks, Mr. Braddock, but that's not why I came." Spencer shifted uncomfortably in his chair. It still wasn't easy talking about Eldridge as a relative. "I wondered if you had heard anything about Eldridge Stoval?"

"What a tragedy. And he was such a credit to his race."

"That seems to be the developing consensus."

"I called his minister over at the Baptist church. He's not aware of any next of kin. As you may know, his wife and daughter both passed on some years ago."

"Yes."

"I called the county and offered my services. I said I would be glad to handle the arrangements and bill the estate later with no interest charge. It's the least I could do since I took care of his parents."

"There might be a slight wrinkle," Spencer offered and began to relate the story of his relationship to Eldridge to a wide-eyed Braddock. He concluded with, "I don't have any financial interest in this, but I just want to see the right thing done by Eldridge and his dogs."

Braddock rested his hands on his desk in the prayer position and Spencer sensed he was struggling to keep from rubbing them together. "In the first place, Doctor, you may very well have a financial stake in this matter. Secondly, I can assure you I will do everything in my power to see that your cousin is laid to rest with the dignity his standing and financial circumstances warrant."

"I appreciate your professionalism." *Here we go again*, thought Spencer. Walker had just uttered the same sentiment as his father's funeral director. He and his mother agreed in principle and the principal of his father's estate became fourteen thousand dollars lighter.

Walker put one finger to his lips and suggested, "I'll tell you what let's do. I'll call the coroner right now and see what the status of the deceased is."

Spencer leaned back in his chair and scanned the walnut bookcases while Walker punched in the numbers and waited. "Hello, Odessa, how are you doin' darling?'" A pause. "And your mamma?" Another pause. "Give her my regards, Odessa. Is Dr. Mitchell available, darling? I need an update on Mr. Stoval. Yes, a terrible tragedy. A credit to his race, yes he was."

Walker waved an arm at Spencer to get his attention and pointed at the far wall where a landscape designer's rendition of the new pet cemetery hung. With feigned interest Spencer got up and approached the framed drawing while Braddock oozed in the background. "I'll hold, darling." A long pause. "Hello, Mitchell, how's your wife? Still in remission? Excellent news. Mitchell, I'm calling about Eldridge Stoval." Pause. "A credit to his race. Yes, indeed. Any ideas when they'll release the body?"

There was a long pause. Spencer turned from the picture to look at Walker whose eyes were now so wide that he suspected that Dr. Mitchell had informed him that he too was related to Eldridge. Finally he spoke again but more subdued now, "Thank you, Mitchell. I'll inform the family."

Walker's hand shook as he hung up the phone. He looked up at Spencer, his face as white as grade-school paste. "There's been a delay, Doctor. Eldridge Stoval was murdered."

"Mr. Braddock, are you all right?" It was Braddock's assistant.

"Yes, I'm fine. I just had some disturbing news. That's all."

"Delwood would like to speak with you. Do you have time?"

Walker looked at his watch. "I have to make a call soon, but Delwood shouldn't take long. He's probably here to apologize."

Delwood stepped into the office, contrite and hat in hand. "Thank you for your time, Walker. I know you're busy setting everything right with your T.V. and caskets, and Clayton and I are sorry for your trouble."

"These are not toys and you're not children," Walker responded.

"We know that, sir."

"Did you know your hair is green? My God, that didn't come from my casket lining did it? That's imported silk from Bangladesh."

"No, sir. This is on a cause of Mrs. Redstone."

"Mrs. Redstone? Is she dead, too?"

"Not that I know of. See, Clayton and me are watching the Redstone place from looters and I borrowed some of her lotion to keep the skeeters away, but it turned my hair green."

"Putting you two on guard for looters is like appointing Bill Clinton counselor at a Girl Scout camp."

"That's not nice talk after all me and Clayton have done for you."

"You've done plenty all right. Now what do you want?"

"I was wonderin' if I could ask you for some business advice?"

"Considering your own enterprise? Now that's admirable, Delwood. You've come to the right source."

"As you know, my daddy once owned a piece of Stoval's land. Since Eldridge has no use for it now I thought I might buy it and become a citrus grower."

"Why would Eldridge want to dispose of his property?"

"On account he's dead."

"My God you must be kidding."

"I ain't. Lightning struck his place and burned him to a cinder. I can't believe you ain't heard."

"This is certainly shocking news to me, but if they don't find the will it could take some time for that property to make the market, Delwood. And even then it will require a hefty down payment," Walker added.

"I should have my FEMA check for the mobile home by then."

"You'll need more than a FEMA check. Besides, most of that government money will be going to Melbourne." Walker paused and studied Delwood and his pea-green coiffure. "I lied to you about Eldridge. I knew he was dead, but did you know he was murdered?"

Delwood looked straight ahead, then asked without flinching, "No, where did you hear that?"

"I just talked to the coroner on the phone. It's really tragic. He was a credit to his race you know."

"So why'd you lie about it? He practically stole my daddy's land. I wouldn't call that a credit to any race. And besides he wasn't pure Neegra anyway. He had some of that animal doctor's blood. You was the one that told me."

"I feel your anger and your pain, Delwood, and you have a point. I hadn't thought of it that way."

"You don't know nothin' about pain. I saw that doctor in here a few minutes ago. You and him better not be figurin' on how to get my land or I'll learn you some serious pain."

"Delwood, relax. The subject never came up."

"It better not. That's my land one way or another, and nobody else had better fuck with my deal."

"That's all you came here to talk about?" Walker reached for his phone to call Lucinda sensing his interview with Delwood was over.

"Yeah, that's about it. I guess I don't need nothing more from you."

"Hello, Lucinda? We need to talk."

"Yes, Walker, what is it? I'm busy."

"The autopsy revealed that Eldridge Stoval was murdered."

"No kidding?" Then silence.

"Are you still there? I said it wasn't an accident. He was murdered."

"I heard you. I'm thinking." A long pause followed by a sigh. "Walker, this doesn't really change our plans."

"Unless someone murdered him because they wanted the land."

"Do you think someone did?"

"Delwood has always had it in for Eldridge. He works for me, and he's the one I told about Dr. Hawley and Eldridge's relationship."

"And he wants the land?"

"He claims Eldridge stole it from his father and it's rightfully his. Lucinda, he threatened anyone who got in his way. I think we should forget about this."

"Get a grip, Walker. I need to do a title search on that property and put my friend Deputy Bob to work on Eldridge Stoval's will. If someone did murder him, the sheriff will have no problem accessing Eldridge's safe deposit box or locating his attorney."

"Lucinda, the Stovals are bad luck for us. Let's let this one go."

"Can't do it, Walker. I've got too much invested in this already. Our signal is breaking up, and I've got work to do before this hits the *Press Journal.* Trust me, Walker."

"But in high school ..."

"This isn't about your major crush on Jasmine again is it?"

"You know better than that. It's a hell of a lot more than that."

"Oh, so we're going to relive the night of the pool party again. The one at your house when your folks weren't home and you got roaring drunk and made a pass at Jasmine."

"She pushed me away and went to you in the deep end but she couldn't swim. It was our fault."

"It was your fault. I tried to save her."

"I should have called the rescue service."

"We were too drunk to think straight."

"But after she was gone."

"You mean dead."

"Fine, after she expired we should have called the police."

"Walker, how many times do we have to rehash this? There were your parents to think of as well as our own asses. Hell, we'd have probably set off a race riot. Who knows how many more innocent people would have been killed?"

"But stripping her naked and dumping her into the river."

"It worked didn't it? No one's ever been the wiser."

"I just can't forget those wide brown eyes as her body drifted from view. That's why I drink you know."

"Oh Jesus, Walker, it's in your genes. If you didn't drink over this it would just be some other damn thing."

"That night has linked us forever, Lucinda."

"If you say so, Walker, but I'd like to think of it with a positive spin. Together we can get away with anything."

"Even murder?"

"Whatever, Walker. We're going to get Stoval's land and finish this once and for all." The line went dead.

When he returned to the clinic Spencer could tell by the look on Missy's face that more bad news awaited him. "Doctor, the sheriff's office called."

Spencer sighed. "Deputy Bob again."

"I'm afraid so."

"I suppose he wants to know if I have proof of my relationship to Eldridge."

"No, that's not why he called." Missy's eyes were red and Spencer could tell she'd been crying. "He called to tell you that Mr. Stoval was murdered."

"I know. I found out while I was at the mortuary. Walker called to find out when they'd release the body and they told him."

"Who would do such a thing?" It was more of a plea than a question.

"I've been trying to figure that out all the way back here, and the best I can come up with is that he ran into some looters when he went home, they killed him, and tried to make it look like an accident."

"But is anything missing? Looters would have robbed him."

"It's hard to tell with the fire and all. Ask Deputy Bob, Missy. I'd sure like to know if that generator is missing because it might be traceable."

"It would have been pretty valuable during a storm like Buzz."

"That's what I'm thinking. Did Deputy Bob say anything else?"

"Yes, he said we'd better not plan on leaving town."

"You're kidding? He's beginning to play like a B detective movie," Spencer said.

"He sounded pretty serious. We're probably the last ones to see Mr. Stoval alive."

"Except for his killer."

TWENTY FIVE

"Come in thirty eight. Over."

"I copy. Over."

"We've got a problem at Gator Lane. Please proceed. Over."

"My E.T.A. is five minutes. Over."

"The gator protesters are under attack from the gator victim's family. Over."

"Are firearms involved? Over."

"We have no reports of gunfire. The family is reported to have in their possession two cases of porcelain souvenir alligator ashtrays. Over."

"Did I copy ashtrays? Over."

"Roger. They are pelting the protesters with them. Use extreme caution. Over."

"I copy. Over and out."

Clayton turned off the scanner and looked at Delwood. "It's getting right ugly over that rogue gator, Delwood." They were sitting in the Redstone's living room on Mrs. Redstone's Ethan Allen couch which emitted the faint aroma of mildew. Delwood had started a fire in the fireplace with the damper closed to drive out the mosquitoes and proceeded to roast half a dozen wieners.

"I hope that gator eats one of those damn do gooders before they shoot him and turn him into Tony Lama boots." Delwood emphasized his point by taking a large bite off a blackened nubbin of a skewered hot dog.

"Well, aren't we in a mood?" Clayton responded in a mock effeminate voice.

"It's gonna get a lot worse if that Braddock and his doctor friend are plottin' to cut me out of the groves. Pass me the ketchup."

"I think we ought to worry more about the sheriff and what we're gonna do now that he knows it was murder."

Delwood grunted. "He couldn't find a turd in an outhouse."

"He figured out Eldridge didn't die of no accident, didn't he?"

"Even a blind pig finds an acorn sometimes, Clayton. Besides, we should have stayed until we were sure old Stoval had been cremated in that fire." Delwood wiped the back of his mouth with his hand and belched.

"Well, we didn't and now they know. We need to get rid of that hammer and generator, Delwood."

Delwood looked up at Clayton, who wrung his hands like a kid about to burst his bladder. "Stop that; you look pathetic. We can throw that hammer in the swamp any old time and we need the generator to monitor the sheriff on the scanner."

"Keepin' the hammer don't make no sense, Delwood."

"What would happen if that hammer turned up at the mortuary in ol' Walker Braddock's tool box? That would put a quick end to Hawley's and his scheme to get my land wouldn't it?"

"You think that would work?"

"When we're done with it we'll put the generator in Walker's shed, too. I gua-ran-fuckin-tee it will work."

"It took a lotta gall to holler at us about a few spilled Cheetos."

"He'll pay for that, Clayton. Don't you worry."

"I can't help it, Delwood. It's my nature."

"I know, Clayton. You want I should make you some more baked beans?"

"No, but maybe we could do some s'mores later."

"Sure thing, Clayton. Let's turn the scanner back on."

"This is thirty eight requesting backup. Over."

"Where are you thirty eight? Over."

"I'm in the fucking patrol car with the doors locked."

"Remain calm, thirty eight, what's your twenty? Over."

"I'm at goddamn Gator Lane where you sent me, asshole. Over."

"What's your situation? Over."

"I have repeated assaults on an officer with a rubber alligator and a threatened anal penetration with a foreign object. Over."

"I didn't copy that last part, thirty eight. Over."

"The perp threatened to shove an ashtray up my ass. Copy that, butthole!"

"I repeat. Remain calm, thirty eight. Can you make an identification? Over."

"I think so. The ashtray is shaped like a swimming pool and has an alligator in a red swimming suit sitting in a beach chair under an umbrella. Over."

"I meant the perp not the ashtray, **deputy.** *Do you copy?"*

"Fuck you over, Roger."

"E.T.A. for backup is three minutes. **Over.***"*

TWENTY SIX

It had been two days since Spencer talked to Walker Braddock about the interment of Eldridge Stoval. His murder made front page news in the *Press Journal*, but no suspects had been identified. From the sheriff's comments, Spencer concluded that he suspected random looters, but he wasn't surprised when the sheriff called and asked if he would stop by his office to answer a few questions.

The unbearable heat and humidity permeated Spencer's being like a slow poison. His damp shirt stuck to the car seat adding further to his ill humor. He had left Missy at the clinic in tears. Her father called from Alabama outraged that she had become her boss's live-in, even though she explained that it was purely platonic and out of necessity.

He threatened her with eternal damnation and loss of her cell phone, not to mention a sexual harassment suit against Spencer. Spencer didn't think the parent of an adult child could sue for sexual harassment, but he reminded himself to tell Missy about Lucinda's offer just in case. Besides, eternal damnation was nothing to scoff at in the South. This Florida heat proved just how miserable Hell could be.

The sheriff's office sat alone on the edge of an abandoned citrus grove across the highway from the Indian River County Fairgrounds. It was a white cinder block building whose only distinguishing features were a tall dispatcher's antenna and an oversized sheriff's badge painted next to the front door. The remote setting had all the ambiance of a scene from *The Last Picture Show*. Spencer fully expected to encounter Ben Johnson in the role of the sheriff.

A cloud of dust swirled then floated to rest on Spencer's truck as he parked next to the only patrol car in the lot. He had an urge to just sit there for awhile and gather his thoughts, but the heat was so suffocating he peeled his wet back from the seat and went inside. A chipper receptionist, apparently unaware that the world was in meltdown, greeted him. Spencer recognized her as a cat-owning client and smiled as he struggled to recall her name.

"Hello, Dr. Hawley. The sheriff is expecting you. You can go right in."

"Thanks. How's your cat?" he managed.

"Just fine," the receptionist giggled as her face flushed. "I'll tell her you asked after her."

"Give her my best," Spencer said and walked into the sheriff's office.

Any illusions of Ben Johnson immediately evaporated as the sheriff rose to greet Spencer. A big man, he must have weighed nearly three hundred pounds, most of which he carried in a paunch that rolled over and hid the buckle of his thick brown belt. His head was as bald as a baby's butt, and his extended hand was the size of Mike Piazza's catcher's mitt. Spencer stuck out his hand and watched with trepidation as it disappeared into the sheriff's grip.

"Dr. Hawley, I'm Sheriff Gibbs. Thanks for coming over. Normally I'd have enjoyed driving up the river to your place, but we're a bit short-handed between the storm and some rioting up on Gator Lane."

Gibbs motioned to a chair and Spencer retrieved his tingling hand and sat down. "It's no problem. I hope I can be of help."

"I hope you can shed some light on this, Doctor." He paused and studied Spencer as if he expected him to spill his guts and hand him the solution to his case. "You were related to Mr. Stoval?" His contemplation of Spencer continued, and suddenly it hit Spencer that the sheriff was seeking a family resemblance.

"It's a distant thing on my father's side. I'm afraid the only proof I had burned in the fire. Eldridge had it recorded in an old family Bible."

"You're from the Midwest I hear." The sheriff opened a drawer and took out a cigar and began to slowly unwrap it.

"Iowa, but my great-grandfather tried to make a go of it down here in the early nineteen hundreds."

"A lot of Iowans came down then. I'm afraid ol' Herman Zeuch sold a lot of land on the premise that he'd discovered a tropical paradise, but that was before air conditioning—and the mosquitoes were as big as sparrows." Sheriff Gibbs leaned back in his chair and licked the end of his cigar before he bit off the tip and spit it in the trash can. "So you came back to reclaim your family's groves?"

"I didn't even know the groves or Eldridge Stoval existed. I needed a change and had an opportunity to buy a practice down here."

Gibbs sat poker faced, his unlit cigar planted between his lips. "It doesn't look like you'll have to prove your relationship to us. Stoval's attorney called and has both the Bible and Eldridge's recent will. Did you know he listed you as the sole beneficiary of his estate?"

If the shocked look on Spencer's face convinced Gibbs of his innocence, he didn't reveal it. "That's going to come in mighty handy for you with all that debt your practice is piling up. Those groves will fetch a pretty price, Doctor."

Spencer shifted uncomfortably in his chair as he realized where the sheriff was headed with his questions. "I had no reason to harm Eldridge Stoval and I certainly had no idea he included me in his will."

"I wouldn't begin to suspect a man with your professional background, Dr. Hawley." Gibbs held a lit match near the end of his cigar and sucked the flame toward the tip. "I believe you were the first one on the scene."

"My assistant and I drove out to see what had happened. Eldridge had been staying at the clinic with us and had driven back to get a generator. Did you find the generator?"

"No, we didn't."

"I think whoever stole that generator is the killer. Find it and you'll have him." Spencer had risen to his feet like a man pleading his case before a jury.

"It's possible, Doctor." Gibbs took a long drag on his cigar and studied Spencer's face again. "If there ever was a generator that is."

"I don't like what you're suggesting, sheriff."

"I'm suggesting nothing, but if I were to suggest something, it would be for you to relax and pay a visit to Eldridge Stoval's lawyer. He's looking for you."

"Thank you, I will if we're through."

Gibbs rose slowly from his chair and extended his hand again. "I'll let you know if we find the generator."

Spencer shook hands again and left the office knowing full well that Gibbs had just set the hook and would play him like snook running for the inlet.

Hamilton Poole's office was the antithesis of Sheriff Gibb's. It was a small converted bungalow on the Twin Pairs near Twentieth Avenue. The Twin Pairs is a couple of one-way streets that extend Route Sixty from Interstate 95 through the heart of Vero Beach to the Atlantic Ocean and back again. Tourists and island residents alike can fly through Vero at forty-five miles an hour completely unaware of the struggling downtown.

Poole's place sat just back off the road on a manicured lawn surrounded by peach-colored hibiscus. Spencer parked his truck around the corner and walked back. He knocked. A high thin voice beckoned him inside.

Hamilton Poole was a stooped elderly black man with short white hair and Ben Franklin glasses. His extended hand trembled, and when he noticed Spencer noticing he said, "It's that damned Parkinsons. But it's not contagious." He smiled and Spencer shook his hand.

"I'm Spencer Hawley."

"I thought you might be. I had hoped to meet you one day but not under these circumstances. Come in and sit down. May I get you some iced tea?"

"That sounds wonderful."

Without another word Poole turned and shuffled down a short hallway. "Can I help, Mr. Poole?"

"No, I'm fine. Have a seat."

Spencer wandered into what was once a small, formal living room. A window air conditioner rattled incessantly and drowned out the BMW's and Jags on their way to their gated beachfront condos. He sat down on a chair perched on a worn oriental rug near an old oak desk. The desk was plain and unassuming, like the ones his grade school teachers used before they tore down Spencer's old school.

Eventually Hamilton Poole, looking for all the world like a butler from an old Spencer Tracy movie, returned with two sweating glasses on a silver tray. Spencer instinctively sprang from his seat to help. "Thank you," he said and reached for the glass.

"It's pre-sweetened. I hope you don't mind."

"That's fine." Spencer took a long draw on the syrupy tea.

"I hear they prefer it unsweetened up North. I could never understand that."

"Sugar is considered self-indulgent."

Hamilton smiled and edged toward his desk where he eased himself into his own chair. With a shaky hand he reached for a Bible and opened the cover. "Eldridge brought me this for safekeeping when he changed his will. There's not much doubt you two are related."

"Didn't he have any other family?"

"Unfortunately he was the last of the line." Hamilton shook his bobbing head and closed the Bible.

"If it's a fair question, what were his plans before I showed up?"

"It is a fair question, Doctor. Eldridge treated his workers fairly and he cared what happened to them. He wanted the land sold to a citrus grower so they would still have jobs, and he wanted his house converted into a day care center to be run by his church."

"I can't believe he changed everything when I came along."

Hamilton picked up what appeared to be the will and passed it over to Spencer. "Black, white, or mixed, blood is thicker than water. He also feared that developers would buy the land out from under the ranchers. If his land were developed, it would have a cascade effect on the whole area. For some reason he trusted you would do the right thing."

Spencer shook his head. "I'm struggling in a near bankrupt practice that only new development could save, and he thinks I'll do the right thing. It's damned amazing."

"I'm sure he thought you would be on your feet before he died. This was a bit unplanned."

"Pardon me for my self-pity."

"That property will turn a nice profit, even if it's sold to someone from the Citrus League instead of a developer. This estate will take some time to settle, but in the meantime you'll be approached with all sorts of propositions. Take my advice and don't make any rash decisions. I have a modest practice and very little influence in this town, but I can help you sort through your options."

"If I can stay afloat that long."

"Once the news of your pending inheritance leaks out, and the sheriff's office is like a colander, you'll be amazed at how substantial your credit is."

"Thanks, Mr. Poole. I hope I haven't sounded ungrateful, but I'm not accustomed to folks having faith in me lately, especially the sheriff and his deputy." Spencer finished his tea and stood up.

"That copy of the will is yours, Doctor. Look it over and call me if you have any questions, and don't worry. It takes time to be accepted down here even if you're white."

"How long?"

Hamilton Poole smiled. "About three generations."

TWENTY SEVEN

Spencer returned to the clinic as a county cruiser drove away. He concluded that Deputy Bob had paid a visit, and that Bob wasn't necessarily looking for him. He studied his rundown building and wondered why he hadn't noticed its condition when he so eagerly bought the practice. He guessed he was desperate for a change of scenery. Now, with the death of a cousin he never really knew, he could afford to fix it up, tear it down, or sell it at a loss and find a better location in Vero Beach. Maybe his great-grandchildren would even be accepted as prominent citizens like Hamilton Poole had suggested, but for now he was an interloper and a murder suspect with one homeless employee and a pack of Boston terriers to support.

He opened the door to Missy's weary smile and the sound of Gidget's toenails clicking across the tile. She had taken a break from her pups. Spencer reached down and scratched her behind the ears and Gidget promptly rolled onto her back for a belly rub. As he rubbed her chest and scratched under her chin he studied her healing wound, relieved it showed no signs of infection. Then he looked up at Missy and asked, "What's new?"

"Deputy Bob just left. He asked a lot of questions about you and where you were during the storm. He also said Eldridge Stoval left his entire estate to you."

"Isn't that a kick in the butt?" Spencer forced a smile.

"They suspect you, don't they?"

"I seem to be high on their list. Did super sleuth mention anything about the generator?"

"No, he didn't. Didn't the sheriff?"

"They seem more interested in pinning it on me. I have a feeling I'm guilty until I prove I'm innocent." Spencer proceeded to fill Missy in on both his visit to Sheriff Gibbs and Hamilton Poole.

"Do you think we should start looking for the generator ourselves?" Missy asked.

"Why not? The governor has privatized every other government function of this state."

Missy bit her lower lip and looked away. "There's another problem."

"There can't be. I'm all booked up on problems until a week from Thursday."

"My father is on the way."

"That's just great." Spencer laughed. "He comes from Alabama with a shotgun on his knee."

"It's not funny, Spencer."

"But it is." Spencer paused and cocked his head. "You just called me Spencer."

Missy blushed. "I'm sorry, Doctor."

"No, that's okay. It sounds more friendly and I could use a friend right now."

"We are friends, Spencer." As she smiled her blue eyes lit up like the Des Moines Younkers store on Christmas Eve.

Spencer reached down and picked Gidget up off the floor. Gidget promptly licked his cheek then stretched over and tried to reach Missy. Just then Eldridge's terriers ran into the room and circled Spencer and Missy. "I get the feeling these are the lost boys, I'm Peter Pan, and you're Wendy."

Missy laughed and Spencer noticed a small tear rolling down her cheek just before she hugged him and an ecstatic Gidget. When she pulled herself away she said, "Captain Hook, Deputy Bob that is, says we can keep the dogs for now."

"Well, I can't keep you with me and risk the wrath of your father. It's amazing but Lucinda saw this coming and offered her place if we needed it."

"Lucinda?!" Missy wailed. "Don't send me there, Spencer. She gives me the creeps. I'd rather face my father than go there."

"Well, I wouldn't. I'm in enough trouble. Besides, Hamilton Poole said something about the development vultures circling Eldridge's land. If anyone would know anything about that, it would be Lucinda."

Missy's face broke into a slow smile. "You mean like a spy?"

"I think any information we can get could help clear me with Gibbs."

Her response was slow and thoughtful. "All right then. But just until he leaves. You can't take care of the lost boys all by yourself."

"I can't cook worth a damn either."

"You don't think I'm going to end up tied to the mast waiting for you and the boys to rescue me from that crocodile?"

"She's an aggressive businesswoman, but she has a heart of gold."

"I think you're a better judge of animals, Doctor Hawley."

Missy scanned the Yellow Pages for businesses that sold portable generators while Spencer walked Gidget back to his office and examined her pups. Gidget sat patiently while Spencer finished, then crawled back into the box Missy had made for her and readied herself to serve lunch. Spencer looked down at his dog and her family and thought about Missy and where their friendship might take them. He concluded that the worst had to be over.

He picked up the phone and dialed Lucinda but didn't get an answer at home so he tried her cell phone. Moments later he got a monotone response. "Lucinda Vickers. May I help you?"

"Lucinda, it's Spencer Hawley."

"Spencer, how are you?" The monotone gave way to exuberance.

"Things are a bit sticky around here, but I think it'll all work out."

"I'm sure you'll be cleared."

Spencer was caught off guard. "I didn't say anything about being cleared."

"One hears things in my business. I hope I didn't offend."

"You must have heard that I'm in for an inheritance also." There was a brief pause at the other end, yet Spencer could practically hear Lucinda's wheels turning.

"Actually I did, Spencer. I think it's wonderful despite the circumstances. It's a very valuable piece of property you know."

"That's what I'm hearing."

"Spencer, who have you talked to?" Spencer took pleasure in Lucinda's panic.

"Hamilton Poole filled me in."

"Oh, him. He's a nice man."

"A credit to his race I'm sure." Spencer was beginning to think Missy was right. He was a better judge of animals.

"Spencer, don't be sarcastic. Hamilton Poole is a good lawyer, but he doesn't have experience with complex real estate deals."

"So you think my deal will be big?"

"Well, not so big. It is just agricultural property, but they're good orchards and should bring a fair price. I could put some figures together for you if you like. It would give you an idea what the average grove sells for."

Average thought Spencer. He'd just gone from a big deal Hamilton Poole couldn't possibly handle to an average grove owner. "I'm not in a hurry, Lucinda, but that would be fine."

"Just do me a favor and promise me you won't talk to anyone else."

"I can do that," Spencer said stringing her along. "That's if you'll do one for me."

"No problem, partner." Lucinda's enthusiasm had returned. It was as if she came with a built-in switch.

"You offered to put up my assistant Missy. I wondered if we could take you up on that?"

"Things a little sticky there, also?"

"Let's not go there, okay?"

"I understand. I've got plenty of room. Consider it done."

"Thanks, Lucinda. We'll get back to you."

"She's a beautiful girl, Spencer. Any time."

My, my, my, said the spider to the fly, thought Spencer as he hung up the phone.

Missy narrowed the immediate possibilities for generators down to three sites between Winter Beach and Ft. Pierce. "We just have to pray he didn't buy it in Melbourne. Who knows if any of those businesses still exist?"

"So where do we start?"

"There's a lawn and landscaping business between here and Vero on Highway One. They sell Hondas and it's the closest."

"Let's try it and then work our way south."

"The dogs are fed and settled. I'm ready."

At first glance Glover's Lawn and Landscape Center resembled a small jungle encroaching on its parking lot and about to devour the highway. The entrance to the obscured building was a tunnel hacked out of the potted palms, hibiscus, and oleander. A sandwich sign next to the road announced a hurricane sale on damaged plants.

The scene didn't dampen Spencer's spirits. He loved everything about greenhouses: the odor of loam mixed with fertilizer, the cool dampness, and the mysterious rare flowering plants tucked under rows and rows of the more common multicolored impatiens, geraniums, and begonias. The whole scene reminded Spencer that, when the time was right, he would direct Walker to display arrangements of fresh flowers for Eldridge's funeral.

Spencer and Missy waded through the greenhouse and found themselves alone in the hardware section. Spencer banged the silver bell on the counter and eventually they heard footsteps approaching from the back of the building.

"I'm Bud Glover, the owner. We're a little short-handed since the storm, but can I help you folks?" Glover was a rotund fair-skinned man with cherubic cheeks and a smile that suggested if he were ninety pounds lighter and three feet shorter he could pass as Santa's elf.

"I understand you sell and service your generators."

Glover laughed as he pulled an oily rag from his back pocket and wiped his hands. "You folks are out of luck. I don't think there's a generator for sale in the whole state of Florida."

"We don't want to buy one," replied Missy. "We want to know if you sold one to somebody."

Glover squinted and studied his customers. "You two don't look like cops."

"We're not," Spencer said. "A friend of mine bought one and now it seems to be missing. We thought he might have purchased it here."

"Why don't you ask him?"

Spencer paused. "He's dead. I think someone might have killed him and stolen the generator."

Glover scratched his bald head and looked around impatiently as if he wondered why one of his clerks couldn't be handling this. Finally he sighed and asked, "Why aren't the police looking into this?"

"They seem to be a little short-handed themselves."

Glover snickered. "Sheriff's department?"

"Yes," answered Missy.

"They always seem to be a little short-handed. Who are we talking about?"

"A citrus grower named Eldridge Stoval. You know him?" Spencer asked.

Glover smiled sadly and shook his head. Then without warning he placed two fingers between his lips and let out a piercing whistle. Momentarily a Boston terrier, who could be a dead ringer for O.J., materialized at Glover's side and sat waiting eagerly for the next command. "This is Glover's Grand Champion Orchid, Orky for short. He won Best in Show in Orlando last fall."

"He's a beautiful stud." Spencer stooped down out of habit and gave Orky a quick exam.

"You look like you know something about dogs, mister."

"I'm a vet. In fact, I raise Bostons myself and this looks like one of Eldridge's."

"He belonged to Eldridge for sure. Orky was payment a few years back on Eldridge's Honda EX4500 XKI generator. It's air cooled with a five gallon tank. Eldridge and I haggled over that machine for a month."

"Would he have still had it?"

"I don't know why not. These suckers will last a lifetime, and they're worth their weight in gold during a hurricane like Buzz." Glover stepped up to his computer terminal at the counter and began to type. "I've got the serial number right here. I always register them for warranty before they leave the shop." Glover scratched out the number on a piece of paper and handed it to Spencer. "I hope this helps you catch the bastard."

Apparently suspecting a new command wasn't forthcoming Orky slumped to a reclining position at his master's feet. He opened his mouth to reveal a broad pink tongue and proceeded to pant. "Why is he called Grand Champion Orchid?" Missy asked.

Glover smiled again, but this time he had a twinkle in his eye. "My doctor said I needed a hobby to release stress, and my wife thought I should raise orchids. Believe me I got no interest in plants when I leave this place, but if I tell the IRS I show *orchids* my accountant says I can write it off as a business expense. So Orky here is my show orchid but that's our little secret." Glover winked at Missy and Spencer was sure she winked back. The corners of Orky's mouth turned up around his pink tongue as if he too got the joke.

Spencer and Missy left Glover and Orky and drove back to the clinic to pick up the dogs. They planned to go from there to Spencer's house to pick up Missy's things before dropping her off at Lucinda's. Reluctant as she was to stay with Lucinda, Missy seemed anxious to get it all done before her father stormed in from Alabama.

Once in the truck their conversation became difficult and strained. Spencer suddenly found himself uncomfortable with this new friendship. At the same time he didn't want her to leave. He had forgotten how lonely it was to live alone with no one to talk to but a dog.

At first they talked about the generator and how to proceed. Missy wanted to take the information to the sheriff, but Spencer thought it wasn't such a good idea yet. When Missy challenged Spencer, he admitted he didn't have a clue what to do with the information. It wasn't as if they could go door to door and ask to compare serial numbers.

They laughed about Orky, the orchid specimen, and Glover, but then got into a serious discussion about how to care for all of Spencer's new dogs. Gidget's puppies couldn't be sold for several months and Eldridge's dogs were technically part of the unsettled estate. His neighbor, Mrs. Helseth, would have a fit when all those dogs began running in the yard.

They both skillfully avoided the issue of Lucinda until they reached Spencer's house. Missy let the dogs in the side door while Spencer carried in the box of pups. "I'll get their food ready, Spencer."

"Fine, I'll get in the mail after I check the answering machine." Spencer pushed the button and heard a mechanical voice report, "*Two new messages.*"

"Hello, Missy, darling. Hello, helloooo? I hope this thing is workin'. If you get this message you'll know I'm in Ocala at the Cracker Barrel. I had a little car trouble but should get in sometime tonight. Don't go to sleep in that man's house until I get there. If that man's a true Christian, I have no truck with him. But if he's not and attempts to violate you, do as your brothers taught you and kick him in the privates. That should incapacitate him until I arrive. Oh damnation, I hope he doesn't hear this first and erase it!"

Spencer instinctively decided not to erase the message. Besides, he wanted Missy to describe her brother's kicking lessons. He pressed the button again.

"Mr. Dr. Hawley, my name is Delwood." A pause followed by a muffled burp. "I'm caretakerin' Mr. T. Pascoe Redstone's estate in his absence and would preci-ate you callin' me back. I overheard the deputy talkin' at the Krispy Kreme that you stand to git Stoval's land. Even though it is rightfully mine I plan to give you a fair price for it. Please call me at 778-1576 tonight." Another muffled burp. "Or I'm comin' over there in person."

My God, thought Spencer, *and this is just the beginning.* Without another thought he dialed the number and waited. "Hello, is this Mr. Delwood?"

"It's just Delwood. Delwood's my first name. Is this Tip? The house is good, Tipper, but the pool is turnin' green."

"Delwood, this is Dr. Hawley. I believe you called about some land."

"Oh Jeeze. It's that doctor," he said to someone else at the other end. "Thanks for callin', Doc."

"I just called to say I have no plans to sell the land at this time."

"Oh Jeeze, let me tell you my plan, Doc."

"I'd love to hear it, Delwood, but I'm on call and I can't tie up the line. I will say that my real estate agent, Ms. Lucinda Vickers, is working on some prelimi-naries and you might try to reach her in a few days." Spencer felt only a momen-tary pang of guilt for dumping the first of what would probably be a hoard of fortune seekers on Lucinda. "Good night, Mr. Delwood."

"Jeeze, g'nite."

Missy entered the room. "I thought I heard Father's voice in here."

"He's blowin' in from Ocala and you're supposed to stay awake and kick me in the nuts if I try anything."

"He didn't really say that. You're joking."

Spencer smiled and hit *replay*.

TWENTY EIGHT

Delwood hung up the phone as he slumped into Mrs. Redstone's overstuffed chair and kicked an empty beer bottle toward the fireplace. Clayton looked up from his reclining position on the couch, but before he could respond Delwood pointed his index finger and cocked thumb at him and farted. "Clayton, they're up to something."

"Who?"

"The doctor and some real estate agent named Lucinda Vickers. They're fixin' to sell that land at a big price I can't afford."

"It wouldn't have to be too much. You can't afford to pay me no never mind."

"Shut up, Clayton. I'm figurin' I might git me a silent partner like Walker Braddock."

"When do you figure to do that?"

"Soon, but first I'm gonna find out what those two are up to. Where's the phone book?"

Clayton pointed toward the fireplace. "Over there. We used part of it to start the fire."

Delwood scrambled out of his chair and crawled to the remains of the phone book. "Let's see—q, r, s, t, u, and v! We still got it, Clayton." Delwood ran his finger slowly through the v's. "Bingo, buddy. We got her." He ripped the page from the book. "Let's go."

Clayton rose from the couch and rubbed his eyes. "What are we goin' for?"

"We're goin' to check her place out and see what we can find out."

"That's the whole plan?"

"We'll just have to wing it as we go, Clayton. Come on." Delwood picked up his keys and started for the front door.

"Just a minute, Delwood, I'm takin' the scanner."

"Come in thirty eight. Over."

"I copy. Over."

"Proceed to Gator Lane."

"Please don't make me do that. Over."

"You have your orders, thirty eight. Over."

"I request backup. Over."

"You don't need it, thirty eight. The judge has granted a temporary injunction against Fish and Wildlife. You're to tell their agent to cease and desist for the present. Over."

"Roger, but I'm proceeding under protest. ETA five minutes. Over."

"Take it up with the union, thirty eight. And bring back the Fish and Wildlife agent. The Save-the-Gator bunch slashed his tires. Over."

"Delwood, we've driven past her place at least six times."

"It's not dark enough to go in yet."

"I gotta pee. We musta sat at that Dunkin' Donuts for three hours."

"I had to think. I know it was the doctor that delivered that blonde to this address. How does she figure into this? That's what I want to know."

"Maybe she's gone now."

"That's what we're gonna find out, Clayton. I'm gonna park in the church lot around the corner and we'll sneak back and take a peek."

Missy leaned against the back of Lucinda's couch and rolled her head from side to side. "The buzz from the Chardonnay actually feels good," Missy called out to her hostess who had retired to the kitchen.

"You probably won't feel that way tomorrow, dear."

"The dinner was divine, Lucinda. I wish I could cook like you."

Lucinda stuck her head around the corner. "It's just Lean Cuisine, dear."

"Oh my," Missy giggled.

"The secret is to scrape it onto good china and ply your guests with wine."

"That's so clever. I'll have to remember that. Do you need any help?"

"No thanks. I'm finished."

Lucinda returned from the kitchen and sat on the couch next to Missy while Missy shifted to make room. Like Missy, Lucinda was dressed for the hot weather in short cutoffs and a loose fitting halter top. As Lucinda tucked one long tan leg under the other and turned to face her guest, Missy giggled again. The wine was working as Lucinda planned.

"Do you think Spencer has decided what he wants to do with the land?" Lucinda asked.

"Noooo. I don't think so. Eldridge told Mr. Pooh, that's his attorney, that he wanted …"

"Yes?"

"Did I say Pooh? Oh, bother, it's Mr. Poole." Missy paused. "What was I saying?"

"Something about poor Mr. Stoval's wishes."

"Yes, Mr. Stoval wanted to save the land for the workers. He even wanted his house to become a day care center. Isn't that sweet?"

"As sugar." Lucinda reached forward and gently stroked Missy's hair. "You have the most beautiful hair. Is it natural?"

"Of course Spencer doesn't know anything about grapefruit if he keeps the groves for the workers. Do you like grapefruit? We're going to have way too much ourselves."

"I'd love to try your fruit."

Missy looked at Lucinda momentarily puzzled, then she smiled and continued. "But I don't know what Spencer is going to do with all those dogs. I think he needs more room, and if there's insurance money from the fire he could rebuild with a kennel and maybe even one of those puppy spas instead of a day care. Did you know that those spas even have puppy Jacuzzis?"

"No, but it sounds like you're planning a life with Spencer."

Missy felt her face flush. "I'm sorry. I didn't mean …"

"That's all right. It's just the two of us." Lucinda patted Missy on the shoulder and let her hand linger.

"Whew! Is it getting hot in here, Lucinda?"

Lucinda withdrew her hand and stood up. "You're right, it is. My air conditioner hasn't worked well since the storm." With that she reached behind her back and untied her halter top.

"Oh sweet Jesus, they're getting naked, Delwood."

"Shhh! Listen, Clayton."

The halter top floated to the floor and Lucinda stood over Missy with her upturned breasts cupped in her hands.

"You're beautiful, Lucinda." Missy gave an anxious giggle.

"So are you, Missy. Get comfortable if you want."

"I'm okay," she squeaked. "Thanks."

"I'm gettin' a boner, Delwood."

"Shhh! Come on, Barbie, take it off for ol' Delwood and join Skipper."

"And I gotta pee."

Lucinda dropped her hands to her sides and contemplated her next move. "That reminds me, I have something I want to show you." She turned and walked into the bedroom.

Missy looked down into her half-filled glass of wine as a drop of perspiration dripped off the end of her nose. "What the heck. It's just us girls." She downed the wine and slipped off her top.

"Oh yeah, Clayton! We be jammin' now, boy."

"It hurts so bad, Delwood. I just gotta pee."

"Don't you do anything, Clayton. This is a once in a life-fucking-time oppor-tunity."

Lucinda's voice echoed from the bedroom. "I found these at Victoria's Secret and I want to know what you think of them." Then she was in the doorway, smiling as she focused on Missy's breasts. "I see you got comfortable and joined the party." For a moment her voice changed. It was sexual and came from deep in her throat. Then she recovered and struck a pose with one arm stretched over her head and against the door frame. "What do you think?" she asked, her voice girl-ish again.

Lucinda posed in a tiny black lace bra that mysteriously cupped her breasts yet concealed almost nothing. The panties were much the same—a sheer revealing panel in front supported by tiny cords that joined to form a thong in back. A deep blush spread from Missy's forehead to the top of her breasts.

"Well, Missy?"

"It does put all your cards on the table, Lucinda." She reached for her own top and began to replace it.

"You are so right, Missy." Lucinda sensed she had pushed her guest too far and too fast, yet it angered her to think she might be rejected. She sat down again on the couch and caught Missy's hand as she reached back to tie her top.

"They're going to feel up each other's titties, Clayton!"

"Oh my God!"

"It doesn't get any better than this."

"Owwww! I'll be right back."

"Git back here, Clayton."

"It's not like you could wear this outfit when you and your boss go trolling."

Missy withdrew her hand and resumed tying her halter. "I guess not. What's trolling?"

Lucinda laughed. "You're being coy. You know what I mean."

"No, I don't." Missy was still drunk but the tone of her voice told Lucinda she wasn't enjoying the game.

Lucinda knew she should stop but she'd been rejected and couldn't resist pushing her point. "You mean he hasn't taken you along on his late-night sojourns?"

"I don't know what you're talking about." Missy backed against the corner of the couch and began to pout.

"You are dense, darling. You don't think he just happens to find all those mutts he brings in, do you?"

"He saves them from being hurt or killed."

"And you never wondered why they were all boys."

"Boys tend to get loose and wander."

"Just like our vet friend."

"I don't like your tone. You're cruel and I don't know what you're talking about."

"He's been taking that little slut puppy of his out at night when she's in heat. He rounds up the boys and brings them in as if he rescued them. It's a hell of a way to build a practice. I've got to give him credit."

"You're lying." Missy began to cry.

"Ask him about that cold bitch in his freezer. She just wasn't up to the task and croaked on us."

Suddenly there was a pounding at the door. Missy jumped as if startled from a dream. Lucinda cursed and dove into the bedroom. Someone pounded again. "What the fuck!" shouted Lucinda. "I've got a doorbell, dammit."

"Missy, it's Daddy. Dr. Hawley said you'd be here."

Missy adjusted her top and swept back her hair before making her way to the front door. The pounding resumed and Lucinda reappeared in a plain terry cloth robe cinched tight at the waist. She brushed Missy aside and opened the door.

"Daddy!" Missy lunged forward and wrapped her arms around her father. "I'm sooo glad you're here. This is Lucinda." She swung her arm in a wide arc toward Lucinda who stood solemnly in the doorway.

Mr. Melnick frowned. "Are you all right, Missy?"

"Oh yes, I'm fine now. I'm sooo glad to see you."

"What the hell is that?"

"What?" chimed both women at once.

Missy's father pointed toward the backyard where a man fumbled with his zipper as he dashed toward Lucinda's living room window. "It looks like one of those peeping Tom perverts."

"Oh shit," said Lucinda.

"Call the police. I'll catch the son-of-a-bitch." With that Missy's father leapt from the porch and started for the intruder.

Missy laughed, but it became a scream as another man materialized from the shadows and struck her father over the head. He slumped to the ground like a hundred-pound sack of peanuts as the two intruders stumbled away into the night.

TWENTY NINE

"How's the Peanut Princess this morning?"

Missy opened one eye then squeezed it shut. "Ohhhh please, turn out the lights." She rolled over and covered her head with her pillow. "Did I talk about that last night?" she asked in her muffled voice.

"No, but your father seems quite proud of your accomplishment. It's all he could talk about in the emergency room. The nurses thought he was the drunk one."

"The National Peanut Princess title capped my short but illustrious beauty career." Missy pulled her head out from under the pillow and rolled over to face Spencer just as Tangela and O.J. bounded onto the bed and lapped her face.

"By the way, I called the hospital and he's doing fine. We can visit him after breakfast if you want," Spencer said.

"Breakfast? You didn't say that did you?" She wiped off her mouth and pushed the dogs away.

"I brought you black coffee and dry toast. And Tylenol."

"Tylenol sounds good. Give it to me." Missy stretched both arms out to Spencer with the desperation of young Helen Keller at the family water pump. "There's a circus midget inside my skull pounding my temples with a sledge hammer."

Spencer handed her the Tylenol and she swallowed the tablets eagerly without the benefit of water. "I don't think spending the night with Lucinda was such a good idea, Spencer."

Spencer sat on the edge of the bed. "Did you learn anything?"

Missy looked at Spencer and raised one eyebrow. "I learned that she's not a very nice person."

"I suspect she has an agenda for Eldridge's property."

"Oh, she has an agenda all right." Missy flopped back on the bed and grabbed her head. "Owww, please stop the little man with the hammer."

"You're not going to tell me about last night are you?"

"Noooo. I don't think so. Maybe in another lifetime." Missy sat up and brushed back her hair. "I need to shower and go see Daddy."

Spencer stood and spoke to O.J. and Tangela, who had returned to see what was holding things up. "Let's go, kids, and give the lady some privacy."

"Spencer!" Missy gasped. "What are we going to tell Daddy now?"

"It's not a problem. Mrs. Helseth is already giving the dogs and me her killer looks. I'll take them down to the clinic tonight and sleep on the couch. You can have the whole place to yourself."

"Oh, I suppose that would be best."

"You sound disappointed."

"I am, but it's about something else. We need to talk."

"Fine, I'll leave you alone with your hangover and shower while I check Gidget and the pups." Spencer closed the door as he left.

Thirty minutes later Missy reappeared. Physically she looked remarkably rejuvenated, but from her facial expression Spencer suspected she was still troubled. "Is the little man with the hammer going away?"

Missy shook her head and frowned. "Last night Lucinda said some things."

"Really?"

"She was angry, and I'm not sure if she felt slighted by you or me, but I suspect it's a bit of both."

Spencer looked over at the dogs who were finishing their chow. "So what did she say?"

Missy paused and swallowed hard. "She said you were a dognapper, that you never found all those stray dogs, and that you used Gidget to attract them. She also said that when Gidget got pregnant you took advantage of poor Beebee, and that's what killed her."

"And you believe her?"

"All the strays were males. You tell me."

"I never planned to hurt anybody or anything. This practice was failing and I couldn't pay my bills. It seemed like an innocent enough plan. It was just temporary."

"Then it is true."

"Yes."

Missy turned her back to Spencer and from the movement of her shoulders he suspected she'd begun to cry. "If I had a place to go, I'd leave, Doctor. When this is all over I'm through. You can mail me my wages but don't bother unless it's honest money."

"But . ."

"That's all I've got to say. Now take me to see Daddy."

Delwood reclined on the Redstone's lounger next to the slime-covered pool. He was in his underwear and wore a pair of cheap sunglasses he'd found in Tip's dresser. Clayton, also in just his underwear, slept face down on the concrete. Last night's sexual tension and the fact that Delwood may have murdered someone else with his ball peen hammer was almost more than Clayton's system could take. Delwood felt sorry for Clayton not being able to enjoy all this. Never before had Delwood felt such a sense of purpose and direction. Contrary to what Clayton thought, everything was falling into place.

Delwood ran his hand through his hair. The green had almost entirely faded. He'd bask by the pool a while longer before he'd shower and shave now that the water pressure had returned. Then he would pick out one of Tip's best silk Hawaiian shirts and borrow his Sunday porkpie hat and pay a visit to his new favorite realtor. She'd certainly be surprised to discover what he knew about her personal sexual preferences.

When Clayton had sufficiently recovered, Delwood had a plan. After its implementation, it shouldn't be too hard to team up with Walker Braddock and buy that property with the lesbian and her doctor partner out of the way.

Delwood looked down at Clayton, who looked more like a wiener on the grill than his new partner. His pink skin had turned to fiery crimson. He'd make Clayton the foreman of his new citrus ranch, and maybe he'd name it Forbidden Fruit after the realtor that was going to help him get it cheap. Clayton moaned in his sleep and Delwood considered waking him, or at least turning him over, but then thought the better of it. He smiled down at poor Clayton and went in to take his shower.

Lucinda looked up at the man who stood in her office doorway. Not her usual customer, this man in his drug store dark glasses, blue Hawaiian shirt, and porkpie hat looked more like a refugee cab driver from *Hawaii Five-O*. "Can I help you?" she asked.

"You certainly can, Ms. Vickers." He stepped into the room and began to close the door.

"You can leave it open."

"I will, but you may want to rethink that when you hear what I got to say."

"Sit down, Mr …?"

"Delwood. Just Delwood for now. How ya doing?" Delwood extended a hand and Lucinda noticed a strange green tint to his hair.

"What can I do for you, Delwood? I already have a lawn service."

Delwood laughed but it was forced. "That's a good one, Ms. Vickers. I like your sense of humor. Keep it while we talk."

"And?"

"I understand you represent Doctor Hawley on the Stoval property." Delwood grinned as if he had just enlightened Lucinda.

"I'm afraid that's confidential."

"Oh no, he told me himself last night and suggested I call you."

"Dr. Hawley did that?" Lucinda brightened at the prospect of officially representing Spencer.

"He did but my partner and I was so excited to talk with you that we drove over to your home last night."

"But I was home all night."

"Clayton and I won't argue that." His grin suddenly lost the thin veil of charm and innocence it had when he walked in. "We saw you had that blonde lady guest and we didn't want to interrupt nothing.'" His persistent grin was starting to annoy Lucinda.

Lucinda let out a sigh of relief. "I appreciate your decorum, Delwood."

"Well that's not all. Actually we sort of appreciated *your* decorum."

"What are you talking about?"

"Clayton and me, well we went to the window to see if we was interruptin' anythin' important."

Lucinda gasped. "That was you, you little son-of-a-bitch?" She started to rise from her chair but Delwood motioned her back.

His smile faded. "I'm a liberal man, Ms. Vickers. My mother was a Unitarian, bless her soul, and I figure what someone does in the confines of their own home is their own business even if they are a tradin' titty grabs."

"What the fuck do you want?"

"First, I remind you that it's important to keep your sense of humor."

"I'm about to shove that little hat up your skinny white ass if you want humor."

"It's probably just another of your perverted sexual fantasies, but I'll let it pass. It would be terrible for your reputation if this sort of behavior were to leak out into the business community."

"You're trying to blackmail me, you little bastard." This time Lucinda did stand up.

Delwood put one finger on his lips and stared at the ceiling in mock thought. "In a word yes, bitch. Now sit back down." Lucinda slumped into her chair with a whimper as she saw all she had worked for float out the window.

"What do you want me to do?"

"Dr. Hawley will be out of the picture soon, and when he is I want you to step in and get that land for me at a price I can afford. You do that and you'll still get your little commission. Is that so hard?" Delwood rose to leave.

"Do I get the pictures and the negatives?"

Delwood paused for a moment. "I'll give you the whole fucking video tape, darling. But if you don't play along, you and your girlfriend will be the main feature down at the VFW."

"Get out!" The murderous quality of Lucinda's voice surprised even her.

"We'll be in touch, Ms. Vickers." Delwood tipped his hat and left.

THIRTY

Missy sat across from Spencer in the hospital cafeteria. Tears rolled off her cheeks faster than the saline from her father's IV bottle. "That's not my daddy in there. He's so confused."

Spencer reached over and rested his hand on her shoulder. "Missy, the doctors say he should continue to improve over the next forty-eight hours."

"Can't they do anything?"

"His CAT scans are normal so all we can do is wait and watch."

"It's all my fault." Missy took the handkerchief offered by Spencer and blew hard.

"The hell it is, Missy."

"Don't be mad at me. You've done enough," Missy wailed. At the next table three nurses, long since desensitized to grief-stricken families, continued to compare their husband's housekeeping abilities.

"I'm not mad at you, Missy, but you didn't do anything wrong. You got me through the storm and helped save my dog and I reciprocated by giving you a place to stay. We never even had sex."

"Shhhh!" Missy blushed and Spencer noticed the three nurses had suddenly become silent and had leaned in unison toward them.

Spencer turned deliberately to the nurses. "Veterinary medicine isn't like *Grey's Anatomy* because it would be wrong for me to have sex with my nurse." He felt a bit sanctimonious in light of his earlier ethical breaches but the nurses turned away in a huff.

Missy frowned. "I can rescue myself, thank you."

"Sorry, I was just trying to help."

"Well don't. Daddy always tried to help, too."

"That's because he loves you and would do anything for you. Sometimes it's hard to get past the parent-child thing, but he should have stayed home."

Missy blew her nose again with a loud honk. "He still sees me as his little peanut princess."

"And the nurses as your royal court."

"That's probably why he went berserk when that male nurse came on duty last night," Missy said. "He began shouting that transvestites had infiltrated America's beauty pageants."

"Maybe he's not as out of it as you thought." Spencer slid his chair back. "He'll be fine, but I won't be if I don't get back to the clinic."

"I don't know if I'm coming back."

"You stay here with your father. The dogs and I can manage." He stood over her now, and even though he hated hospitals he didn't want to leave her. Maybe ever. "I'm sorry about everything I did, Missy."

Missy looked away without responding.

"Maybe I'll see you later."

"Fine," she whispered.

Walker's visit surprised Lucinda. Usually she sought him out, but here he was sitting in her office. He didn't look well. His hands trembled and his skin had the pale waxy shine of one of his customers. "You look like you could use a drink, Walker. I've got some bourbon in the drawer." Lucinda opened the drawer and removed a bottle of Wild Turkey and a glass.

"Aren't you going to join me?" His tone sounded needy.

"I had enough last night, thank you." She poured a generous amount into the glass and shoved it toward Walker. "Sorry, but I don't have any ice."

"Straight up is fine, thanks." Walker took the glass with both hands and downed half the contents.

"Easy, boy, that's sippin' whiskey you got there."

Walker set the glass back on the desk. "Sorry."

"Walker, I haven't seen you look this bad since you got overcharged for that shipment of Chinese-made coffins." Lucinda leaned forward and whispered, "What's wrong?"

"I can't do this Stoval deal, Lucinda. I thought I could but I can't. I don't care how much we make. We're cursed."

"Cursed?" Lucinda sat back in her chair.

"He knows about his daughter now and he's cursed us from the grave." Walker took another drink then wiped his brow with his handkerchief.

"You're talking crazy talk, Walker. Next thing you know you'll start believing your own shit about armadillo protection."

"I'm serious, Lucinda. Today one of my own workers approached me and demanded I loan him the money to buy the place. He wants me to be his silent partner or he's going to report certain business practices of mine to the state board."

Lucinda sat upright and demanded, "What's his name?"

"The board president?"

"No, the son-of-a-bitch who's blackmailing you? Was he wearing a blue Hawaiian shirt?"

Walker gasped and almost dropped his glass. "Delwood! How did you know?"

"The little peckerwood thinks he's got something on me and wants me to broker the deal. Dammit, Walker, we've got to do something about him."

"It's Eldridge's revenge. We're cursed." Walker rose from his chair and slammed his glass down on the desk. "I'm going to the police."

"Sit down, Walker," Lucinda snapped. "You're not going anywhere."

Walker slumped back into his chair. "Tell me, Walker, what rock does this slime ball live under?"

Spencer twisted and tried to get comfortable on his office couch as he listened to the sound of distant thunder. He craned his stiff neck and checked his watch. It read 10:00. He must have fallen asleep reading journals.

O.J. and Tangela snoozed in the pockets of available space between his knees and feet while Mismark lay curled up under his chin, snoring rhythmically into his face. The heat generated by the dogs made him feel like a slow-roasted chicken on a spit.

As he extricated himself from his ovenmates he heard a car door slam in the parking lot and footsteps approach the front door. Cautiously he crept toward the reception area and cursed himself for forgetting to lock up. As the door opened into the darkened room, Spencer grasped the nearest weapon he could find, a plastic dog bone from the toy rack.

As the intruder slipped into the room, he arched the Nylabone over his head and in a hoarse whisper inquired, "Who's there?"

"It's me, Missy." She flipped on the light switch and momentarily blinded Spencer in his defensive stance. "Were you planning to beat me senseless with that bone?" she asked.

Spencer looked up at the bone suspended over his head then back at Missy. "I forgot to lock up and I thought you were a burglar." He put the bone down on the counter as O.J. wandered into the room and sniffed Missy's feet. His curiosity satisfied, he yawned and walked back down the hallway to bed.

"Some watchdog you are," Spencer accused as O.J. snorted and continued on his way. Spencer turned back to Missy. "What are you doing here? Is everything all right with your father?"

"Daddy's fine. By the time I left him he made as much sense as he ever did."

"He's alone now?"

"With his Bible and the Christian Discovery Channel. He likes to talk back to the preachers on the screen." Missy slumped into one of the waiting room chairs. "I went back to your place and Bob called. Then it got dark and started to thunder."

"Did you say Bob called?"

"I was scared to be alone," Missy said addressing no one in particular.

"Deputy Bob?"

"What about him?"

"What does he want now?"

"He'd finished his shift and wanted me to meet him at Dunkin' Donuts to talk about the case." Missy stood up and marched past Spencer toward his office and the dogs. "Bob gives me the creeps. I've decided to stay here."

Spencer turned and followed with a mixed sense of relief and panic. He didn't like the idea of her staying at his place alone, but he didn't relish having to face a religious zealot who argued with television evangelists and blindly chased down window peekers. "But what's your father going to say?"

"It's time Daddy learned I can make my own decisions."

"Who cares what he says to you. What's he going to do to me?"

When he caught up with Missy she was already remaking his bed on the couch. "I threw your couch cushions and some pillows into my car. You'll have to get them."

Spencer left and returned with the armload of bedding and found Missy curled up on the couch. O.J. and Tangela, not particular who they shared a bed with, had returned to their old places. "I can set up my bed in the lab."

Missy shook her head and pointed to the floor. "You can sleep here where I can keep an eye on you."

Spencer spilled his cushions onto the floor and began to arrange them next to Missy's bed. Mismark and Eldridge's other pups looked on with curiosity.

"You don't need to be this close," Missy said.

"The dogs will keep me honest."

"Like I'm going to trust your accomplices. Move it, mister."

"Fine, I can take a hint." Spencer dragged his cushions across the room and turned off the light. Mismark and the pups eagerly joined him. While the others sniffed the cushions, Mismark preoccupied himself with Spencer's face.

The windows rattled softly with the approaching thunderstorm, and the dogs nestled in against their human protector. Then, except for their snores, it was silent.

Spencer lay there looking up at the ceiling. He wasn't much of a protector and he didn't deserve Missy's or the dogs' loyalty.

Spencer listened for the noise that awakened him. It wasn't the storm or the dogs.

"I can't see for all this rain. What are they doing now?" asked Walker.

"I think they backed their truck up to the rear of Hawley's clinic." Lucinda reached forward and rubbed the windshield with her hand. "Turn on the defrost, Walker."

Walker restarted the car and pushed the defrost button. "If they break into that clinic we should call the police and go home."

"I told you, we need to know what they're up to. We're not going to involve the sheriff."

"This is a bad idea, Lucinda. My head aches, my clothes are wet, and I want to go home to bed."

"Shut up, Walker. Where's the flashlight?"

"Don't tell me we're going back out in this rain!"

"Quit whining, Walker. I get so tired of carrying you when things get tough. If those good 'ol boys enter that clinic I plan to find out why. If you want to drive over and park next to them so you can stay dry go right ahead."

"What do you mean you're always carrying me?"

"You know damn well what I mean." Lucinda didn't look at Walker, but instead tried to peer through the rain toward Delwood and Clayton. "I think they're trying to lift something out of the back of the truck."

"I did my part. Who else would have?"

"Sure, Walker, sure." Lucinda said only half listening to him. "Do you think that's a bomb? It looks too big to be a bomb."

"I can't tell. They've got it covered."

*   *   *   *

"Be careful, Clayton, this is one heavy bastard."

"Tell me about it, Delwood. It's slippery, too." Clayton strained against the generator as it slid to the back of the truck. "We shoulda' bought a couple of two by sixes and slid it down them."

"Just lift. Ugh! And set it down. Slowly, Clayton! There we go. Now let's push it toward the door."

"This rain is like fire on my blisters. How are we going to get in?"

"Like I said, lobster back, I'll jimmy the lock and we'll store it inside. Then we'll mess the place up a bit and steal a few things to make it look like a robbery. When Sheriff Gibbs comes to investigate, he'll find Stoval's generator and the hammer in Hawley's possession, and we're home free." Delwood leaned hard into the door and jammed his screwdriver between it and the frame. As the wood splintered Delwood exclaimed, "God, this is easy! In three months you'll be fore-man of my new ranch, Clayton."

Spencer and O.J. sat bolt upright. Missy stirred but continued to sleep, and Gidget peered over the wall of her box just long enough to make sure someone would take charge of the investigation. O.J. emitted a low growl and started for the back door. "Wait, boy," Spencer whispered but it was too late. O.J. had rounded the corner. Spencer untangled himself from his blanket and followed.

Before Spencer could reach the light switch O.J. had begun to bark and he could hear voices. *Yark, yark!*

"It's a dog!" *Yark, yark!*

"Of course it's a dog. Does it look like a fucking sea bass?" *Yark, yark, yark!* "Shut him up!"

"I ain't grabbin' no rabid dog. You shut him up."

Spencer found the light switch. As the light flooded the room he shouted, "What the hell's going on here?"

"Oh shit," someone groaned.

As Spencer's eyes began to focus in the bright light he could make out the two drenched men alongside a red Honda generator. "What do you want?" *Yark, yark!* "Be quiet, O.J." Of all the thoughts that ran through Spencer's mind at that very moment, the one that would stick was, *Why would a man wear a luau shirt to a break-in?*

"They're inside."

"That's it, Lucinda, call the police."

"No, the lights just went on. Spencer must have been waiting for them."

"They may have turned them on themselves. These two aren't the brightest bulbs on the marquee."

"We've got to find out what they're up to. Let's go." With that Lucinda began to rummage through the glove compartment. Once satisfied that she had found what she was looking for she jumped from the car and ran toward the clinic.

"My God, Lucinda. Where'd you get a gun?"

Delwood reached under his shirt and produced a small caliber pistol which he pointed in Spencer's direction. "Pick up that dog and shut him up."

"Delwood, you've got a gun!"

"And if you pull my finger I'll fart. Of course it's a gun, Clayton."

"But Delwood ..."

"While you're at it why don't you write our names and phone numbers in the doctor's guest book."

Spencer swept up O.J. and struggled to contain him as he noticed Missy standing in the doorway frozen like a doe in headlights. "We don't have any money, so you'd better leave."

"Oh lookey, Clayton, we've interrupted the doctor's slumber party."

Clayton rubbed his eyes and squinted at Missy. "Delwood isn't that the same one from last night?" His eyes focused on her breasts and he smiled.

"I believe you're right. I never forget a pretty titty."

Missy gasped. "You two are the ones."

"And you must be AC/DC. First Xena the Princess Warrior, now Dr. Doolittle. Maybe when we're done with the doctor and his funny-looking dogs, you'd be a sport and play a little two-on-one with Clayton and me."

"You're sick. I'm calling the police." Missy turned to get the phone just as Delwood fired a warning shot into the ceiling.

The room fell silent as plaster dust floated gently to the floor. "Nobody moves unless I say so."

"Was that a gunshot?"

"Shhhh. I can't see. I'm going to get closer to the back door."

"Delwood, this wasn't part of the plan. We need to talk about this."

"Sure, Clayton, we'll just call a time out and step into the bathroom to formulate a plan while you pee. I'm sure you have to pee by now, right Clayton?"

"I wish you hadn't brought that up, Delwood."

"Jesus, Clayton. Where's your facilities, Doc?"

"Just off the waiting room," Spencer answered and nodded his head in that direction.

"All right, Clayton, you go pee, and I'll cover everyone and think up a plan."

"Okay, Delwood, but I think we should just pack up the generator and leave."

Spencer looked over at Missy then back at Delwood as Clayton ran down the hall past them. "If you've got Eldridge Stoval's generator, I think you'd better put down that gun and let us call the sheriff. You've got some explaining to do."

"Clayton's got a big mouth and you're too smart for your own good. The sheriff is going to find that generator right here with you two lying next to it."

Missy gave a short cry. "Spencer, what does he mean?"

"I mean you two are about to have a lover's tiff over the fact that the doctor here murdered Stoval."

"But he didn't."

Delwood smiled. "She's a beauty, Doc, but a little slow on the uptake."

"Your partner's brain may be no bigger than his bladder, but I don't believe he'll go along with this."

"You let me worry about him, Doc."

"What's happening, Lucinda? I can't hear."

"Delwood killed Stoval and he's about to do these two in and frame Spencer for the murder."

"I told you we should call the police. I'm getting the cell phone."

"There's no time for that now, Tonto. I'm going in."

Lucinda grasped her grandfather's Colt 45 firmly in both hands just like she used to see on *Cagney and Lacey*. Planting her feet in a wide stance she extended her arms and nodded to Walker to fling open the back door to the clinic. "FREEZE, MOTHERFUCKER!!!"

Lucinda's surprise was complete. Delwood spun around and instinctively fired, but his shot was wide and to the right. Lucinda squeezed off a round in response which ricocheted off Hawley's sterilizer and imbedded itself in Delwood's right arm.

With the roar of the Colt 45's echo still reverberating throughout the hallway, Spencer dropped O.J. and dove for Missy driving her back into the office and out of Lucinda's line of fire.

Delwood dropped his gun and clutched his bleeding arm. "Bitch!" he screamed.

Lucinda stood her ground and smiled, "Asshole!" She fired another shot at Delwood and laughed wickedly as it careened off the tile between Delwood's legs.

"Claaay-ton." Delwood broke into a dead run for the front door as Lucinda emptied the revolver in the direction of his retreat. As Delwood struggled for the handle O.J. appeared from out of nowhere and sank his teeth into his exposed ankle. Delwood kicked frantically and sent over-matched O.J. skidding across the room into the steel leg of a chair.

Lucinda ran down the hallway and flung the empty gun at Delwood only to hit the door as it closed. "Dammit," she panted as she heard the door slam on the pickup. "That other one got back to the truck."

"I called the sheriff and they're on the way." It was Missy. Lucinda started for her, but stopped as Spencer stepped in, putting his arm around Missy as she leaned into him.

That's when they all turned to Walker who stood squarely in the back doorway clutching his abdomen with a bloody hand. "I've been shot, Lucinda." With that he collapsed to the floor.

"Walker!" Lucinda screamed as she ran to his side.

Walker opened his eyes and looked up. "I'm hit, Lucinda. Am I going to die?"

"Oh, Walker, you can't leave me now. Someone call for an ambulance for Christ's sake!"

"There's no time, Lucinda. My funeral instructions are in the Grecian urn in the living room at home."

"Don't be so fucking melodramatic, Walker. You're going to be fine."

"I've got a guaranteed price on a teakwood casket. You hold them to it."

"We've called an ambulance. Hold on."

"It's on the way," came Missy's voice from the other room.

"I'm in that long tunnel, Lucinda. I can see the light. Lord, I can see the light, but I have to confess my sins and receive the sacrament."

"Walker, listen to me. You're not going to die. Besides, you're not even a damn Catholic."

"I killed that girl, Lucinda. I can't go to my grave with that on my conscience." Walker coughed and the patch of blood surrounding the small hole in his shirt began to radiate from its center. He looked down at his wound and began to cry. "I'm so sorry I killed that girl, Lucinda."

"You didn't kill her, Walker. I did, and you were too obtuse to ever figure it out."

"What do you mean, Lucinda?"

"I loved her more than anything but she rejected me. That night in the pool I decided if I couldn't have her no one else would."

"But you couldn't ..." He coughed again.

"She couldn't swim, Walker, and I let her drown. I've never had the decency to tell you. Forgive me, Walker." Lucinda struggled to wipe away her tears as she clung to Walker.

"I don't believe you, but dying in your arms is consolation enough. You deliver the eulogy, Lucinda." Walker coughed again but this time he managed to smile. "It's in the urn, too. I wrote it." With that Walker slipped into unconsciousness.

"Wake up, Walker, don't leave me!" Lucinda's voice was small and faint like the squeak from a new kitten.

Spencer knelt beside Walker and took his pulse. "It's okay, Lucinda. He just passed out." With that Spencer proceeded to lift Walker's shirt to examine the wound. "It looks like he was hit by Delwood's small-caliber gun. He may need surgery, but he'll be all right."

They could hear sirens in the distance. "Thank you, Spencer." Lucinda stroked Walker's forehead, then softly kissed it. "You must have been delirious with fear, darling," she said to her unconscious partner. "I don't know what you were talking about." Lucinda looked up again at Spencer. "I just went along with him. I didn't know what else to say."

"You did the right thing, Lucinda."

"Jesus, you're bleeding, Delwood."

"That real estate bitch kicked in the back door and shot me. She meant to fuckin' kill me." Delwood struggled to pull out his handkerchief.

"What are we goin' to do now, Delwood?"

"I'm thinkin'.... Just drive."

"Well, you'd better think fast because those are flashing lights approaching us from the south."

"Turn in here and get off the highway."

"You don't look so good, Delwood. Maybe we should get you to a hospital."

"I think I'm gonna' be sick."

Clayton pulled over on the side of the road as Delwood struggled with the door handle. Finally he kicked the door open and, clutching his wounded arm, stumbled toward a nearby canal. "Where are we?" he asked over his shoulder.

"The sign said Gator Lane, Delwood."

THIRTY ONE

Walker regained consciousness by the time the paramedics arrived. As they started his IV, he remained calm and seemed ready to accept his fate. Lucinda stood in the corner near Deputy Bob. He wore a Dodger's cap and a tight navy-blue T-shirt that advertised both a local gym and his physical progress. Deputy Bob was off duty but heard the commotion on the scanner while making a beer run in the patrol car and thought he might be needed. Lucinda reached out and touched his forearm as she explained her grandfather's vintage Colt 45 and why she didn't have a permit.

Gidget left her pups in the box and trotted to the waiting room with Tangela to look for O.J. Now they were both whining. "The dogs need to go out," Spencer said to no one in particular. He was trying to comprehend why the killers were after him and how Lucinda and Walker knew about it.

"I'll take them," Missy said as she proceeded toward the sound of their whimpering.

Spencer started toward Lucinda and Deputy Bob, but before he could speak Missy called to him from the waiting room. "Spencer, come quick! O.J. is hurt."

O.J. lay on his side near a chair. He lifted his head briefly to look up at Spencer, then let it fall back to the floor. His respirations were shallow and his eyes had the glassy look of a drunk heading for a coma.

Spencer knelt at O.J.'s side and ran his hands carefully along the ribs. O.J. twitched with pain and tried to lift his head again. "He's got broken ribs and they might have punctured his spleen."

Missy knelt down near Tangela and Gidget and stroked O.J.'s head. "Can you fix it?"

"Let's move him to surgery where I can perform a better exam and start an IV." Spencer carefully lifted O.J. and looked up to see Missy retreating down the hall toward surgery at full speed. By the time he reached the table she was connecting IV tubing to a bag of saline solution.

Spencer palpated an area above O.J.'s right front ankle as Missy uncapped the needle and passed it to Spencer. O.J.'s pulse was weak and thready, but Spencer managed to find the vein and thread a tiny catheter into place. Missy passed him the tape to secure the site and opened the valve to the line. "Let it run wide open," Spencer ordered.

Once convinced the flow was sufficient Spencer proceeded to examine the injured dog's abdomen. He looked over his shoulder as he palpated and noticed that Gidget and Tangela had gathered Mismark and the others. They all sat in the doorway and patiently waited for Spencer to work some magic.

"Can you feel anything?" Missy asked.

"I'm not sure but I think his abdomen might be filling with blood. I'm going to need a nineteen gauge butterfly catheter on a syringe to puncture the abdomen. Then get me more saline so I can flush the peritoneal cavity and find out what's going on."

O.J. barely responded to the penetration of the needle as Spencer introduced it through the abdominal wall. He flushed the attached tube with the saline-filled syringe and shook his head at the bloody return. "Get the anesthesia ready, Missy, and break open an emergency abdominal tray. He probably needs a splenectomy."

Spencer scrubbed his hands briefly and threw on a surgical gown. By the time he returned to the table, Missy had opened the tray and started to prepare for the anesthesia. Spencer began to arrange the instruments and said, "Just barely put him under since he's in shock."

"I'm ready," Missy replied.

"Then go." Spencer picked up his scalpel and made a midline incision. "Suction on?"

"Suction is ready, Doctor."

"There's a lot of blood, Missy," Spencer said as he passed the sucker tip into the open cavity. "Once I've sucked it out I'll pack a sponge against the spleen to temporarily stop the hemorrhage." With his free hand and a pair of long forceps Spencer reached for a small cloth sponge. Then he put down the suction and gently retracted the bowel to expose the spleen. "This is the spot." He blotted the surface again to get a better look. Multiple lacerations spread over the spleen from a central contusion and reminded Spencer of a car windshield that had been struck by a rock. "The spleen is fractured and I'll have to take it out."

"His pulse is steady."

Spencer retracted the bowel with moist sponges, then began to dissect away the tissue covering the splenic artery and vein. "I've got the vessels exposed and am ligating them now. That should stop the hemorrhage."

Spencer, who had been the best surgeon in his class, worked quickly to finish the task. Like the hands of an orchestra conductor, each movement was precise and purposeful. In just minutes he laid the small bloody mass of a spleen on the table. "There are no other signs of bleeding, Missy. I'm going to close."

"Will he live?" It was Lucinda, who stood over the dogs in the doorway.

"I hope so, but he's lost a lot of blood. We'll give him some plasma post-op."

"Come in thirty eight. Over."
"This is thirty eight. Over."
"We have a sighting on the suspect's truck in your vicinity. Over."
"I copy. What's the twenty? Over."
"We have a report from Gator Lane. Over."
"Dammit, not again!"
"What's your ETA thirty eight? Over."

Spencer finished closing the wound and directed Missy to place a dressing over it. When he reached the hallway Lucinda was already on her way out the back door. "Lucinda, wait. Where are you going?"

She stopped and turned to face Spencer as tears streamed down her face. "I've got to go to the hospital and check on Walker."

"Why were you here in the first place, Lucinda?"

Lucinda brushed away a tear. "Those mental midgets worked for Walker and he thought he overheard them plotting, so we followed their truck."

"You saved our lives, but you could have just called the police."

"We weren't sure. Besides we didn't expect we'd find the two of you here."

Spencer handed Lucinda his handkerchief. "You're a lousy shot but thank you."

"I watched you two in there." She motioned toward the surgery suite. "You make a good team."

"Thanks, she's a good kid."

"You do realize that she loves you?"

"There was hope until she discovered I was a dognapper," Spencer mumbled.

"I'm sorry I spilled that. I guess I was jealous, but my guess is that she'll come around if you don't say something stupid and lose her."

"You and I weren't ..."

Lucinda reached out like a big sister and patted Spencer on the shoulder. "You and I never happened. We're alike in an odd sort of way that scares the hell out of me."

"Thanks, Lucinda. I owe you one."

"Just remember I'm your agent when you decide to sell that land."

"Sure thing. And thank Walker for us, too."

THIRTY TWO

"This is thirty eight. I'm at the abandoned truck and will investigate. Over."
  "Switch to your shoulder mike, thirty eight, so we can monitor. Over."
  "Roger. Over. There's blood on the seat of the truck. Over."
  "Proceed, thirty eight. We are sending backup. Over."
  "I hear something in the area of the canal. I'll wait for backup. Over."
  "Proceed to investigate, thirty eight. That's an order. Over."
  "We left a twelve foot gator down there!"
  "Then proceed with caution. Over."
  "Asshole."
  "I copied that. Over."

"Delwood, Delwood, where are you?"
"I'm down here takin' a leak in the canal."
"Nooo, Delwood. He doesn't like that. We gotta get back to the truck."
"Clayton, I'm a wounded fugitive on the run. I really don't care who I piss off."
"But Delwood ..."
Delwood heard the loud hissing sound first and thought someone had let the air out of all four tires on the truck at the same time. "Clayton?" Then he became aware of the cold lifeless eyes of the largest gator he had ever seen. Before he could even consider *How fast can the big fella be?* the beast slid forward and swallowed his right leg up to his knee. *He's pretty fuckin' fast,* Delwood thought in the millisecond before the grinding began. "Ayeeeeeee!"

"Don't let him pull you into the water, Delwood!"

For all the good it did Clayton might as well have said *Have a nice day.* Delwood clawed the bank with his good arm sinking his fingers into the soft earth. But this attempt to delay the gator's fast food stop only angered him more and he shook Delwood loose, like a puppy's chew toy, and retreated further into the canal. "Heeeelp, Clayton!"

"Thirty eight to base. Over. We've got another alligator attack at the canal. Over. I think I'm going to be sick."

"I copy thirty eight. I'm sending backup. Over."

"Arrruuughh!!"

"I copy thirty eight. As soon as this is over we'll get you into PTSD counseling."

"Don't quit, Delwood. The deputy's here." A pause punctuated by Delwood's excruciating screams. "Jesus, Delwood, the deputy just tossed his doughnuts and coffee."

"Ayeeeeeii." Gurgle.

"For Christ's sake shoot him, deputy!"

"I can't. The gator's under a protective court order. I'd have to get it lifted first."

"Oh, shit. Delwood?" Clayton choked back a sob. "He's gone."

"Was he your friend?" Uuurrp."

"Hell yes, he was my friend. I'm sorry, Delwood."

"Maybe you should get some counseling, too."

THIRTY THREE

Spencer awakened from his nap on the living room couch. The sun streamed in through the window and he could hear the soft whir of the ever-present air conditioner outside. Gidget had left her pups to join him while Tangela maintained her vigil over O.J. recuperating in the kitchen. Mismark and the rest of Eldridge's pups flopped alongside Missy on the floor where she lay reading Sunday's *Press Journal* in her short shorts and halter top.

Spencer's eyes followed a line from her calves past her thighs and focused on the exposed hollow of her arched back. Now that he no longer thought of himself as her employer he relished the thought of studying her body and discovered he loved every part of it. She wore her hair long now, but she was considering cutting it short. Even the thought of her new look aroused him.

As if she sensed his gaze Missy turned and looked up at him. "You're awake."

"I just had a nice dream." Gidget stood up, stretched and hopped off the couch to go check on her pups.

"Was it about us?"

"Maybe. I'll tell you later after the news." Spencer pointed toward the scattered paper.

"Walker Braddock is recovering nicely and should be released from the hospital tomorrow. There's another picture of Lucinda holding her grandfather's Colt 45 and rumor has it that *Playboy* has already made her an offer for a nude layout."

"I'm not surprised. She's a striking woman and she certainly redefines the term *Survivor*."

Missy made a face and continued. "There's also a picture of Deputy Bob next to the Honda generator. I think he's cute."

Spencer reached for his pillow and tossed it at Missy. "Deputy Bob is one bullet short of a six-shooter."

"That's not nice." Missy grabbed the pillow and tucked it under her chest. "There's a story here about that other deputy, the one that apprehended Clayton on Gator Lane."

"What about him?"

"He went postal and tried to kill the dispatcher the other night."

"No kidding? I wonder what that's all about?" Spencer walked into the kitchen and stuck his head into the refrigerator. "Do you want some orange juice?"

"Sure."

He returned shortly with two Star Wars glasses full of fresh juice and handed one to Missy.

Missy sat up and contemplated her glass. "What will you do, Spencer?"

"I thought I'd stab my employees with a tiny scalpel. Guns are so noisy."

"No, seriously. What are you going to do about the oranges? Those groves are surely yours now."

Spencer sat on the floor next to Missy and Mismark. "I'm no farmer, and all I know about oranges I read on the concentrate can. When Eldridge is properly buried I'll talk to someone at the Citrus League. I'd like to keep the land in the family and rent out the groves."

"You were wonderful in the operating room with O.J." Missy smiled and leaned over to kiss Spencer. "But you taste like oranges."

"It looks like I'm going to smell and taste like oranges for a long time."

"Until we're old and gray, Doctor." With that she stood up and took Spencer by the hand and led him past Mismark toward the bedroom.

"Does this mean I'm forgiven?"

"We'll see."

Mismark sat and looked after them, his head cocked to one side as they shut the door. When he was certain they weren't returning, he leaned over and lapped up the juice from the Darth Vader glass.

EPILOGUE

▼

After Missy and Spencer were married, they continued to raise and show Boston terriers. With the money from the grove rental, Spencer closed his Winter Beach clinic and started a surgical specialty practice in Vero Beach. They rebuilt Eldridge's home with a front porch and a swing so they could sit out at night and smell the orange blossoms. Missy converted the shed into a puppy spa which became a much-sought-after venue for the rich and famous of Premiere Island.

Walker Braddock recovered and graciously interred Eldridge at cost. He later joined the rest of the local citrus growers in contributing a large sum of money toward the Eldridge Stoval Day Care Center for migrant children. His pet cemetery never got off the ground, but he eventually made a fortune selling his patented armadillo repellent to mortuaries throughout the South.

Clayton is doing ten to twenty in the Panhandle. He and his cell mate Bubba plan to decorate their love nest in early Tina Turner and Madonna with mauve accents.

Eldridge's pups as well as Gidget's all were sold to good homes and have shown well throughout Florida. Mismark was Spencer's engagement gift to Missy, and since his surgery has served as the faithful eunuch at the puppy spa.

T. Pascoe Redstone ran for the U.S. Congress on the family-values platform and pledged strict FDA review of the false safe-sex claims by condom manufacturers.

He won by a landslide, and in just two years sexually transmitted diseases increased one-hundred and fifty percent in his district alone.

Lucinda Vickers took the proceeds from her *Playboy* layout and moved to Orlando where she landed the part of Johnny Tremain's mother in Disney's multimillion dollar remake of the movie. The movie flopped, but she married the director and moved to Beverly Hills. That marriage ended when he caught her with his secretary.

978-0-595-47875-0
0-595-47875-1

Printed in the United States
144153LV00003BA/8/P

9 780595 478750